The Free Verse Society

The Free Verse Society

DELALI ADJOA

PEACHTREE
Teen

Peachtree Teen
An imprint of Peachtree Publishing Company Inc.

Printed and bound in November 2025 at Toppan Leefung, DongGuan, China.
Edited by Ashley Hearn
Book design by Lily Steele
PeachtreeBooks.com
First Edition
ISBN: 978-1-68263-840-8 | 1 3 5 7 9 10 8 6 4 2 (hardcover)
ISBN: 978-1-68263-878-1 | 1 3 5 7 9 10 8 6 4 2 (paperback)

Library of Congress Cataloging-in-Publication Data is available.

EU Authorized Representative: HackettFlynn Ltd, 36 Cloch Choirneal, Balrothery, Co. Dublin, K32 C942, Ireland. EU@walkerpublishinggroup.com

For me at sixteen.

No matter what happens next,
you did it!

—D. A.

CHAPTER ONE

Jae

After months of muggy heat, a cool breeze passes through to say goodbye. It curls around me like a snake, smooth and slow. I clasp the handle of the suitcase by my waist, recounting everything I packed inside like a memory game: clothes and toiletries; a vintage postcard of Georgia, brown around the edges; a photo album; Mom's faded Bernie Mac tee; and as many books as I could fit inside.

I never paid much attention to the sidewalk, to the way it curves perfectly around the bend. This corner was always a *passing-through* place, a nowhere on the way to somewhere. To catch the bus for school, for the clinic, or to meet up with Austin Green. Now this is where I'll pass from one world to the next.

The phone in my pocket vibrates. I pull it out to read the message from Uncle Rowan: Just a few minutes.

Soon, a sleek black Cadillac pauses at the four-way stop before making a turn and pulling up beside me. The windows are tinted so dark they nearly blend in with the body of the car. The engine cuts off, the door opens, and Uncle Rowan's shiny brown head emerges from the driver's side. He's wearing dark sunglasses, and he walks toward me in a gray suit that shimmers like a new quarter in the sun.

He comes close to give me a quick pat on the back and says my name, *Janelle*, like it's a greeting. I see the tiredness stained red in the corners of his eyes, from a full day of visiting clients and old friends on the way to pick me up. *I have people to see along the way,* he'd said. As if they were the ones that made the stagnant hours on the road worthwhile.

I don't realize my fingers are wrapped tightly around my suitcase until he tries to wrestle it from my fingers.

"Did you cram the whole house in here?" he asks as he opens the trunk and heaves the suitcase inside. He grunts, dusts off his hands as if they've gotten dirty, and slams the trunk shut. We both look toward the empty apartment complex, and stupidly, I wave at the time-battered bricks.

Call me if you need me, Mom said this morning before leaving for her nursing shift. But we both know I won't call. These days our words are so sharp they could cut our own tongues. This is my chance to leave everything behind, including her voice.

Uncle Rowan says, "Let's get a move on," and nudges my shoulder.

I open the passenger-side door and pause, one foot hovering over the mat inside. The Georgia dirt clings to my black shoes like a final goodbye. I pull my foot out again and kick the curb, watching the dirt pepper the street.

When I step into the black-and-silver interior of the car, with all its gleaming gadgets, I feel like I'm stepping into the future. And I finally understand what a new car smells like. I've never ridden anywhere without the smell of cigarette smoke clinging to the seats, the smell of gasoline thick in the air, the smell of unwashed bodies sitting too close.

“We’ll be home in about eight hours,” Uncle Rowan says.

The word *home* rattles me. I remember that the place we’re driving away from isn’t home anymore, that it stopped being home a long time ago. Today my family name, my father’s name, feels like a mockery. Afenyo. *Home is good.* A reminder of what’s been broken, what I no longer have.

I wrap my arms around my stomach and listen to Uncle Rowan talk about his legal practice and his new office in the heart of Delray Beach. An easy commute, he says.

I *uh-huh* and *hmm* to show interest while I watch the houses with yellowed siding and chain-link fences pass by the window with increasing speed. Then we’re on the highway, where Uncle Rowan sinks back comfortably in his seat and turns on music that makes me think of Afros, bumping hips, and bell bottoms. I’m relieved not to have to fill the silence with small talk.

Quietly, I pull out my copy of *The Best American Poetry* and try to forget what I’m leaving behind.

☽

Raise your right hand for me.

My eyes flutter open when I hear the familiar voice. I expect to find myself sitting in a red plastic chair in a small office, but all I see are the dashed white lines of the encroaching road. Uncle Rowan yawns beside me. The bumpin’ oldies music is now gentle classical, which had lulled me to sleep.

We’re driving through the city Uncle Rowan calls home. I stare out the window at Delray, and Delray stares back with bright, unblinking streetlights. Palm trees hover over colorful buildings, and dark shadows walk past. There's a quiet energy that makes me want to take it all in.

Soon, the houses get greedier, taking up more and more space, some peeking coyly through wrought iron gates. Uncle Rowan's house stands behind a white stone wall. We roll slowly around a circular driveway, at the center of which stands an illuminated statue: A woman with hair round like a halo carries a jar on her shoulder. She looks steady, but the jar is tilted, and I'm sure at any moment it'll fall to the ground and shatter. The yard is full of towering trees, lush palms, and flowers brilliant even in the dim light. It reminds me of the gardens Mom and I would visit every Sunday when I was little. She would talk about the wisteria she wanted to plant someday when we got a yard, a garden. The wisteria would line a stone walkway, hanging over like a canopy of purple raindrops. I wonder if she envies Uncle Rowan for having the garden she never had.

Without a word, he turns off the car and steps outside. I realize I'm staring wide-eyed at the house—which looks like it belongs in Europe somewhere, with all its arches and glinting glass—when he knocks loudly on the passenger window and walks away, towing my suitcase behind him.

The front door opens to reveal a thin, dark woman standing in the light of a chandelier. She's wearing a blue maid's uniform and a white smile. Uncle Rowan disappears inside, and when I finally get to the door, the woman sticks out her hand and shakes mine.

"You can call me Ms. Rosette," she says in an accent that feels familiar. "You are Janelle?"

"Jae," I correct her. Uncle Rowan doesn't know I shed my old name like I shed so much else.

"A pleasure to meet you, Jae," she says. But in her mouth, *pleasure* sounds like *pleh-jah*. Her words come out slow and purposeful, like she's polishing them to a shine before placing them down.

I hesitate as I step inside, staring at my shoes and the spotless floor.

"You can leave them on," she says, flicking her hands like she disapproves. "That's what people do here." I'm staring at her, overcome by how similar she sounds to Dad, until she points me to the bathroom to wash my hands for dinner.

I can't shake Mom's voice as I walk across the shimmering cream tiles in my boots: *Does it look like we have a maid in here? I am not gonna pay another carpet-cleaning fee.* I almost laugh out loud. Well, there is a maid now.

Ms. Rosette ushers me down the hall with her hand against my back. "He is waiting in the dining room," she says.

I find Uncle Rowan sitting at the head of the table. I sit beside him, and it's just us and the silence. In front of me is a wineglass filled with water, a red napkin folded up like a pope's hat, and more forks than I need. There's an empty silver plate on my mat, but no food at the table to serve myself.

Just then Ms. Rosette walks in carrying two bowls of salad and sets them in front of us, right on top of the large silver plates. No one can read my thoughts, but I'm embarrassed that I feel so out of place. Back home, we eat dinners in front of the TV so we can stream *The Bernie Mac Show*. You don't need all the extra silverware for TV dinners. Seeing the table set like this, I agree with Mom. Uncle Rowan's too rich to be an Oakland.

"Eat," he says. His glasses are halfway down his nose and he peers at me over them.

I look down at my salad, suddenly remembering that I'm hungry, that I only ate a handful of cereal in the morning as I did some final packing, and then only picked at my drive-thru fries at lunch. I remind myself that rich people don't eat much, that this salad is probably all I'll get for dinner and I should try to enjoy it. I reach for a fork, but my hand hovers, unsure.

"Start with the fork on the outside. Then work your way in," he says.

We eat in silence until Ms. Rosette picks up our empty salad bowls. I'm surprised when she brings in plates of rice and chunky red sauce.

I poke the slab of meat drenched in bloodred.

"Lamb," he says.

I haven't eaten meat in years. Not since the day I opened the deep freezer in the African market and saw a goat. A whole goat. It was the meat Dad used in his Ghanaian light soup, and there it lay with its eyes wide open and frozen, staring back at me. Now I look up at Uncle Rowan's expectant face and cut into the lamb swimming in sauce on my plate. *I'm sorry*, I tell the lamb. *Go easy*, I tell my stomach.

Uncle Rowan clears his throat. "You start school tomorrow," he says. "Bellwood is in a different league academically. You'll have to work hard." He says this like I'm some kind of slacker. Like I'm not a straight-A student. "You'll need to start thinking about college applications as well."

I pause and lower my fork. "I'm only a junior."

"If you want to get a leg up, you need to start now. Research schools, attend college fairs, build relationships with your teachers so you can ask for recommendation letters. Have you thought about extracurriculars?"

"Not yet."

He shakes his head. "Not surprised. Coming from that school where all you kids care about is who's dating whom. And who's got the newest Air Jordans. The flyest snapbacks. When I was young, I seized the chance to be somebody, to pull myself out of the hood and make something of myself. I saved every penny I could. Learned how to invest. There wasn't any opportunity that could present itself that I wouldn't be ready for." He shakes his finger at me. "Your mom, she always asked for handouts. And look at where we both turned out, the victim and the victor. And if it weren't for your so-called father—"

I sigh and drop my fork onto my plate. Uncle Rowan ignores the loud clatter and continues, but I'm done listening.

There's nothing he can tell me about Dad that I don't already know. I know that he up and left. Took his notebooks full of physics and poetry. Took his prized mounted bass from that precious fishing trip with his boss. And left every single picture of me behind. My body still remembers his leaving, the clench in my heart, the sweat in my palms. It sits in the pit of my stomach always. So when it comes to Dad, that's all I need to know.

I watch quietly as Uncle Rowan drags a chunk of meat through sauce.

"Where is Ms. Rosette from?" I ask, desperate for conversation that has nothing to do with me.

"Togo," he says, and my mind goes white for a second. Togo sits next to Ghana, Dad's country, arms touching like close kin. "I think she speaks your language. I mean, your dad's language," he corrects himself. And he's right to, because Dad never bothered to share E*v*e with me. Uncle Rowan sweeps his finger in the red sauce and pops it into his mouth, the most normal thing I've seen him do all day. "Anyway, she came highly recommended. It's the illegal ones that are the problem," he says. "They steal jobs from our people, and we do nothing to stop it."

This is where Mom and Uncle Rowan would have a fight. *Your uncle lost his religion in all that money*, she said once. She would quote the Bible to him, chapter and verse, something about kindness to strangers in a new land. She loves the Bible, even though the last time she went to church was when Jesus turned water into wine.

We sit in silence as Uncle Rowan sips from his glass and sighs absentmindedly between bites. I take note of the lines across his forehead, which weren't there years ago.

Raise your right hand for me. Do you understand that once you sign, you will have given up all your rights?

I push the voice away again.

Uncle Rowan takes a sip of his wine, pats his mouth with his napkin, and returns it to his lap. "I think you'll do fine here. It's a chance for you to grow up and face real responsibility. Responsibility you can't just hand over to someone else."

I snap my mouth shut to keep the words in. My face flushes from the heat of unsaid things. I heap shovels of coconut rice into my mouth, just to keep my tongue busy.

Ms. Rosette shuffles into the dining room, her dark hands stuffed into the pockets of her blue apron. "How does it taste?" she asks, looking hopefully from Uncle Rowan to me.

"Good, good." He nods. "The lamb is a bit too red for me, but we shouldn't get trichinosis."

She shakes her head. "You want apple pie or cherry pie for dessert? Both are ready to go."

I can feel his eyes on me. "What would you like, Janelle?"

Pie or no pie, I can't spend another minute at the table with him. He's not the Uncle Rowan I used to know, the one I used to curl up with on Christmas morning with hot cocoa and marshmallows. The one who read *How the Grinch Stole Christmas!* with all the voices, making me laugh until I cried. This Uncle Rowan doesn't laugh. He doesn't smile. And he thinks the worst of me.

"Can I be excused? I need to get ready for school tomorrow."

He nods. "Good for you. Rosette, I'll have some apple pie."

"Yes, sir." She leaves the room.

Upstairs in my new room, a very pink room, I stand on a rug the size of my old bedroom in Atlanta. I stare at wall-to-wall bookshelves and wall-to-wall curtains, and a bed big enough for six of me. I feel small, like there's not enough of me to fill up this new world.

Uncle Rowan would agree. I'm the daughter of Paula Oakland and Kofi Afenyo, and I'm a walking statistic. The shame of it throbs like a fresh wound. I'm surer than before that no one in Delray needs to know my whole story.

Raise your right hand for me.

I pull my phone out of my pocket and find the saved number that I think about calling every day but don't. I press the call button and it goes right to voicemail.

"Hey, Sherry. It's Jae. Janelle Afenyo. I just wanted to check that you got the email about my address change. Did you? Um . . . Please tell Anne I'm looking forward to seeing the picture. I can't wait to see it. Thanks. Thank you."

I hang up the phone, and in the space of quietness, my guilt grows. *This is all on you. Don't forget that*, it says. But I could never forget. I wear the memories in stitches, in pain that takes its time. The body remembers everything.

Blinking quickly, I clear the wet haze of the bedroom.

Then, hungry for new air, I walk toward the curtains and pull them aside, and the world outside takes my breath away. There's the ocean, and the water is a black mirror with the moon glowing on its surface. Sailboats float past like mystical clouds. I push the window open and the breeze sweeps the water, kisses the moon, and makes the curtains dance. It brushes my skin with its warm fingers, making me think of Georgia and last goodbyes.

CHAPTER TWO

Jae

It's my first day at Bellwood High, and my body and mind are in two different places. My feet take me from room to room as I match the numbers on my schedule to the numbers on doors, getting lost in the flow of students who know exactly where they're going.

But my thoughts wander to a small air-conditioned room. Red plastic chairs. Cold. The serenity prayer on one wall, a glossy horse poster on another. And flowers. Lots of flowers. For thank-yous and sorrys and goodbyes. Whenever a teacher calls my name, I'm dropped back into my body, my feet on pristine tile, my back pressed against straight wood.

Soon enough, the second lunch bell rings and I find myself planted in the bathroom stall, leaning against the brick wall, listening to voices float through the hallways like smoke. I survey the stall door where phone numbers, names, and body parts are scribbled in black marker beneath the words *junior hos. sharing is caring*.

The words, not meant for me, still inject themselves like viruses into marrow. They multiply, until I forget that the words are written on gray metal and not under my skin.

Avoiding the pee spots on the floor, I shuffle my feet to ease the numbness, to feel my body be mine again.

There's chatter in the hallway. I instinctively hold my breath, put the toilet seat down, and step up, tucking my dress behind my knees. A woman's voice calls for the drifters to hurry to the cafeteria, and I'm left facing an imaginary Mom, who kisses her teeth, gives me a sour look, and says I'm just like Dad, hiding when things get too tough. *You need to be pressed if you want to be a diamond, Janelle.*

So much for leaving her voice back in Atlanta.

I jump when the bathroom door swings open and slams against the wall. The thud echoes in my chest and sends my heart quick-stepping. Heat surges through my body, fear clenches my lungs. *Breathe, Jae, breathe.*

The squeaky shuffle of shoes passes the first two stalls and stops when a body slams into the wall closest to me. I flinch, hug my knees closer.

"What the hell were you doing at my house, Tillman?" a voice asks in a sharp whisper. My brain slowly registers that it's a deep voice.

"Look, dude, I have no idea what the big deal is," another voice responds, cracking.

"*Dude*?" Shuffling feet. "Did you just *dude* me, Tillman?"

"Sorry, sorry. No need to get upset."

"Nobody knows where I live."

"*I* had no idea where you lived. Had I known, I would have said, 'To hell with it! I'm not delivering pizzas to that house!'" This voice rises like it's full of helium.

"Are you trying to be smart?"

"Smart? Not me. Dumb as a block."

The silence is filled with agitated breaths. I tell my heart to settle. Nobody knows I'm here.

"Derek, come on." Tillman's voice trembles. "This is a classic case of projection. You assume I'm feeling what you're feeling, but I'm not, I'm really not!"

"I know what projection means."

"You *really* think people will stop liking you if they find out the truth? Any therapist worth their salt—"

"Shut up, Tillman."

"Did you know *salt* and *salary* share a Latin root?"

"Tillman. Shut up!" Thud. "Say a word to anyone, I'll pluck the braces off your yellow teeth and make you swallow 'em. You know I can do that, right, book freak? You'll regret the day you met me."

"Already happening."

"Then get the hell out of here. Go eat your freaking cheese sandwich."

I hold my breath for another body slam, but there's only the sound of retreating feet and the thud of the door. I let out a long sigh of relief.

I think I'm alone until feet move toward the other side of the bathroom. The tap turns on, running at full blast. Then there's the sound of water splashing, an agonized "*Shit!*" and sobs. They're almost inaudible, drowned out by the water, and for a moment I wonder if I'm just hearing things. What kind of bully cries after threatening his victim?

I'm stuck, afraid to move. But still, drawn to the familiar ache of tears. Like the way I cried when I realized Dad wasn't coming home again. Or the day I signed away the most beautiful gift, not understanding the breadth of *forever*. The pain is so tangible I can almost hold it in my hands.

Trying to squelch my fear, I slowly step down from my crouched position on the toilet seat and grab my I LOVE LUCILLE canvas bag from the hook. *Sometimes sadness is loud and it needs to be heard,* I tell myself. I open the stall door, and the boy at the sink looks up into the mirror, startled.

I'm startled too. My feet won't move. My brain had conjured up an image of a boy on the other side of the door. A generic, everyday boy. Brown-haired and lanky. But my expectations have been demolished, completely ground into fine dust. There's nothing generic, nothing average about him. Boys like him make you think of dark and beautiful things.

He turns off the water, turns away from the mirror, and stares at me with eyes that remind me of black water and aching lungs and sinking deep. They're lined with dark lashes, shadowed by thick eyebrows. He shifts a white baseball cap over shiny black hair, and I can't tell if he's Latino or Indian or Middle Eastern or something else. As Dad would say, I can't tell where his parents are from.

He purses full lips. "What are you doing here?" His voice is still sandpaper, his eyebrows knit together. The muscles around his sharp jaw pulse. He turns quickly to the sink, holds his cap in one hand, and splashes water on his face with the other. He turns around, pulls up the bottom of his shirt to dry himself, muscled torso on display. My insides swim, and I forget why I left the stall in the first place.

"I thought this was the girls' bathroom," I finally answer, feeling my face warm. "I mean, it might be. I probably shouldn't assume . . ."

My voice trails off at the squinty, just-drank-spoiled-milk expression on his face.

"Chill. Our school's not that progressive." He points over his shoulder to urinals against the wall, right before the first stall.

"Wow," I whisper. How did I not see them? My face is burning up. I pray for a sinkhole to swallow me. I read they were all over Florida, and yet none has come to take me.

When I finally get the nerve to look at him again, his expression has shifted to one of curiosity.

"You're new?" he asks.

I nod. "Jae. With an *e*."

"You're scared of the cafeteria or something?"

It's not the cafeteria; it's all the kids in it. But I respond, "Something."

"So you're spending lunch in the bathroom." He's squinting at me again.

Embarrassment holds my tongue. Nothing comes out.

He lets out a dry laugh. "You're . . . different." He pauses. "And I mean that in a good way." He crosses his arms over his chest and examines my face, like he's trying to memorize it. Then his gaze drops lower, sweeps slowly over the neckline of my dress, my waist-length locs, my meticulously moisturized legs. I watch every flicker of his eyes, how easily they move over me, like the world could be ending and he would still take his time.

I shift from foot to foot under his gaze. "Different? Why do you say that?" It's not like I'm the only Black girl in school. There was a group of them standing at the lockers, straight hair, curly hair, and Afro meeting in a huddled circle. And there was one in my Advanced Placement Biology class, though she avoided eye contact. Maybe she thought talking to me would make her Black too.

"I dunno," he says. "Just a feeling. Like, everyone here basically looks the same, talks the same. They wouldn't be caught dead in that, for sure."

"A little rude," I say. "What's wrong with what I'm wearing?" I look down at my white cheesecloth dress tied with a braided belt. My cocoa-colored legs end in sandals. My white canvas bag hangs over my shoulder.

"Besides the fact that you'll need something more substantial than a tote bag for all your books? Nothing. I like your look, actually, it just doesn't scream *Hey! I'm desperate for your attention*. And your hair. I like it. It's nice." He pauses. "Hey. Gotta go. But . . . good luck." He gives me a tight-lipped smile and turns to the door.

"Wait!" I blurt out, because he's about to leave and the fog has finally lifted. "Are you okay?"

He stops and faces me again. "What do you mean?"

I bite my lip. "I heard you—"

"You didn't hear anything." The edge is back in his voice.

"No, I heard you," I insist. "I'm not *judging* you, I just . . . I heard you crying. You sounded extremely sad and I just . . . I wanna know if you're okay."

He inhales and exhales, nostrils flared, slow and deliberate like he's trying to stay calm. But his eyes are piercing, as if by staring at me hard enough, he can make me disappear.

I shake my head, turn to leave, right as the bathroom door flies open and a tall boy with a tilted yellow hat strolls in. "Derek, come on, man. We're . . ." His voice trails off when his eyes fall on me. "What the fuuuu . . . ?"

I'm waiting for Derek to say something, but he looks down, takes off his hat, and runs his hand through his hair. A frivolous waste of time when he could have been explaining things.

His friend stands between us and crosses his arms. His eyes flick back and forth from Derek to me, and he laughs. "Valeria's not gonna like this."

"Not gonna like what?" Derek huffs. "We're not dating anymore. If you could finally get that through your sister's head, I'd be grateful." He starts walking to the door. "Miguel, let's go. Nothing happened here."

His friend grunts. "Be for real, man." Then slowly, a thin smile inches across his lips. He looks at me with an eyebrow raised, a shiny silver hoop pierced through it. "What are you doing in the bathroom? You just wait around for guys or something? Who's next?"

His voice is far away and tinny, like I'm falling, like I'm looking at the bathroom through a tunnel. This is the sinkhole. And Derek's not going to pull me out. He's like stone, his jaw locked shut.

"I thought this was the girls' bathroom," I say, my voice finally resurfacing.

Miguel laughs. "Yeah. Okay." He points to the urinals.

Derek shakes his head. "Come on," he says, and opens the door. "I told you, nothing happened."

His friend follows, glancing back at me one last time, his eyes dancing. "Ho," he says, the word like a sharpened dart that meets its target.

The door closes behind his laughter and I'm left standing alone, screaming at myself for stepping down, for leaving the stall, for trying to help. I press my lips together to keep them from shaking, tell myself to breathe.

My fresh start is gone. I'm right back where I used to be. The bathroom stall. The names and numbers.

This is how a blank slate gets covered with words that can never be erased.

genesis. again.

i am:
whoever you say
i am

the creation
of lesser gods

CHAPTER THREE

Soccer practice ends. The team heads to the locker room, I go to the bike racks. Miguel Montero's eyes are watching me, I can feel it. I throw on my backpack, jump on my bike, and pedal out of the parking lot toward the gravel road.

Miguel's not all bad all the time, but he loves to have fun at other people's expense. So if I don't stick around, they can't give me a hard time about Jae, the girl in the bathroom.

Are you okay?

How is it a perfect stranger seems to care the most?

The sound of crunching rocks beneath my tires is numbing. My mind wanders to—Jesus Christ—the look on Tillman's face when I got home last night.

I rode up to the front yard. He was walking back to his car with the pizza delivery sign on the roof. Mom was following him, and I heard everything she said. I recognized him right away, even in the dim light: his wire-framed glasses, his narrow eyes, his copper-colored hair. I'd known Tillman my whole life, and he'd never looked at me with pity. *He* was the outsider, the one with his nose always in a book, the one always scribbling his mysterious notes. Now he knows my secrets, and he can look at me the same way I look at him.

I ride until mansions become bungalows. Some of them you could say, *I bet a sweet old granny lives there*. But not the other ones. You ride faster past those ones. You wonder what really goes on in those ones.

I roll up to our pink house, where a dark blue pickup truck is parked. My hands form a death grip around the handlebars. It's Peter Manganelli, Mom's boyfriend and all-around douchebag. He doesn't come around much these days because his wife is starting to ask questions.

The gate to the front yard screeches and scrapes the sidewalk. The path is overgrown with grass. I lock my bike to the paint-chipped porch, and when I reach for the front door, it swings open with ease. How many times do I have to tell them to keep it locked? Just a few doors down, sweet old Mr. Jefferson was robbed at gunpoint. He was eating meat pies in his tighty-whities.

Inside, the kitchen linoleum is stained with yellow and brown splotches. A lonely stick of incense on the counter fights to overpower the smell of smoke and booze.

"That you, kid?" an ogre-ish voice calls from the living room over the blaring TV. I don't respond. He'd know it was me if he'd locked the door.

My stomach growls. I open the cereal cupboard and find an industrial-sized canister of garam masala sitting right in front of my box of Coco Rocks. I'm annoyed that Mom would buy any spice at all when she barely cooks anymore—she barely does anything—and I'm annoyed that it's not in the spice cupboard where it belongs. I push it aside and grab my Coco Rocks, and the box feels unbearably light. When I shake it, I'm greeted with the hollow rattle of two or three chocolaty pieces. Peter.

Jerk.

I reach into the fridge for some ginger ale and ease my hunger with large gulps before grabbing my backpack, heading to my room, and slamming the door.

Let there be light. I flick on the switch, and white orbs of light float like ghosts over glow-in-the-dark constellations on the ceiling. A Milky Way mural spans each wall, dark blues and blacks and purples, and stars twinkling in every hue. A giant solar system lamp with round globes arches over my bed. And a spaceship lamp on my desk illuminates the posters behind it: *Star Wars*, *Interstellar*, *Koi . . . Mil Gaya*.

It's a shrine to the cosmos, the closest I might ever get to religion. Maybe it's my attempt at harnessing all the creative energy of the universe.

On my desk sits a box of my half-baked movie scripts and loglines. Screenplays I might write one day. I haven't had any fresh ideas in weeks, and I'm hoping something will come to me.

But what if it doesn't? Maybe I should be like Mom and try different mediums, except not with colors. With words. A short story, maybe?

I toss my bag somewhere and push my chair up beneath the door handle, forming a barricade.

"Derek?" Mom calls from down the hall. She sounds good. Happy. But why can't she be happy when it's just the two of us?

I see her now, all spindly, stumbling a few steps before finding a windy path to my room.

Three tentative knocks sound on the door. "Derek?"

Maybe if I'm quiet she'll forget I'm here.

"Derek?"

"Yeah." My bed frame moans as I sink into it.

"Where were you?"

"Guam."

I could remind her every day for the next year I have practice after school. It wouldn't make a difference. Mom doesn't really care where I am or what I do anymore.

There's silence on the other side. And then she shuffles back to the living room. Hey, at least she put in her best effort, right?

With an hour to kill before my shift at the diner, I reach for my bag and pull out my history book, the only reading assignment for today. I flip it open and try to focus my eyes on the chapter headings, the dates, the pictures that should be telling a story but mean nothing. I can't focus on history when shit is going to hit the fan *today*. Because in this house, happiness never lasts.

Mom used to date this doctor. She wasn't so bad then. She still looked like Mom. Her hair was a long bright auburn. Her face was sharp and stunning. And her eyes weren't sunken and dark-rimmed like they are now. When I was younger, I thought she looked like a princess, but I'd rather kiss a horse's ass than tell her that.

I don't know why she broke up with Dr. Rai, but after him, she brought home Peter the Degenerate. He has the temperament of a constipated gorilla. *Me angry! No poop to sling!*

"What do you see in him, anyway?" I asked in one of our Peter-related tiffs. "Dr. Rai was great. He was normal. He smelled good. He brought you flowers. Remember him?"

"Well, it sounds like you have a crush on Dr. Rai."

"Gross. But see? Peter? You got nothing."

Maybe Mom got rid of Dr. Rai because he made her feel guilty about my lack of Indian culture. "He's lost," he'd said once. "Completely confused. Doesn't know Hindi."

"He's Gujarati," she'd snapped back.

If it was anyone's duty to teach me Gujarati, or Hindi even, it was my dad's. He was, after all, the Indian one. But when it came to his culture, Dad was always too practical to be proud. *This is America*, was his answer to everything. He'd been that way since he and Mom met at Georgetown University, where frat boy Dad downplayed his Indian heritage. To him, India was like a distant relative, one he loved but didn't miss very much. He preferred the version of it that didn't require a plane ticket: frozen samosas popped into the oven, the occasional festival (if Mom dragged us there), or any movie with an A. R. Rahman soundtrack. So without Dad's insistance that I was Indian, I never felt like I was, and *he's Gujarati* never really sunk deep for me.

A hard knock on the door interrupts my thoughts. "I'm out of cigarettes. Run and get me a pack, will ya," Peter says from behind the closed door.

"That's illegal," I say. "I'm not eighteen yet. Plus, homework. You know, *kid* stuff."

There's a THWONK so hard I expect a hairy hand to break through the wall. I jump up to open the door.

The first thing I see is Peter's gorilla chest, the hair smothering a gold chain hanging from his neck. His graying black beard is oiled and man-scaped within an inch of its life. His nose is so delightfully freckled and his eyes so dreamy gray, there must have been a glitch at the hell factory that spawned him.

He's the kind of guy people talk about on the news: *He was such a nice man, I never thought he'd do such a thing.*

Peter drops a bill into my hand and I head outside to Mr. Brown's store a couple of blocks down. On the sign, DISCOUNT CORNR SHOP has no *e*. Everyone complains about it, says the sign makes the whole neighborhood look bad. Have they *seen* the neighborhood?

I walk in and Mr. Brown says, "Derek, Derek, Derek," with a cigar dangling out of the corner of this mouth. Guy always says my name three times, and he always has a cigar in his mouth like it's been surgically attached.

"Hey, Mr. Brown." I wave and head down the aisles. I grab a pack of ginger ale, some Coco Rocks, and a couple of TV dinners and diet sodas for Mom.

I drop the items on the counter, scoot my fake ID toward him, and point to Peter's favorite brand. "Two," I say.

Mr. Brown gives me a look.

"For my mom's boyfriend," I explain.

"No can do, Derek."

"Hey, Mr. Brown. This guy has, like, giant hands. And he's just looking for a reason. You know what I mean?"

His brown eyes stare at me unblinking, and then he snatches his cigar and shakes it at me like a thick finger. "Now, don't you come asking me again," he says, before popping the cigar back in his mouth and turning to unlock the glass case. "Make me lose my damn store."

As soon as I step outside, I crumple the receipt and shoot a three-pointer into a trash can. I glance down the street to the house and figure I have five minutes before Peter loses his shit.

Somewhere a dog is barking and a woman's shrill voice yells, "Minnie! Quiet!" A car drives past, blaring country music from behind tinted windows.

The houses on this street are almost identical. They might be different colors, but they're all really the same. Dusty lawns scattered with toys or broken furniture, screen doors that couldn't keep an insect out, let alone a human. There is one exception, though: Miss Carol's baby-blue house. She spends most of her time outside, planting flowers, trimming bushes, and cleaning windows. It's not enough to make the street look better, but I appreciate the effort.

I open one of the cigarette packs and pull out a lighter from my pocket. As I light up, I suddenly remember me and Dad on the veranda of the old house, how he passed a cigarette to me and watched as I inhaled and choked. His version of a PSA to never pick up the habit. He laughed and kissed my hair, which was dark and wavy like his.

Dad was never close to his parents, so he overcompensated with me. Presents on every occasion, including Bs on my report card, and an embarrassing shower of kisses. I secretly loved it. He was like my best friend. If best friends kissed your forehead and called you *beautiful boy*.

I imagine him watching me now, and I grind the cigarette into the concrete. *I'll stop*, I promise him. *At least I'm not vaping like all the other kids. You can't quit a habit when it's flavored Berry-gasmic Explosion.*

Bullshit, Dad says.

Back at the house, I drop the spare change into Peter's Godzilla-sized hand.

"Where's the receipt?" he asks.

"I tossed it." I want to say something snarky about a delivery fee, about him being stupid enough to send me out with his money, but I don't. I turn into my room and barricade the door.

The TV blares. Cops? Could he be any more predictable? I grab my phone and turn on a playlist. I've never been good at studying with music on, but I try anyway. For the next ten minutes, I read, not remembering the pages I just read. Finally, I turn off the music and toss my phone across the bed.

I open up my laptop and search through my movies for something mindless. I settle for *Koi . . . Mil Gaya*, because it's good in a cringy way and I'm feeling nostalgic. In the movie, a little blue alien named Jadoo heals a brain-damaged kid who goes on to have special powers. And of course, it's full of musical numbers and hip-hop dancing. Amazing.

But right before the first song, complete with a dancing-in-the-rain motif, the TV quiets and voices drift in from the living room. I close my laptop and rest my head beside it, staring at the ceiling. "Ladies and gentlemen," I whisper to the sticker constellation above me. "The show has just begun."

They're talking about the three-foot glass vase Mom painted. At the bottom are baby birds that slowly transition up the side until they're adult birds in flight. It's the only thing in the house that looks expensive. When I told Mom how much I liked it, she said, "It's yours."

"That's something else, Nancy," Peter says. "That's really something else. You got some real talent in those hands of yours. Never seen anything like it. Look at how the light hits the little bird there."

I can almost feel Mom's pride swelling from behind the door, and she says something I can't hear.

Peter's quiet too. I imagine him taking a drag on his cigarette. His sparkling gray eyes becoming storm clouds. And then all I hear is Peter's voice changing and changing some more.

. . . think I'm gonna give you studio rent? . . . Becca's watching the bank account like a hawk . . . nickel I spend, she's asking me why . . . probably your fault anyway . . . hand's shaking . . . hold a goddamn paintbrush . . . losing too much weight, told you that already . . . the haircut? Grow it out like you had it when I met you.

All the air's sucked out of me and I can't breathe.

Mom's yelling now, "You have no idea how much pain I'm in!"

"Oh, give me a break," Peter scoffs, and I know the fuse has been lit.

Mom starts screaming about Peter bringing alcohol into her house. I clench at Peter calling Mom a bitch, and wince at the loud crash, the sound of birds shattering into pieces.

Then silence. Even the silence is deafening.

I jump at the footsteps thundering past my room and out the front door. The door slams, and the soccer trophies on my desk tremble. Seconds later I hear the burbling engine of Peter's pickup disappearing down the street.

I pull the chair away from the door. "Mom?" I run to the living room and she's on her knees, picking up shattered pieces of the vase from the floor. There's a hole in the wall and glass scattered on the orange floral sofa below it.

Mom doesn't look at me, so I kneel beside her and turn her face, my heart beating hard in my chest.

"He didn't hit me," she says in that way, like Peter never would.

He wanted to.

"I got it," I tell her. She dumps the broken glass into my hands and kisses my forehead before shuffling off to the kitchen.

I pick up one of the larger pieces of glass with a whooping crane still intact, its wings arched in flight. I place the crane on the old splintered coffee table and wonder why he had to break the only beautiful thing we had.

I have a single thought, on repeat. *Bring Dad back. Bring Dad back. Bring Dad back.*

A new logline comes to me. I try not to forget it. I hold it as carefully as I'm holding the glass.

Logline #134: When kindhearted Nita lets loose a caged bird on the planet of Peril, bad luck falls upon her family.

Are you okay?

Jae. Her voice hovers in the silence as I drop the broken birds into the trash can. A glass splinter digs into my hand and leaves a small, swelling red mark when I pull it out.

Are you okay?

I look up at the ticking clock on the kitchen wall. I can't be late for my two-hour shift at the diner.

Are you okay?

I rip off my jersey and jump into the shower and try not to think about her dark eyes shining like glass. I try not to think about the dimples that appear like magic when she talks. I wonder if I could ever make her smile and how deep her dimples would get. I wonder what would happen if I touched her, or if I ever should.

Maybe she'd break like everything else.

CHAPTER FOUR

Jae

I never should have left the bathroom stall.

His eyes feel like black water. Like something to sink into. To lose your breath for.

There's more than one way a body can drown.

The first time it happened was the summer after Dad left, on a weekend with no school and no money for a babysitter. Mom took me along to old Mrs. Higgins's house, which sat up on a hill at the end of a cul-de-sac where Confederate flags fluttered proudly from front porches. The house was so big I was shocked to see Mrs. Higgins's small, bent frame standing in the front door, wrinkles snaking through white skin. A taller woman with a stern face, Mrs. Higgins's daughter, came and stood behind her.

Mom and I made our way up the winding driveway, and it seemed like the steps to the front door went on forever. Inside, I ran my curious fingers along every shiny surface, along crystal vases and marble counters, shiny wooden seats and gold-framed mirrors, until Mom finally grabbed my arm and dragged me to the backyard, where she dropped me like an unwanted package.

"Just sit over there and don't move," she said, pointing to a table underneath an arching peach umbrella.

As I made my way across the yard, she closed the screen door and the voices inside floated toward me.

The younger Higgins said in a slow and careful drawl, "I'll be here on the weekends to watch her, but we need you here every night from Sunday to Friday, without exception. I live hours away, you know, and I can't just drop by if you decide not to show up for work."

It was a miracle that Mom got the job considering what happened later that afternoon. Maybe the Higginses felt sorry for her.

I turned away from the voices coming from inside the house and looked down at the grass beneath the table. The brightest green I'd ever seen. Full like a carpet, with no broken glass or plastic littered around. I pulled my feet out of my shoes, stepped out from under the umbrella and into the sun.

I kept walking, feeling the different textures beneath my feet, until I stepped onto the smooth stone pathway that led to the pool.

I stood at the edge of the water, ripples whispering over smooth glass. A small seven-year-old stared back. Dark, thick lips, quiet eyes. Two braids rested at the collarbone with purple balls holding the ends together. I must not be pretty, I thought, if Dad could leave my pictures and leave me.

As I watched the water, I wanted nothing more than to be someone else, something else. Even a fish, like the one Dad had mounted up on the wall. He loved that fish more than anything, couldn't leave it behind. I imagined myself with skin that glistened in the light. Silver. Feet that wiggled and propelled me through water so fast he'd have to use all his strength to catch me. I touched the surface of the water with my toe, and the water changed shape and I disappeared. And when it settled again, smooth like glass, there I was. I waved my toe and erased my reflection. And then suddenly, like I really had become a fish, I plunged in.

Water and time slipped cold through my fingers. I begged and I couldn't hold them. There were fleeting moments of a captured breath, a vicious, hungry breath. And then it all slipped, and I disappeared, blackness surrounding blackness.

I woke to the sound of beeping machines in the hospital, to Mom frowning with her eyes wet and bright and red. "I told you not to leave the table."

The second time I drowned was after Austin Green leaned against my locker and said, "Hey, let me take you out." He was the tall basketball player with hair and eyes that said he was more than just Black. Everyone thought he was something special. And anyone he liked became something too. The whole world tried to tell me I was beautiful. But when Austin said it, I heard it. He caressed me with words I always wanted to be true.

He took me everywhere. To the movies, where he held my hand and whispered in my ear. To the ice cream parlor, where he scooped minty-chocolaty spoonfuls into my mouth. To his house, where I learned how real another person's skin could feel beneath my fingers. I learned how a body could scream without making a sound. Clenched thighs. Clenched breath.

But the day he stood with his friends and laughed, his eyes dancing, his lips saying, "It was only a dare," I found everything beautiful about me gone.

I realized I was drowning when I found myself staring at a bottle of Mom's painkillers in the cabinet. I remembered the blackness surrounding blackness. The beautiful quiet. I wondered if I should let myself sink deeper, if I should come up for air at all.

I emptied the pills into my hand and busied my mind with counting them, trying to keep my hands from shaking. I counted more pills than good memories. More pills than years with Dad. More pills than people who would listen.

My phone rang and I closed my eyes to it. If I could just remember what it felt like to be gone, maybe I could do it. Be gone. Quiet.

There was silence again, and I wondered who had called. Who was on the other line waiting for me to pick up? What would they think if they could see me right now, with a bottle emptied out in my hand?

Each second in silence made me more afraid, like that moment before you step off the edge and free-fall.

The phone rang again, and this time it didn't stop.

Leave me alone, I whispered, hoping for silence that wouldn't come.

I made my way to my room, the pills still clutched in my fingers.

"What?" I asked, pressing the receiver to my ear. "What do you want?" I didn't know I was crying until I heard it in my voice.

"What do you mean, *what*?" Mom barked on the other end. "Is that how you answer the phone? What is wrong with you?"

"Nothing, Mom."

"Doesn't sound like nothing to me. Are you okay?"

I wiped my runny nose on my sleeve. For some reason, I had at that moment the distinct memory of her standing over a pot of newly planted portulacas that had quickly drooped and died. She was heartbroken. *What did I do wrong?* she asked herself as she yanked the dead stems out of the pot. *I must have done* something *wrong.*

I heard Mom's sigh on the other end. "I'm using the hospital phone right now, can't find my purse. Don't know if somebody took it or what. But I might need you to let me in when I get home. You hear me, Jae?"

"Okay."

She hung up the phone, and I stood at the door, waiting until she knocked.

I stayed because she needed me.

But Mom's not here now. I only have myself and this second chance. And that might be gone now too.

So I never should have left the bathroom stall.

Those dark eyes. Those pretty eyes.

thoseeyescould d r a g m e

u

n

d e

r

CHAPTER FIVE

My shift is nearly over. I'm putting a stack of paper napkins in the cupboard for my boss, Gina. I'm a whole foot taller than her, even with her piled-high Dolly Parton curls. My phone buzzes.

hey, at ur house, u home?

I feel like I'm on one of those drop-of-doom rides at the theme park. I'm strapped in, and my lunch just might come through my nose.

Miguel doesn't know where I live. But if he's at my house, that means I'm screwed. "Shit." I stare at my phone screen. "*Shit.*"

Gina looks up. She's wiping tables down, singing Aretha Franklin like she's a paid background vocalist. Without missing a lyric, she reprimands me with her blue eyes caked in layers of mascara.

coming now don't go in, I text back.

Then I apologize to Gina and I'm out the door by the time she yells something back. Within seconds I'm blazing down the street on my bike like it's the Batmobile. Then I'm in my old neighborhood, a place I never go unless I'm feeling morose. It's the picture-perfect world Mom and I left behind months ago.

On the day we moved, summer was painfully bright. We sat in the U-Haul, and shouts of *Cannonball!* and splashes from the neighbor's pool filtered through the windows. I would miss the ease of summer nights here, the stream of glitter sprinkling the ocean from shore to sun. Boats cutting through the shimmery trail, carrying girls and fun and laughter. As we pulled the U-Haul out of our street, the palm trees fanned the houses—three and four stories high—like they were regal. Then we drove away and parked the van in front of a pink bungalow that was nice enough, but would always be empty.

The problem now is, I haven't told the guys we moved yet.

I see Henry Lee's hair first. It's like an upscale landscaping in itself: jet-black, gelled into a Mohawk, and shaved on one side. Sometimes he sprays color on the tips. Freshman year, he had wavy hair with bangs and looked like a model. Sophomore year, he buzzed it short and bleached it blond. And now it's junior year and a whole different Henry.

When I pull up, neither he nor Miguel says anything. They're staring at my head.

"Shit," I say again.

"What's with the origami hat?" Henry asks.

"And the dumb vest." Miguel points at my chest like it's covered in snot.

I swing off my bike and lean it against the iron gate. "It's called work," I say, with the greatest nonchalance I can muster. "Wouldn't hurt you guys to get a job too."

"Damn. You sound like my mom," Henry says. "*You need a job, Henry! You don't know the value of money, Henry!*"

"Why get a job if you're not, like . . . poor?" Miguel asks.

Poor. The word sits on his tongue like a spoonful of sewer sludge sprinkled with roach juice and beetle dung. I want to punch him.

"Guys, it's no big deal," I say. "Just trying to learn a little responsibility. Wouldn't kill you to do the same."

"Mm, I disagree," Miguel says.

A bad day for the guys is being grounded from yacht privileges. They have no idea things are different for me now.

Dad was always cool about paying for our hangouts and parties, even taking Miguel's family with us on a cruise. So they're not going to understand how bad things are now. I can't tell them that Mom financially destroyed us, and that without my new job, I wouldn't have any spending money, which includes school lunches. And more importantly, I wouldn't have enough money to apply for college without a fee waiver. They wouldn't understand. Or worse yet, maybe they would, and they'd stop hanging out with me.

Bottom line is, Miguel and Henry are all I have left from Before. They're my only anchor to the past where I wish I could have stayed.

I look toward the house, and I can almost see our ghosts through the walls: me and Miguel and Valeria, running down the basement steps to play foosball; Mom and Dad, dancing barefoot on the kitchen tiles, blasting Bon Jovi; birthday hats; barbecues; board games; family dinners. Maybe we left pieces of ourselves in there. A lost game token down the vent, a forgotten box in the attic. That potted vine that hung in the kitchen that Mom forgot to take. Maybe we're still in there.

The driveway is empty now, the curtains drawn. I'm praying for the front door to stay closed, for whoever lives there now to not be home.

"Why are you here?" I ask the guys. "I told you already. Mom doesn't want anyone over."

"'Cause she's grieving? It's been two years, man," Miguel says.

"So what? Grief isn't linear."

"Yo. Whatever. Just change out of those ridiculous clothes. McAllister found the keys to his dad's bike. We're gonna take it for a spin."

On any other day I would have laughed at how dumb Brody McAllister's dad was, but I'm feeling kind of dumb myself. Miguel and Henry are eyeing me, waiting.

"I can change later," I say, walking toward Henry's Benz parked at the curb.

"Ho-ho, no way!" Henry waves his hands in objection. "You're gonna scare away all the chicks. Just go change."

"Don't feel like it."

"Hey, you wanna hang or not?" Miguel adjusts his hat over his shiny eyebrow ring. "Seriously, you look fucking ridiculous."

I look at the house again. Did I see a shadow move inside?

"I'll just change here," I say, pulling my shirt out of my backpack.

"How about those?" Henry points at my creased white pants. "No offense, but I don't wanna see your balls. Just change inside, dude. Is there something you're not telling us? What's the problem?"

"Fine. Fine." Sighing, I sling the bag over my shoulders. "Stay here."

I push the wrought iron gate. Locked, of course. I hoist myself up onto one of the ornate spirals and pull myself over, then drop to the ground, feeling a slight tweak in my ankle, and bend down to rub the pain.

"Why didn't you just use the code, genius?" Miguel asks.

"If I knew the code, I would have used the code. Genius," I say. "Mom changed it. Changes it all the time and forgets to tell me. I told you. She's not well."

I shake out the pain and make my way up the stone driveway, past the gushing fountain, a wave of emotions riding me.

I miss this house. I miss everything about it, how it used to be. The curtains are a powdery blue now. Ours were striped gray and white. The rug used to say PEACE, not HOME SWEET HOME. I look at the drawn curtains before picking up the rug where the spare key used to be. It's gone. Of course it is. I look over my shoulders at the guys. Henry is peering through the gate like a jailed man looking to freedom.

"Come on!" he yells.

I press a finger against my lip and make a sign like Mom's sleeping. Then I make a last Hail Mary and wiggle the front door latch, push and pull fast, hoping the people who live here now put off fixing the door like we did. I push and pull again. Again. And finally, the front door swings open.

I'm in.

CHAPTER SIX

Jae

It's first period English and the teacher, Mrs. Aldana, is pacing the front of the room. Her long green skirt flows around her like waves.

"Twain began writing the manuscript in 1876," she says. "What was significant about writing *Huckleberry Finn* during that time?"

She speaks in that accent of hers—a confection of Spanish and Quebec French—that some of the boys make fun of when she's not in earshot. But I think it's beautiful. Her lips are bright red; her hair tumbles in dark curls over her shoulders; and she drapes herself in scarves despite the muggy Floridian heat. She looks like a statue that belongs on the helm of a great ship, wind-blown, sun-kissed. With her talkative hands and her pacing and her fast speech, she holds everyone's attention.

Except for me. My mind is an unleashed thing that wanders, and soon I've lost myself in a field of memories and *what-ifs*, plucking regrets like flowers. Today I see Mom's dimply smile as my tiny hands slap a mound of dough, sending flour like smoke into the air. I see Dad sitting under the dim kitchen light with his notebook, his hand scribbling furiously, turning poetic phrases like the easy turn of a leaf. I see Austin with his honey-colored eyes that are anything but sweet, and I remember the way he touched me and made my skin feel new and beautiful. I see a small office with red plastic chairs and a woman telling me to raise my right hand and make promises I can't understand.

"Jae Afenyo?"

My eyes refocus on Mrs. Aldana's face.

"Did you hear the question?" she asks, her eyes bubbling with energy.

I did hear the question. Didn't I?

The students sitting in the front rows swivel their necks around to stare at me. A hundred pairs of eyes. I feel like a circus animal expected to perform an amazing trick, but I don't know what it is.

The girl behind me whispers, "Is that her?" And I remember seeing her when I sat down, a dark-haired beauty who could play Selena Gomez in any biopic. I think her name was Valeria. But the question, *Is that her*, derails me.

How does she know me?

"I'm sorry. Could you please repeat the question?" I ask Mrs. Aldana.

Her smile is patient. "Of course. I asked about the significance of Twain writing the novel in 1876."

"Um . . ." I swallow. I know this. I've not only read *Huckleberry Finn*, but all of Twain's books.

But the weight of a thousand stares could make someone forget their own name. In my old school, I wasn't the only brown face in class. There was someone to share the embarrassment with when the class talked about race. But here, it's just me, pretending to feel just fine talking about Huck and the runaway slave Jim while curious eyes watch me every time someone says *N-word*. I wonder if the white kids feel heavy too, or if the weight of it is all on me.

I hear a voice to my right whisper, "Reconstruction."

Suddenly, my brain starts working again. I clear my throat. "Twain was writing during the Reconstruction period, just a decade after the end of the Civil War. There was still so much racism and terrorism then, and his own views on slavery had changed over the years. So maybe he was exploring the concept of freedom and what it meant to that society."

Mrs. Aldana nods and smiles. She turns to write on the board. "Any other comments?" she asks the rest of the class.

I turn to my right to look at the boy who whispered to me. His shoulder-length blond hair is pulled into a ponytail.

"Nice answer," he whispers.

I give a slight smile and try to refocus on Mrs. Aldana. But out of the corner of my eye, I see a boy with a tall Mohawk shaved on one side staring at me. I turn my head to look at him. He wiggles his eyebrows, and his eyes twinkle as if he finds me amusing. The way he's looking at me reminds me of the other boy in the bathroom yesterday with his yellow hat and eyebrow ring. Miguel, was it? I quickly look away and stare down at the book cover, at Huckleberry Finn and Jim floating away on the Mississippi.

Soon the bell rings. I shoot up, eager to pack my books and run off to second period. Eager to get away from the boy who seems to know something about me.

"You didn't need my help," the blond boy says. His words come out in a thick English accent that I didn't notice before. He's putting his reading book in his backpack.

"She caught me off guard," I explain.

"Well, Mark Twain is one of my favorite writers. I'm quite a fan of witty abolitionists. Did you know he also wrote under the names Josh and Thomas Jefferson Snodgrass?" He smiles and points to my white canvas bag, hanging on the arm of my chair, with I LOVE LUCILLE written in fluid, romantic letters. "And you're a fan of Lucille Ball."

I turn the bag over to the cartoon drawing of a brown-skinned, halo-haired woman. "Lucille Clifton. She's one of my favorite poets."

"You like poetry." His eyebrows spring up and he reaches across the aisle for a handshake. "I'm William Shakespeare Huntington."

"Shakespeare?"

"Not as good as Thomas Jefferson Snodgrass, but it is my real name."

"I'm Janelle Aƒenyo. Everyone calls me Jae."

"So, Jae," William says in a way that makes me feel like he knows me already. The room has cleared out by now and we start walking through the rows of empty seats toward the door. "What are you doing after school today?" He stops and looks at me with intent blue eyes.

"Um . . ." I shrug.

"Well, then, I'd like to formally invite you to our first club meeting," he says, pulling out a yellow piece of paper from his bag and placing it in my hand. "It would be good for you to have some camaraderie. Even Hemingway had friends. Think about it, Jae." He pats my shoulder and heads into the hallway.

I glance quickly at the paper, slide it into my bag, and make my way to my locker. Maybe this is just what I need. A club. A group of built-in friends. Like a college sorority for readers. I could get along with people like that.

Luckily, my locker is right outside the English classroom, which means it's not one of the plain yellow ones. It's painted like the spine of a book cover. Mine is *Everything I Never Told You*, smack between *The Hate U Give* and *The Kite Runner*. It's strange that these painted lockers can make me sigh in relief, make me feel a little more like myself.

As I try to remember my locker combination, I hear laughter behind me. I look over my shoulder and my heart nearly falls out of my chest.

There he is.

Miguel, with his yellow hat tipped to the side. And the same boy with the Mohawk who was watching me in class. And Derek.

He's not laughing like Miguel, but he doesn't look happy to see me, either. Gone is the look of calm and quiet brooding. His arms are crossed over his chest and he looks like he'd rather be anywhere else.

I fumble with my lock, hitting the wrong numbers each time, telling myself to breathe easy. After a few attempts, I finally get the combination right and open the door, and it knocks the bag off my shoulder.

Laughter.

I bend over to pick it up.

More laughter.

"Come on, guys," I hear Derek say.

I breathe through the heat burning my face. What exactly are they laughing at?

I see Austin's face flash before my eyes and that familiar wave of panic makes me grab my stomach. The sinking feeling. I'm washed in a flood of memories, from different times, different spaces.

You'll never know what this means to us.

Austin, what's going on?

Come on, it was all a joke. You had to know it was all a joke.

You made the right choice, Janelle.

Raise your right hand for me.

When the voices quiet down, the wave of panic recedes. I'm standing in front of the lockers again. I can feel the boys still watching me and I avoid looking over my shoulder. I look down at a piece of paper that floated to the ground when I opened my locker door. I don't have to pick it up to see what it says. In large block letters are the words: *MEET ME IN STALL 3*. I look up. Miguel breaks out into uncontrollable laughter and the boy in the Mohawk tries to hide his smile. Derek's face is frozen like stone.

I turn away, pretending to look for a textbook, and blink away tears. I let my own words drown out the noise outside me.

LightShadowRainSunBreatheDeepCarryOnLightShadowRainSun-BreatheDeepCarryOn.

My breath begins to slow down. My heart begins to calm.

Light, shadow, rain, sun. Breathe deep. Carry on.

Light, shadow, rain, sun.

Breathe deep.

Carry on.

CHAPTER SEVEN

Derek

It's after lunch. The junior counselor, Mr. Corrigan, calls me to his office. He's sitting at his desk in front of a long window. Half-closed blinds let the sun slip through. Outside, the gravel road is laid out like a dark ribbon and shadowed by trees. Mr. Corrigan leans across his desk and folds his hands on the shiny mahogany. It's hard not to notice the shape of his head, how it's as close to a perfect sphere as humanly possible, with round glasses perched in front of his eyes to make things worse.

I collapse into a cushioned chair across from him just as he says, "You were in my office four times last semester. Are you trying to break that record? Getting a head start?" He sighs. "It's the second day of school, Derek. You shouldn't be here already."

Yeah? Whose fault is that? I want to ask. But I settle for something less snarky. "I'm not too pleased about that either, Mr. Corrigan." Between the two of us, I'm more tired of seeing him than he is of seeing me, I'm sure of it.

He sits back in his seat and crosses his arms over his chest. His brown eyes pierce mine. He doesn't say a word and neither do I. He's waiting. Waiting to see if I'll get uncomfortable and start talking. So I turn away and scan the titles on his bookshelf. *Helping the Struggling Adolescent. Teens in Therapy. The 7 Habits of Highly Effective Teens.* I try not to snicker, but the idea that these books could fix any of my problems is comical. I'm not the one who caused them.

The second hand on the wall clock is gliding around the circular face. Once. Twice. Three times. I think Mr. Corrigan's face would make a nice wall clock. I think the guys would appreciate that thought.

Finally, I sigh. "Okay. You win. Why am I here?"

"You don't know?"

I shrug. "Because you like me?"

Without taking his eyes off mine, he grabs a nearby pen and taps it against the desk. "We have reason to believe you broke into the house of one of the faculty yesterday evening."

I lean forward. "Faculty?"

"A teacher," he says, almost smug.

"A *teacher*?" I'm squeezing the life out of the cigarette box in my pocket.

He leans far back in his seat and it creaks beneath his weight. "That's a serious crime. Worse than anything you've done already."

By crimes, he means silly pranks. Like stringing the school mascot, Oluf the Wizard, up on the flagpole with a trail of condoms dangling behind him. Breaking into a teacher's house wasn't that. I was between a rock and a hard place, and it's not like I stole anything. I changed my clothes and ran out as soon as I heard footsteps upstairs. The most import thing is the guys still think I live there.

"How can you be so sure it was me?" I ask.

"I'm not going to indulge you, Mr. Patel. You know you did it, I know you did it, and most importantly," he says, leaning over the desk again, "the video cameras on Mrs. Aldana's property know you did it."

Dammit.

Just then the door opens. I turn to see a tall, thin woman walk in and close the door behind her. She's wearing a skirt the color of a Christmas tree. "Helluuu, Mr. Corrigan," she sings with a bright smile. She lowers herself into the seat next to me and a waft of air like fresh rain envelops the room.

"You must be Derek," she says with one hand on her chest, the other extended, like she's greeting a dignitary. "I recognize you from the security footage."

Uneasy, I shake her hand, absolutely sure she has some loose screws somewhere.

"So, what did I miss?" she asks, almost cheerfully.

"I was just telling Derek about the video cameras."

I wince again, kicking myself. I forgot about the cameras because we never used them. Mom stopped paying the security service long ago.

"I would never have known it was you," she says, patting my knee. "By the time I made it down the hall, you were already running out the door. My husband thought you might be a student, and the school was happy to check the video for me."

Mr. Corrigan nods. "Now. What do we do with you?" he asks me.

I shrug. A part of me doesn't really care.

"My door is always open if you need to talk," he says. "I keep telling you that, but you never come. Until you get in trouble, that is."

I wouldn't come at all if he didn't summon me like a peasant.

There's a knock on the door.

"Come in, Mrs. Patel," Mr. Corrigan says, and my heart drops.

Mom?

She opens the door too quickly and almost falls through. Her face is sweaty, her eyes bloodshot, and her short hair sticks to the moisture on her forehead.

"Hello," she says. "Sorry to be so late. I had to rush here from the art studio. Short notice, you know." She nearly falls into one of the chairs.

I lower my head. She's wearing slacks that are way too baggy on her now, and her white blouse is wrinkled, with a yellow stain on the shoulder.

She doesn't ease into the tirade. "What were you *thinking*, Derek? Breaking into a teacher's house? I don't know what to do with you. What do I do?"

I wash my hands over my face and let out a loud groan. "Why does everyone ask me that? You're the adults here, aren't you?"

She looks from Mr. Corrigan to Mrs. Aldana. "I'm doing my best," she says to them, and her voice catches in her throat. "I didn't raise him to be this way. I taught him to ask questions, but never to be disrespectful. He was a good boy. The sweetest thing."

"Oh, I think he still is," Mrs. Aldana interjects. She's beaming at me.

I laugh involuntarily. "How do you know?" I'm surprised by the meanness in my voice, how it pops up when I least expect it.

"I've learned to trust what I feel about people." She pauses and presses her bright red lips together, as if feeling for the right words. "And Derek. You were in a hurry, weren't you? You left a note anyway. I think that makes you a good person."

I blink. Look down.

"I believe you need a place to unleash your thoughts. An outlet," she continues.

"I'm not doing counseling," I say quickly. I look at Mr. Corrigan with the hardest glare I can muster. "I'll save you the time. *Derek, how does that make you feel?* Like shit, Mr. Corrigan. I always feel like shit."

"Derek!" Mom whisper-yells. She hates hearing me curse, even though she and Peter curse like teen gamers when they fight. God forbid if I do it. Typical adult hypocrisy.

Mom suddenly clamps her mouth shut and the muscles around her eyes tense. She leans forward and presses her hand against her temple.

"Are you okay, Mrs. Patel?" Mr. Corrigan asks.

"Just a headache," she says, her voice straining. "It's what happens when you have a son who causes so much trouble. Don't worry, it will pass."

"That headache's not my fault," I mutter.

"You be quiet," Mom snaps.

Mrs. Aldana leans over to put a gentle hand on Mom's shoulder. "I can get you some Tylenol from the office."

Mom smiles through her pain. "Thank you. I have my meds at home. Just as soon as we're done here . . ."

"Sure! Let's conclude this matter so you can get going," Mrs. Aldana says. "Derek, the reason we brought you here is to help you." She's looking me straight in the eyes. "You're full of potential, I can see it."

"It's just gas," I say. God, why is she being so nice at a time like this? And why does it feel like she can see me—really see me? It makes me want to run for the hills.

Mr. Corrigan ignores my quip. "We wouldn't be helping you if we let this go unchecked," he says.

"Then why don't you just have me arrested?"

Mrs. Aldana finally stops smiling. She frowns like I've said something ridiculous. "You don't need to be locked up, you need to be set free."

I clamp my mouth shut to hold in the laughter, but it shoots out in a blaze of salivary glory. I wipe my mouth with my sleeve. Can they blame me? I mean, lady, come on.

Mrs. Aldana continues. "I'm mentoring the poetry club this year. We'll be hosting a free verse poetry reading—"

"Free what?"

"Free verse poetry. I think—*we* think it would be a good idea for you to join the club this semester. The other option, Derek, is community service."

"I'd rather play leapfrog with unicorns."

"You'll need to go to the office after school today and sign up for one or the other. Leapfrog is not an option."

In a mere second, my friends' faces flash before my eyes. A poetry club? Community service? Either way, they'll never let me live this down. I'll be the laughingstock of the soccer team. I'll never get any girls ever again.

"I can't," I say. "I have soccer practice every day after school, remember? I'm the best player on the team. Can't miss it."

"We've already talked to the coach and he believes, as we do," says Mrs. Aldana, "that you could stand to miss practice on Tuesdays."

"Every Tuesday?" My jaw drops open on its hinge. I'm swimming for excuses, anything to get me out of this. *It was just a joke, a stupid prank gone wrong. And I left a note! FIX THE STRIKE PLATE. Doesn't that count for anything? There's no reason to sentence me to social purgatory.*

After what seems like hours of trying to find the right words, only one comes to mind.

"Fuck."

☽

I follow Mom out to the parking lot, staring at the hair plastered against her neck.

"Mrs. Aldana's kinda weird, huh?" I say to her back. "I can see the headlines now: Teacher disappears teen poets." My laugh is awkward, but Mom's not listening anyway. She's walking fast toward the farthest end of the lot, where Peter's blue truck is parked. There's movement inside.

"You guys made up already?" I ask. Depending on how big their fights get, they can stop talking for weeks. But Mom's car is at the shop after she hit a tree, and it doesn't look like she'll be getting it back anytime soon. Not if she keeps losing art students. Looks like she'd rather make up with Peter than ask someone else for a ride.

"That's none of your business," she says, walking faster. "You need to think about your own life. Before you end up in jail."

I stop walking, which makes her stop. She turns to face me and I stuff my hands in my pockets. I'm so used to seeing distaste in her eyes, it shouldn't bother me anymore, but it still makes me want to shrink till I'm invisible. And that makes me want to fight back, because who is she to make me feel so small?

"What, Mom? You forgive Peter for being a dick all the time. But you can't give your own kid a break."

"I don't know what you have against Peter, but I wish you'd just let it go."

I want to scream. *Bring Dad back. Bring Dad back.* It feels like a million waves are crashing in my head and all I can do to quiet the noise is close my eyes and breathe deep and grit my teeth. When I open my eyes again, Mom is walking away.

"Do you even care about me?" I ask. I don't mean for it to come out this way, like I'm fourteen and scared again.

"Of course I care," she says, frowning.

"As much as you care about Peter? And your pain meds?"

Mom's face is bright red now, and her lips are pressed into a tight line like she's trying to keep herself from blowing up. But I don't care. I'm not the one who smashed her vase into a thousand pieces. Maybe I'm a stupid kid and I do stupid things, but at least I don't try to hurt the people I love.

"You believe in past lives? Rebirth, right? Maybe in your next life, you'll love your son, too." I swallow a lump in my throat, turn away, and pull a cigarette out of my pocket. *Sorry, Dad.*

Mom calls my name as I walk past the school doors toward the grove. "Derek, where are you going? Don't play the martyr now. Get back to class."

I finally stop and look at her. Her hand is holding her purse strap in place on her shoulder. Even from where I'm standing, I can see her hand shake.

"I'm not the one who broke your vase," I say. I leave her in the lot and walk into the quiet woods.

When I'm in the thick of it, I sit on a tree stump and rest my elbows on my knees. Let my eyes fall to the space between my feet. Somewhere there's an open classroom window. The sound of laughter filters through. I try to remember the last time I felt that good.

☽

The school's main office looks much nicer than any high school should. It's dimly lit, with light fixtures installed in the dark wood panels along the walls. On a table is a small fountain, and the sound of trickling water interrupts the silence. One of the student volunteers, a senior, is sitting behind the secretary's desk.

"Hey, Derek," she says as I walk in.

I almost stop in my tracks. Should I know her? Her strawberry-blond hair falls around her shoulders and she has a light spattering of freckles on her nose. There aren't many girls around here that look like that.

"Uh . . ." I squint, searching through my memory bank for her name.

"Sarah?" Her upper lip curls up, revealing teeth. "You don't remember me?"

"I, uh . . . I wish I could say I do."

"You kissed me at Miguel's party? Your freshman year?"

I'm starting to notice that every statement she makes rises like a question. "Hm." I don't remember her or her lips. I did a lot of kissing my freshman year. Including with Valeria, which, in hindsight, was a mistake. It's hard to shake her off once she sinks her teeth into you.

Sarah drops her head to leaf through an open notebook. After she's made a point of ignoring me, she snaps, "Can I help you?"

"Yeah, I need to sign up for community service. Or a poetry club."

"I hope you don't think I'm going to decide for you."

"Well, do they have information sheets or something?"

She riffles through a large accordion folder sitting on the desk and pulls out a few flyers. "This is the sign-up sheet for the Green Planet Club."

"You mean Green Earth?"

"*Nooo?* This is the Green *Planet* Club. They do a lot of fundraisers for environmental causes, but mostly they pick up trash on the beach or along Atlantic Avenue."

I clench my teeth. If I have to do something wholesome with my time, I'd prefer it not to be so public. "Do they wear orange jumpsuits, too?"

Sarah rolls her eyes. "Yes or no?"

"Any other options?"

"Tutoring at the local church."

"How far is it?"

"Probably fifteen minutes."

"By car?"

"Of course."

I sigh. Right now, the best option seems to be the poetry club. At least I could get away with no one finding out. The meetings would be in one of the classrooms. I could slip in and out without anyone knowing. "How about the poetry club?"

She slaps a paper in front of me. On the top is scrawled *The Free Verse Society*, and there are two names on the list. William Huntington. Jae Afenyo.

"Wait." I hold up the sheet and point at the neat cursive at the bottom. "This girl. Did you see her?"

"Um . . . yeah?"

"She's this high?" I put my hand at chest level. "Long hair? Super cute?"

Sarah sits back and frowns again. “Black. She’s Black.”

I grab the pen on the desk and scribble my name on the bottom, right beneath Jae’s name. “Hey, there’s no room number here.”

“They meet in the grove?”

“The grove?”

I push the paper toward Sarah and give her a genuine smile. “Thanks.”

I head to my locker, feeling a little better. No, it’s not ideal. The poetry club is still social exile. But Jae will be there. For a minute, I let myself indulge in thoughts of her. The soft eyes. The cute dimples. The milky voice. *Are you okay?*

I open my locker and start planning my first poetic masterpiece.

There once was a naked mole
Who slid down a stripper pole
He felt rather stiff
Attempted the splits
And tore him another black hole

CHAPTER EIGHT

Jae

I step into the cool shade of the grove and feel the soft grass bow beneath my feet. The sharp whistles from the soccer field are far away now, and it's eerily quiet. The only voices I hear are the birds tweeting from their branches overhead. I wonder if I'm in the right place.

Then I see the gold flash of Mrs. Aldana's scarf. She's sitting on a giant log behind a huge fire pit. A white boy with carefully coiffed red hair is lying on a blanket on the forest floor with an Asian girl. She's wearing a jean jacket that looks like a scrapbook of her favorite things: buttons, feathers, colorful patches, and pins. Her eyes are lined with thick black eyeliner, and she has leopard-print makeup on her eyelids. William's sitting on a tree stump nearby and waves me over like he's been waiting to see me all day. He nods toward an empty stump next to him and I sit down and drop my bag with a thump beside me.

"You made it," he whispers, leaning sideways. "Welcome."

"Thanks."

“As we wait for our last student,” Mrs. Aldana says, “let’s take in the beauty of what surrounds us. There’s a reason so much poetry is written about nature.”

There isn’t much time to take in any beauty before I hear a twig snap behind me. The birds silence overhead. Someone gasps. The footsteps stop and I turn around to see him standing there, as unexpected as the first time I saw him.

“There you are! Our star student,” Mrs. Aldana sings. “Take a stump, Derek!”

Derek walks past me, his head lowered, staring at the ground through dark lashes. The air around him smells like cigarettes and I’m glad I’ve found another reason to dislike him. Besides the fact that he failed to stand up to his friends for me—not once but twice. Or that he threatened to beat up a kid in the bathroom. Why did I ever leave the stall to talk to him? Why didn’t I just let the jerk cry?

He sits down and leans over with his elbows on his knees and stares hard at the ground.

“What are you doing here?” I hiss under my breath.

“Hell if I know,” he answers, not even sparing me a glance.

Mrs. Aldana is saying something, but my mind is spinning like a marble in a drain and I can’t hear a word. He’s not supposed to be here. This is supposed to be my place to get away from people like him.

“You can’t be here.”

He laughs.

“What’s so funny?” I snap.

“What’s funny is you actually think I wanna be here.”

Mrs. Aldana claps her hands together. "Welcome to the Free Verse Society, everyone! I promise I won't be here long. I'll soon leave you to your own devices—for better or for worse. But first, I always like to begin the introductory meeting with a small exercise. So settle into your seats and close your eyes. Breathe deep. Fill your lungs with fresh air."

"More like toxic ashtray," I mutter.

Derek guffaws and I cross my arms over my chest and lean away from him. I don't want to breathe deep and all that. Not just because Derek stinks of old casino, but because I didn't sign up for a meditation circle. I didn't sign up to get inside my own head. I don't like it in there.

I just don't have the time for this mess. There's calculus homework today, which will probably take me twice as long to complete as everyone else because we didn't have calculus at my old school. *Bellwood is in a different league academically. You'll have to work hard.* When Uncle Rowan asks me what I was doing after school, what will I say? I was taking deep breaths and touching trees?

"If you're feeling resistance to this, it's normal," Mrs. Aldana says quietly, and I peek through one eye to see if she's hovering nearby, maybe sucking up my energy, reading my thoughts. But she's sitting calmly on her tree stump. "Just take a few minutes to observe all those thoughts wandering through the corridors of your mind like uninvited guests. Watch them come and go."

My arms are still crossed, but I take a deep breath. I can't leave. After what happened with Derek's friends, I need someone. I need this group. And I can't let Derek ruin this for me.

And then there's Dad. Dad loved poetry. His poems sat at the kitchen table with his physics books, side by side like the contradiction he was. I need poetry like I need memories of him. I burrow deep, hoping someday I'll find him in a title, at the end of a stanza, at the signing of a poet's name.

So I take a deep breath, and I observe.

The corridor of my mind is dark and it's full. Thoughts wander in and out like lost souls. One stays long. It's familiar. It says, *They can't love you if they know you.* It says, *Everyone stops loving you eventually.*

I see Uncle Rowan's face. His stern eyes, his bald, shiny head. At any moment, he could disappear. He could decide I'm too much trouble and send me away. *A disappointment.* That's what Mom's eyes said for the past year. And now Austin's looking at me with that slippery smile and his face is getting closer to mine until it disappears too. Then I'm riding the bus to the hospital, wearing nothing but loneliness around my skin. I'm standing at the street corner where my world changes again.

"Good," Mrs. Aldana says, and I'm sitting in the grove, surrounded by people who don't know what I am or who I've been.

She reads us a poem, "The Meadow" by Kate Knapp Johnson, and asks us, "What's your interpretation of that line? What does it mean to leave thinking for thought?"

"It's complete drivel," Derek says. "Doesn't make any sense."

"To you," I snap, and my face flushes. "Sorry. I mean, it does make sense if you think it through. To me, the word *thinking* feels active here. It's something you do with intention. But the word *thought* feels passive. It's something you get lost in."

Mrs. Aldana nods, looking back and forth from me to Derek. "In your silence, how many thoughts did you *plan* to think? Of course, that's not how thoughts work. The beauty of writing is paying attention and exploring the thoughts that are worth our time, letting go of the thoughts that aren't. Giving our thoughts their proper weight. The page is where we can re-create ourselves into who we want to be."

It's not that easy, I think. *You can't write away the truth.*

"We can't always know what a poet means," she continues. "Our only job is to approach the text with curiosity. Keep this in mind when you read each other's poems."

Mrs. Aldana reaches into a large tote bag and pulls out a stack of small notebooks. She walks around the fire pit and gives one to each of us. I look at the notebook on my lap, lit by the sun peeking through the canopy. It's a beautiful dark blue with white swirls. I look down at my high-waisted blue pants and white shirt. Each notebook is different, and each one seems to belong to the right person.

"You'll have five minutes at the beginning of each meeting to write a free verse poem. Can someone tell us what free verse is?"

"It's poetry without a prescribed form," William says.

I smile at how the word *form* fills his English mouth.

"Right." Mrs. Aldana nods. "It's poetry that has its *own* form. It creates its *own* rules. Your five-minute poem is where you can unleash your thoughts without judgment. You cannot ask questions about anyone else's poem. Understand? You'll have other opportunities to critique and give feedback. With that said, I want you all to write your first poem right now. This is your attempt to answer the question Who am I?"

Derek lets out a slow, loud sigh. He's rude, but I agree. I didn't come here to talk about me. The last thing I want to do is talk about me. When I signed up for this club, I saw myself in a beanbag chair in a brightly lit classroom, reading the works of famous poets like Langston Hughes. Not the inner thoughts of Janelle Afenyo from Georgia.

Mrs. Aldana claps her hands together and her shoulders spring up to her ears. “Begin!”

I open the notebook to a lined page. I lift my pen and press it down, over and over again, deepening the single dot. What can I say without saying too much?

I sneak a glance at Derek, who’s turning his blue-and-yellow notebook over in his hands. It’s the school colors, and I wonder if he’s some kind of jock. Unfortunately, when he pulled up his shirt in the bathroom, I saw abs that could have been spray-painted on. Very unfair.

His eyes snap toward me and I look down at my notebook.

Five minutes pass like five seconds.

“Ready?” Mrs. Aldana asks. “William? Will you share first?”

“Certainly,” he says, picking up his notebook. It’s a serious gray, but when the light hits it at different angles, it glimmers like a kaleidoscope. He stands up and tucks a stray wisp of blond hair behind his ear. His mouth is moving, but my heart is thumping too loud to hear him. *Am I reading next?* He’s saying something about his name, but before I realize, he’s already sitting down again and everyone is clapping. I join in, sorry I didn’t really hear.

Mrs. Aldana extends her hand to the girl on the blanket. “Ready, Swan?”

Swan crosses her legs and confidently takes in the whole group before beginning.

i can't remember the streets
i never walked
my Seoul
is empty
of memories
Korean American
but i don't think i can be me
sometimes
Cho Su Hwan / Swan Cho
i am neither and i am both
when i find my Seoul
maybe i'll know
who i am

Everyone claps. Derek gives his notebook half-hearted pats.

"CJ?" Mrs. Aldana calls.

All eyes turn to the red-haired boy sitting up on the blanket. His green eyes blink wildly behind rectangular glasses, and he glances around the group like a mouse at an owl convention.

"CJ?" Mrs. Aldana's voice nudges him gently.

He starts reading and his voice quivers.

Derek is leaning back, head cocked sideways like he's hanging on to every word CJ says. When CJ's done, his breath comes out loud and shallow and Swan whispers something into his ear.

"Are you all right, CJ?" Mrs. Aldana asks.

"Just . . . uh . . . an-an-anxiety."

"Take a moment. We'll move on so you don't feel pressured."

"In four, out six," Derek says.

CJ's eyes snap to him. "Huh?"

"Breathe in four counts, breathe out six," Derek repeats, then crosses his arms. I realize I'm staring at him when his thick eyebrows knit together beneath his white cap. "What?" he says to me.

I turn away. Whatever I just witnessed, I don't want to care.

CJ rips a sheet of paper out of his notebook and folds it with intense focus, like he's doomed if he stops moving his hands. He doesn't seem to hear Mrs. Aldana when she speaks again.

"And who are you, Derek? What can you share with us?"

"Um. Not a poet, apparently," he answers, holding up his notebook. "Didn't write anything."

"Oh! It's always good to make an attempt. We're not here to judge."

"Well, you kind of are," he answers with a smile and a shrug. "Otherwise why bother being here, right?"

"With time, I think you'll learn to see yourself more and judge yourself less. I for one am just so happy to have you in our group."

"Absolutely," William adds. "The more the merrier."

I clamp my mouth shut to not yell, *It's about quality, not quantity!*

"Ready, Jae?" Mrs. Aldana smiles eagerly, but the butterflies in my stomach pick up speed. I look around the grove, at the faces speckled with bursts of sunlight. Blue eyes. Green eyes. Brown eyes. Dark eyes. Derek's looking at me now, and his face reads apprehension. Curiosity. Everyone seems to be holding their breath, leaning toward me.

I stare at my notebook. I can read the poem on the left, which is passable. It says I cared enough to write something. Or I could read the poem on the right, which is real. It tugs at my insides, hard, knots up my throat, squeezes my gut.

I take in a deep breath. I read.

nobody knows my name, or
　　　　they don't know how to say it so
　　　　they call me New Girl.
but moving from there to here
　　　　can't make everything New for real

Mrs. Aldana's smile stretches wide. "Wonderful job, all of you!"

I sneak a quick glance at Derek. He's still staring at me, and he won't look away. I pretend to adjust the blue straps of my wedges. It's his stupid eyes. I could look at them all day. Sometimes beautiful things are cruel.

Mrs. Aldana stands up. "Wonderful. I'll hand over the rest of the meeting to your president, William Huntington." She pulls her shawl tighter around her shoulders, steps over the fallen log, and begins to walk through the maze of trees.

"You're leaving us?" I ask.

"Oh, this is your club, Jae. I'm just here to cheer you on." She cocks her head to the side. "You're in good hands, but you're welcome to join me for a walk if you'd like."

I look around at everyone else. Potential friends, save one. "No. I'll stay."

"Don't we need supervision?" Derek's voice is low and accusing.

"I trust you won't burn the grove down." Mrs. Aldana winks. Her footsteps crunch as she makes her way through the trees. She touches each one she passes, brushing her hand along the trunks and staring up at the leaves.

"Jesus," Derek mutters.

CJ sets aside the paper he folded into an intricate frog. He pulls out another sheet, and without looking at us, starts folding again.

William stands up and shakes his hair out and pulls it back into a tight ponytail. “First of all, I’d like to welcome everyone to another school year, another semester of the poetry club. This year we’re focusing on free verse poetry, and thus the name, The Free Verse Society. We’d like to extend a special welcome to our newest members.”

“I’m not really a member,” Derek says quickly. “I’m just here for a little bit.”

William taps his finger against his lips. “Have I seen you around?”

Swan scoffs. “You’re the only person in school who doesn’t know Derek. He’s on the soccer team, but we won’t hold that against him because he actually has brains. He scored in the ninety-seventh percentile on the PSAT without even studying.”

The last thing she says catches me off guard and I look at Derek. He’s looking down at his feet.

“Impressive. Thanks for the quick briefing, Swan,” William says. “We’ll be putting out a literary journal at the end of the spring semester, but for this fall, our goal is to host a big event. We’ll expound upon that later.”

Derek groans and rubs his eyes. “Hey. Is there any way to keep the club membership under wraps?”

“What do you mean, Derek?”

“I mean, I’d prefer if nobody else knew I was here. With you all. You know what I mean?”

“Yeah . . .” Swan frowns. “You think we’re a bunch of losers you don’t want to be associated with.”

“Hey, hey,” he says, holding up his hands. “Those are not my words. I’m just asking for a little discretion.”

“Yeah, whatever,” Swan says, waving a dismissive hand. “We

really don't have time for your ego, you know? William, I think it's a good time for club rules."

"Absolutely." He nods and sits back down on his stump.

Swan stands up slowly on the blanket, as if she's about to make the most important speech of her high school career.

"Our club can only work if there are certain rules in place. Rule one. Be on time for meetings. That's obvious. We start precisely at three o'clock, not a minute later. I keep strict attendance and report it to Mrs. Aldana when she's not here."

Derek sighs. "Attendance for what? Isn't this an extracurricular?"

"Rule two. You must read at least one literary work per week. Not stupid teeny books or fluffy romance."

Swan's so wound up, I don't think a little romance could do her any harm. *Reading doesn't have to be a struggle*, I want to tell her. A book has value because it's the heart of a human being, not because it's complex. But instead, I say, "You're not following us around, so how do you know what we read?"

"Stagnant vocabulary. Lack of insightful commentary." She looks down at her notebook. "We have a three-strike policy—"

"We decided against that," William interjects.

Swan gives him the side-eye. "I think it's especially necessary this semester." She crosses her arms over her jean jacket and stares directly at Derek. "Three strikes and you're out of the club."

"Oh?" Derek says with feigned excitement.

William shakes his head. "You can't be against three strikes in the criminal justice system but completely for it in a club that you're running."

"Those are two different things," Swan says.

"No, they're not. What you're proposing is a hypocrisy. An abuse of power. Each situation needs to be reviewed on a case-by-case basis. And the only rule that's relevant is the first." William looks around at all of us. "Please be on time."

"Fine." She drops her leopard-print notebook on the ground like a hot potato. "It's on you if our club falls to pieces. Let's get to the first order of business, then. We need to plan for our big open mic in December. I think it's appropriate that the newbies head that project." She looks from me to Derek and back again.

"What?" My voice comes out squeaky.

"We'd prefer an interesting venue, something we haven't done before. You will, of course, have the club budget to work with. We raised quite a lot of money selling journals last year."

"Wait. I . . . I just moved here. I don't know anything about the city yet."

"Then it's a great chance for you to learn. Besides, you'll have Derek to help you."

"Derek? That Derek?"

Swan squints. "Can you do it or not?"

I bite my lip. Derek doesn't say anything.

I know how this goes. I've always been the overachiever grouped with slackers. The whole project will be on my shoulders. But no matter how much I don't want to do this with Derek, I won't spend another day hiding in the bathroom. The Free Verse Society is my place. I can see myself fitting in here. And I won't let him ruin this for me.

"Okay," I say quickly. "I'll do it."

Raise your right hand for me. Do you understand that once you sign—

I shake my head to clear the voice that found its way in again. It's always there, like a harsh wind screaming outside a closed door, moving in through the cracks.

I tell myself there's no reason to feel anxious. This is a small commitment. I don't have to sign my name. It won't break my heart and it won't keep me up at night. We'll plan the open mic, and then I'll never talk to Derek again.

Raise your right hand for me.

The poem on the right:

<u>*Georgia Dreams*</u>

I've got dreams,
Georgia dreams,
dreams of mothers and daughters,
    lost mothers and daughters;
I dream of smiles,
and little hands,
and little feet,
and words like "I'm sorry."
I've got Georgia dreams
that keep me from sleep,
and dreams of you
that keep me from me.

CHAPTER NINE

The meeting ends. I jump up and grab my backpack. William yells, "See you next week, Derek!" and I give a wave over my shoulder, step into the sun.

I keep my head down, skitter like an ant along the side of the building till I get to the bike racks. I'm unlocking my bike when I hear a whistle from the soccer field. I look over my shoulder. Yellow-and-blue jerseys sprint across the grass. Like he can sense me there, Miguel looks over, and I duck my head.

The story is, I have to miss practice once a week because Gina gave me more hours at the diner. But if the team sees me hanging around an hour after school ends, it'll blow my cover.

My phone dings, and I expect it to be a text from Miguel: haha caught you! But instead, it's Valeria. I mean, a *lot* of Valeria in very few items of clothing. I sigh, almost delete the picture. Then I imagine her standing at the edge of a building, mascara streaming down her face, yelling, "You didn't like my picture!" Because since her parents' divorce, she looks to me for complete validation of her existence.

I hit the red heart.

Me: i think you sent this to the wrong person.

Valeria: omg! Embarrassing! But do you think it's a good picture to send Tommy?

Me: who's tommy?

Me: nevermind. you look nice. you always look nice, so you don't have to keep sending me these pictures.

Valeria: I didn't mean to

Me: cool.

Valeria: You don't think the angle's wrong? My neck looks kinda short, right?

Me: you have the neck of a gazelle. it's lovely.

I put my phone away, wheel my bike out, and push it through the grass until I turn the corner. I finally take a deep breath and follow the gravel road, where voices are still coming from the dense trees. I try to catch a glimpse of Jae's white shirt. Instead, there's a flash of gold.

I jump when an engine roars past and a yellow Ferrari spits gravel into the air, filling my nose with its earthy smell. Two seniors stick their heads out of the windows and yell, fists pounding to heavy bass. I cover my eyes and wish I could melt into the rocks and disappear forever. I was supposed to get a Ferrari for my sixteenth birthday. Instead, I'm riding around on a two-wheeler.

The bike pedal clips my calf and I wince and throw the bike into the gravel.

Just then footsteps approach. I glance behind me. Fluttering high-waisted pants. A braid hanging over one shoulder. Her short legs are moving as fast as they can, and she reminds me of Henry's dachshund. I pretend not to notice her and bend down to pick up my bike from the dirt.

"Hey," she says in a clipped tone. "When do you want to meet?"

"For what?"

"*For what?* We have to find a venue. We're supposed to plan the whole thing."

"Hey," I say as nice as I can. "I know this means a lot to you. Honestly, it's cute. I just don't care, okay? So whatever you want is cool with me."

"Well, I know this means nothing to you, and it's *not* cute. But this isn't about you or me, it's about the club. I could plan the whole thing myself, but I don't think I should have to."

Another car blasts past, sending dirt into the air. I half expect to see Miguel and Henry.

"Let's get outta here," I say, picking up the pace.

She lets out a long sigh but follows. "Slow down, Derek," she says, working double-time to keep up. I do. Her face says she's on a mission and she'll kill to accomplish it.

"Frankly, I'm surprised you even want to talk to me," I say.

"Well," she answers.

"You hate me?"

She cocks her head to the side and smiles. Her dimples are like wells you could drown in, but it's not the kind of smile I was hoping for: Her eyes are ready to impale.

"Why would I hate you?" she asks.

"Come on."

"No, you come on. They say you're supersmart."

"That's what they say."

"Then I don't get why you're asking me dumb questions." She stops walking and balls up her tiny little gerbil hands and plants them on her hips.

I'm not a genius but I'm not dumb, either. I know why she's mad. "It's because of my friends, right?" I say. "Look, they're being idiots and I don't think it's funny. I told them to leave you alone. But Jae. I'm not responsible for what those guys do."

"It was my first day here! My first!" Her black eyes are sparkling as if she's about to cry, and honestly, it makes my heart ache a little. Before I can say anything, she hurries ahead of me, almost in a run.

Explaining things wouldn't make a difference. She wouldn't understand. Dad's gone, and in a way, so is Mom, and the guys are the only sense of normal I have left, even if we have less in common than before. It's like looking for food in the same empty cupboard, over and over again, hoping there'll be something there the next time. It's not that I want to be friends with them. I need them.

It's almost too easy to catch up to her. "Jae. My friends—"

"I don't want to know anything about you or your friends. This is strictly business. So do you have an idea for a venue or not?"

"How about the school gym?"

She actually growls and stomps her foot. "I can't with you. I can't."

"Fine. There's another place. We can meet Friday if you want."

"Same time? Three o'clock?"

"Can't. I have soccer practice. I can stop by your place when I'm done. Around four thirty or five."

"My uncle's house?" She's shouting even though she's whispering. "No way. Let's meet at your place."

"No way. Just meet me there. Atlantic Dunes Park. It's not too far from here. You just head down that way. I can meet you at the pavilion."

She nods.

We reach the end of the gravel road and Jae takes a sharp left. I know she can hear me behind her, my bike wheels whirring softly, but she doesn't say another word. It's like I'm pulled along on an invisible leash. I want to look at her as long as I can.

Soon we're all the way on Ocean Boulevard, where the mansions overlook the water. And I realize that Jae lives close to my old house—Mrs. Aldana's house.

We pass a cream-colored stone wall, then Jae walks through a black ornate gate, past a black car parked on the circular driveway, and up the front steps of a sprawling palazzo. She opens the door and looks over her shoulder with an expression I can't read. I suddenly remember her face in the boys' bathroom, how much she cared. *Are you okay?* For a second, I wish she could see the Derek I used to be. Because there's nothing I want her to know about the Derek I am now. If she knew how bad things have been, she'd feel sorry for me, and the only thing worse than hate is pity.

CHAPTER TEN

Uncle Rowan's voice roars from the dining room. "Janeeeelle!"

"Coming!"

He's sitting with papers spread out in front of him on the table. His back is toward me, his head gleaming from a fresh shave.

"Where have you been?" he asks without looking up. His pen is frantic against a yellow legal pad. He opens a giant tome and the hard cover smacks against the table. He wets his finger and flips through the pages. "Well?"

"I had a club meeting."

"Oh, yeah?" He stops now and looks at me and there's a whisper of approval in his eyes. He clicks the top of his pen twice. "What club?"

My stomach clenches. "The Free Verse Society."

"The what?"

"It's the poetry club," I say, looking down at my pants and ironing out invisible wrinkles.

When I look up again, his shoulders drop and he rubs his face with both hands. "We'll talk over dinner," he says, shaking his head and turning back to his work.

I shouldn't be surprised by his complete lack of enthusiasm, but I am. Mom would be happy I joined any after-school club at all. She worries that I hide behind books because of social anxiety. But I hide behind books so the real world can't disappoint me. When I read, I can skip the chapters I don't like, or close the book altogether and move on. Life isn't like that.

Halfway up the stairs to my room, Ms. Rosette's voice calls from the kitchen.

"Ja-*neeelle*! Please, come, come."

I pause, not sure what this could be about. She's already in the middle of cooking dinner.

I head back toward the smell of food downstairs. I step into the vast white of the kitchen, its granite countertops shimmering in different shades of pale. The light from the bay window hits the gold retro lanterns hanging over the kitchen island. Ms. Rosette is standing at the stove, her apron tied over her blue dress, her hair pulled into a puff at the nape of her neck. Her hair could never hold a perm because when she cleans, she sweats. She yells at stains as she kneads fabric between closed fists and she scrubs the floors with a vengeance.

Right now, her arm is muscling like she's stirring cement. I see the white dough and immediately know what it is.

"Come. Va," she says, and I stand beside her body, tinged with the smell of a sweet citrus cleaner. I stare into the pot. Her arm turns and turns the deceptively fluffy dough. *Wap, wap, wap*. She's breathing through her nose, lips pressed together, focused. A slight sheen of perspiration crowns her forehead, from the work or from the heat or both.

"Uncle Rowan eats this stuff?" I ask.

"Ke? This *stuff*? Fufu?" She gives me a glance. "You cannot take *this stuff* from his hands."

"I didn't mean it like that," I mutter.

"Do you speak E*v*e?"

"No."

She continues the *wap wap wap* without taking her eyes off the pot. "You should learn it. Your name. A*f*enyo. You know the meaning?"

"Home is good."

She looks at me sideways. "So. Home is good for you?"

Oof. I suck in my breath. Why does it feel like I've been hit in the chest?

Her dark eyes sink into mine. "You don't want to talk about home? I can talk about mine. I left Togo two years ago," she says over the sound of bubbling soup on the far burner. "My husband and I, we came here. We left our girls in Lomé. Three beautiful girls. I worried for them so much." She stops pounding the fufu and wets a small bowl to gather its stickiness, then drops the round mounds into several serving bowls. "We worked, and then when we could, we sent for them. They were very angry with us. With me. They did not understand the sacrifice." Her voice trails off. "Mothers have to leave sometimes."

I swallow a lump in my throat and watch her open the lid of the bubbling pot and stir. She scoops into it and brings the spoon to her mouth, closes her eyes, and smacks her lips. "Home is good, but a country cannot hold all that you are. A language, too. Try," she says, blowing on the hot ladle and offering it to me.

"It's good," I say, savoring the ginger, the anise, the pepper. "Very good."

She nods. "It tastes like home. Do you know why home is good? Home is with your people. Now, you go rest before dinner." She leans in and whispers, "I do not think dinner will be easy for you."

I want to hug Ms. Rosette, to feel the same warmth in her arms that I feel in her voice, but I step back. I don't need another mother. Mothers don't stay.

She was right about dinner.

Uncle Rowan rests his forearms on the side of his plate and stares at me as I cut fufu with my spoon—a sacrilege in Dad's book. He ate it with his hands, and the hotter the soup the better. Wincing and blowing on his torched fingers was part of the ritual that made it delicious.

Uncle Rowan clears his throat. "Where do you think a poetry club is going to take you?"

I scoop a mushroom cap out of the okra soup and stare at it. I don't know where the club will take me, but everyone needs to belong somewhere. At least there's a misfits collective at Bellwood.

"I've always wanted to be a writer," I tell him. "Since I was little, remember? I wrote that Christmas story for you when I was twelve—"

"'An ATL Christmas Tale,' yes." He leans back in his chair. "It's a cute story. I still have it, you know."

My jaw drops a little.

"But that's all it is, Janelle. Cute. It won't get you anywhere. Now. You left your mama in Atlanta and came all the way here for a fresh start. Is this the amazing fresh start we were hoping for? What are you going to do with your life?"

My whole life? I don't know what I'll do tomorrow.

"When it's time for you to move out and make it on your own, what are you going to do? Write poems and tack them on telephone poles? Fold them into origami and sell them at craft shops in the Bahamas? I mean, how are you going to support yourself?"

"I don't know!" The words burst out like flames from a blowtorch and I quickly cover my mouth. We're staring wide-eyed at each other like time has frozen us both. I slap my hand over my heart. "I'm sorry, Uncle Rowan. I'm so sorry."

And I am. Maybe Derek has me all wound up because I'm not the talking back or yelling back type. I think Uncle Rowan knows this, so the anger in his eyes abates almost as quickly as it rose.

"Hm." He shakes his head and picks up his spoon. "You're a lot like your mama. You can't tell a dollar from a cent." He pauses and clears his throat. "Your grades start slipping, you won't be in that Kumbaya club anymore. You hear me?"

I bite my lip. Doesn't he know that I've always been a straight-A student? Even during the years when I lost the people I loved?

"Janelle."

"I hear you, Uncle Rowan."

I retreat to my room without dessert again and close the door with a sigh. I need to make sense of things. I need to read and write. I need to let words flow through and spill out.

I'm making a beeline for the bookshelf when I notice a courier envelope sitting on the desk. I pick it up. The *from* address reads *Anne Lawrence.*

When the envelope rattles, I notice my hands shaking. I drop it onto the desk. It's what I've been waiting for. For three months. So why can't I open it?

I stare again at the name scribbled on the outside. I pick it up and head over to my bed, sit on the edge, and feel the envelope for what I know will be there. Slowly, I pull the tab, taking in a deep breath and letting it out, and when I reach inside for the picture I know I'll find, there's June Baby, as small and juicy as a plum. The photo is taken from right above her, and she's on her back with her feet in the air. It feels like I could reach down and pick her up. She's smiling so wide. Do babies that small smile so big? Is her joy that big?

My lips start shaking and I press them together. June Baby. I breathed and she breathed. I ate and she ate. I slept and she . . . well, she did everything but sleep. I kept her for nine months, and then the world took her away.

I mean, I *gave* her away. *I* did that. I gave her to somebody else. Someone I didn't even know. And I never got a formal goodbye. My adoption counselor, Sherry, suggested an entrustment ceremony. It would give me a sense of closure, she said. But June Baby had her new parents, and her new parents had each other, and I had no one. How could I get through a ceremony like that without anyone by my side, *on* my side? So after forty-eight hours of holding June and rubbing her soft stomach and kissing her soft cheeks and smelling how sweet she was, I handed her over to Anne and Jermaine Lawrence and she was no longer mine.

I didn't even give her a name. I called her June Baby because that's what she was. The sweetest little joy born in June.

I tell June over and over that I'm sorry. I whisper Lucille Clifton's words, and I wonder if anyone will ever read poetry to my lost girl.

But June doesn't worry about poems and apologies. She smiles back at me.

I reach into the envelope again and find a letter from Anne, her adoptive mother. Her mother.

Dear Jae,

You're holding this letter, so you know I got your email. And Sherry at the agency got your email and your call. I know you were worried about not getting the picture, or it getting lost in the mail, so I rushed it to you. I don't want you to ever worry about not having contact with Sarah.

I stop reading. Sarah? How could she be anything but June Baby to me? I know she needed a name, a real name, but *Sarah* doesn't capture that gummy smile or those bright black eyes.

This letter is hard to write because I don't have the words to thank you for what you did for me and Jermaine. We are so blessed that you chose us to take care of your sweet baby girl. I know it's hard for you sometimes. If I'm honest, it's hard for me. Because you will always be Sarah's mother, no matter what I do for her. No matter how much of a mother I am. You brought her here. You gave her life. And for that, I can only thank you.

Sarah loves her tummy time. She drools and pees and poops and cries, and Jermaine dances with her to Bob Marley and the Wailers, and they both wail together. She is everything to us. I wish I could explain what a joy you've given us. The least I could do is send you her smile, which she gives us every day. For such a young girl, you had to make such an adult decision, and I know it wasn't easy. I hope you find your peace. And when you are ready to be a mother for the second time, if you are, I hope you know that you are worthy of that joy.

We will love you forever.

The three of us.

CHAPTER ELEVEN

Derek

My boss, Gina, she showed up at our house some months ago. I opened the door to see her eyelashes thick like giant tarantulas. It was almost as bad as seeing a teacher outside of school. Maybe worse. Like the diner, she looked like she belonged somewhere in the past, with her big blond curls and straight bangs. She craned her neck to look around me and into the kitchen. Her head jutted this way and that.

"Hi, honey, where's your mother?" she asked. "She didn't show up at the art studio and I waited for twenty minutes and then I called and called and called," she said, holding up her phone as proof. "She was supposed to start teaching me how to paint the mountain scene with the little lake and all. You know, the one with the white-spotted deer taking a drink." She leaned in closer. "Where is she?"

I licked my lips, trying to think of a cover-up that wasn't really a lie. "She came home early. Sleeping off a nasty bug or something."

"Yeah? Is that right?" Gina turned her head to the side and looked at me with small eyes.

I stared at her staring at me, and she was quiet. She grabbed my waist and pushed me to the side, walked through the kitchen and down the hall. "Nancy? Naaaancy. It's Gina. I . . ." Silence. Rattling pills. Maybe she was counting the number of bottles on the table. Maybe she was counting how few pills were left.

"Nancy?"

I walked into the living room to see Gina bent over Mom on the couch. She waved a hand over her face, but Mom didn't respond.

"Nancy, it's Gina," she whispered close to Mom's ear, then again, louder. Mom swatted and turned away from her, and Gina stood up straight and whirled around to look at me. "Dear God almighty, Derek, does this happen a lot?"

I nodded.

"Well, do you know if she's okay?"

"I counted the pills. She'll wake up soon. Don't worry." But I couldn't keep the worry out of my own voice.

I followed her into the kitchen and watched her grab a towel and soak it under a stream of water. She wrung it out and marched back to the living room, where she slowly wiped Mom's face, moving away tendrils of red hair. Mom muttered something like *Leave m'alone ung sleep.*

Gina tsked. "Nancy, this has gotta stop. You've been getting mighty thin. And irritable!" She looked at me. "My God, will she snap at you if you mix the wrong colors. I had my suspicions, but then I thought, *No, not Nancy*. But I should know better. Addiction doesn't have a face. It runs in my family, you know. My daddy was a drinker. Got mean and nasty and one couldn't stand to be around him most of the time. And it made him a complete dimwit, too. Thought he saw a wolf walking through the yard at night and shot it. Turned out to be the neighbor's little boy. Barely lived, poor thing. Mama drank too, but I think she did that to deal with Daddy's drinking. And me, I've been sober for thirteen years." She looked up at me and smiled. "So I sure as hell know what I'm talking about. Now," she said, pushing herself up from the couch, "you tell your mother to call me when she sobers up. I have some information I can share with her."

I shook my head. "Gina, she doesn't want it, trust me. And she won't be happy that you saw her like this."

"Well. I can't help her if she doesn't want to help herself. That's the God-honest truth." She paused. "But I don't want you to ever give up on her."

She walked back into the kitchen and began opening cupboards, muttering to herself. "Just a little bit . . . macaroni . . . good ol' Southern . . . warm it up." Then she straightened and brushed out her clothes. "All right, honey, I'll be by later with my famous casserole. Maybe two. You can freeze one and heat it up later."

"I'm okay, Gina." I was planning on living on sandwiches and cereal until I moved out, anyway.

"No, you're not. You're not okay." She looked me straight in the eyes and I swallowed a lump in my throat. "I can't fix this situation, but I can at least make sure you're fed." She patted my cheek. "Okay, honey, see you in a few hours."

When she left, I felt more alone than before.

It's like the eerie feeling you get standing over a body in a casket. You think that any second, their eyes will open, and they'll sit up, and they'll be just like the person they were before. They'll tell you to grab the remote. They'll say, *Hey, let's go on a road trip, just you and me*. But it's just a body. An unfeeling, empty body. And you're alone.

Gina was right. The answer to Jae's question is *no*. I'm not okay.

CHAPTER TWELVE

Jae

The cafeteria is a sea of rectangular tables and unfamiliar faces. My stomach rocks gently like I'm on water. I make my way through the buzzing room where every student has a place, and I feel the weight of a thousand stares. I stop at the end of the cafeteria line and grab a wet tray. *This is easy*, I tell myself. *Just get your food and if you can't find the club members, grab an empty seat anywhere. Smile. Make small talk.* God, I hate small talk.

The line moves forward and I take a small step. I fight back a yawn, thinking about my sleepless night with Anne's letter and June Baby's picture, and then I realize I'm hugging the tray to my chest like a shield. I look down to see a giant wet spot over my boob, reminding me of suckling lips and baby smells and colostrum. Perfect. I turn my attention to what I can see, not the feelings roiling in my gut and chest and throat.

The food counter is separated from the rest of the cafeteria by a short wall, so when I get to the front of the line and finally see the food display, my heart sinks. Sloppy green beans. Fried chicken with moisture spots. Mashed potatoes thinned out with water. I didn't expect Bellwood's cafeteria to be just like my school's back home.

An orange-bearded man with a hairnet scoops the food onto a plate and drops the plate on my tray. He gives me a warning look that says he's heard too much complaining already. I plaster on a smile and thank him and move down the line to the register where a fluffy woman, pink from sunburn, holds out her hand and mumbles, "Three fifty." I rummage through my wallet and drop the change into her beckoning fingers.

She shakes her head. "Can't take that, honey. Where's your meal card?"

"I don't have one."

"Well, you need one." She drops the money onto my tray. The sound of the clattering coins makes my face warm.

I lean toward her. "I'm new here. Can I pay with cash? Just for today?"

"No can do." She shakes her head. "You'll need to go to the office, get a meal card, and fill it up."

"By the time I do all that . . ." I sigh. Lunch will be over. Resigned, I hold out my tray to the bearded man, who shakes his head as he reaches for it. But before he can grab it, someone else does. My heart can't decide whether to sink or soar, because it's Derek. He's standing over me, his eyes shadowed by a baseball cap, and he pushes the tray back into my hand.

"Here. Use mine." He holds out a card and I stare at the half-smiling picture of him on the shining plastic.

"What?"

"Just take it."

"You're paying for my lunch?"

He adjusts his hat and looks over his shoulder. His mouth is moving around a piece of gum and I get a wave of mint from his breath. "Come on. Don't make a big thing out of it."

The pink lady behind the register taps the counter impatiently with her nails. "Use the card or get out of line, honey," she says. "We've only got fifteen minutes left and you're taking up all of it."

I give the lunch lady the card and she swipes it twice and hands it back. She waves us away.

We step out of the line and I hand the card back to Derek. "Thanks," I say.

He nods and walks away. Around the wall, I see him heading to a table filled with laughter and big voices. I notice Miguel in the group, and the girl who sits behind me in English class. Valeria, I think. For a brief second, her eyes are narrowed at me, and then she turns away. I keep moving, drop my head to let my locs fall like a curtain.

My eyes scan the room for a familiar face, a kind one. I can't find the Free Verse members anywhere, and I decide they're off on their own somewhere, leaving me to fend for myself. There's a Black girl named Shayla I saw in one of my classes, and when I meet her gaze, she quickly looks away. She leans over to share wide-eyed secrets with her friends, and I don't think there's a place for me. There's an empty seat next to a teacher and I decide it's better than standing in the middle of the cafeteria for the next fifteen minutes. I begin to make my way there, realizing I'm nowhere closer to making friends than I was yesterday.

"Jae!"

My head snaps around in search of the voice calling my name. In the far corner of the cafeteria, William is standing and waving his arms. I let out a sigh of relief and make a beeline to the table.

"I was trying to get your attention when you walked in," he says, sitting back down.

CJ is shoveling a spoonful of sloppy green beans into his mouth. He salutes me. "Your eyes are all puffy."

"Thanks," I say sarcastically. "I didn't sleep much. Where's Swan?" I plop down and begin spreading the green beans around my plate.

William sips on a box of chocolate milk. "She's prepping for a presentation to the school board. On minimizing the effects of financial disparity in the student body. Basically, she's trying to convince them to implement uniforms so the poorer students don't get bullied."

I take a bite of my green beans. It tastes like the flavor was completely boiled away and salt was added to compensate. I clear my throat and pour a cup of water from a plastic pitcher at the table. I think about Swan's colorful jean jacket, her dark eyeliner and leopard eye shadow. "She doesn't seem like the type to go for uniforms."

"She's not," William says. "She's proposing it for next year."

"I'm guessing Swan graduates this year?"

"Yup."

"Then why even bother?"

"In regard to Swan, the more fitting question is, why not? She will literally do anything—"

"Except calculus," CJ interjects.

William nods. "Except calculus. Math in general, actually. Don't ask her to count her fingers."

I think about Swan and CJ during the club meeting, how he rested his head on her stomach as she stroked his hair. "Are you and Swan—"

William chokes on his milk and sets down the carton, thumping his chest. "CJ and Swan? What? Boyfriend and girlfriend?" He shakes his head and laughs.

"We're the very definition of amor platonicus," CJ says.

"Oh." I turn back to my plate and push aside the chicken. I'm still not crazy about eating meat. Not when I don't have to. I sweep my fork through the runny mashed potatoes and try to scoop up as much as I can.

There's a chorus of *ooo*s at the other end of the cafeteria and we all crane our necks to see. It's Valeria. She stands behind Derek with her arms around his neck, hugging him close. Her black hair falls over his shoulders and she plants her red lips on his cheek. He's as still as glass. Even from where I sit, I see the tension in his jaw. Slowly, he removes her hands from his shoulders, fills up a cup of water, and drinks it until it's empty.

CJ lets out a big puff of air, his cheeks chipmunk full. "Derek Patel," he says simply, then pulls out a piece of paper from his notebook and starts folding it.

I stare at my potatoes like they're a Jackson Pollock painting. "He paid for my lunch."

There's silence. I look up to see CJ's hands frozen midair.

"Huh? Derek?" he asks.

"Yeah. I didn't have a meal card, so he paid for my lunch."

His hands get back to work, folding quickly until he's made a 3D star. "Well, he was a nice kid in middle school. Maybe he's coming around again. Or maybe he just hit his head and forgot he's supposed to be a complete asshole." He pulls out another sheet of paper and folds quickly, as if talking about Derek makes him anxious.

We're all quiet and I poke the chicken with my fork, sad that Uncle Rowan ruined my two-year vegetarian streak, annoyed that Derek's wearing a girl around his neck instead of sitting with us. Annoyed that I give a damn what Derek Patel is doing.

As I watch CJ make another star, I suddenly remember how small Uncle Rowan made me feel. *What are you going to do? Fold them into origami and sell them at craft shops in the Bahamas?*

I carefully unfold CJ's star. I write: *Poetry is when an emotion has found its thought and the thought has found words. —Attributed to Robert Frost.* CJ reaches for it, reads it, grins, and pushes it toward William.

Then we're all quiet, writing words on sheets of paper and letting CJ fold them into origami.

"We'll leave them around school," William says, his tongue sticking out the corner of his mouth as he writes. He writes his lines, signs them *TFVS*.

CJ pulls out another paper from his notebook. My eyes fall on his name written across decorative tape in the upper corner: Christopher James Tillman.

"Wait . . ." I close my eyes and try to reach for a memory that's taking shape. First day of school. Shuffling feet. Heavy breaths. *What the hell were you doing at my house, Tillman?*

I slap my forehead. "You're Tillman!"

"Huh? Yeah." He shrugs, still folding. "Why?"

"It was you. You got into a fight with Derek in the bathroom."

He stops and falls back against his seat. Looks at me with his thin green eyes. "How do you know about that? He told you?"

"I was there."

"Huh?" he and William say at the same time.

"It was the first day of school and I was too nervous to come to the cafeteria alone, so I hid in the girls' bathroom. Embarrassing, I know. But it turns out it wasn't the girls' bathroom."

"Holy shit on toast," CJ says.

"So why did he do it?"

"What?"

"Threaten to beat you up."

CJ pauses. He blinks wildly behind his glasses. His lips start forming words he never says, until finally he bends over his folding again, quiet.

William's shaking his head and rubbing his temples. "Ay yay yay."

"It's okay, CJ," I say. Because I'm not telling them the whole story, either. That I heard Derek sobbing and left the stall to talk to him. That my heart nearly stopped when I saw him because, behavior aside, he is quite possibly the most beautiful person I've ever seen. And I don't tell them that my stomach flip-flops when I see him, and how much I hate it. Maybe I want to have a little piece of Derek to myself, even if it's just his secrets.

"Well, have you and Derek decided on a venue for the poetry reading?" William asks.

"I'm meeting him after school Friday," I say. "Hopefully the first place we find will be perfect and we can move on." *I can move on*, I think.

William and CJ carry on with a conversation I can't follow. All I hear is *What the hell were you doing at my house, Tillman?*

CHAPTER THIRTEEN

Derek

It's late Friday afternoon, but Atlantic Dunes Park is mostly quiet. Except for the waves and seagulls. They bring back memories of weekend beach days with Mom and Dad. Naps beneath blue umbrellas. Feet sinking into warm sand.

I walk across the wooden pavilion. Jae's leaning against the railing, her back to me. She's wearing another white dress, maybe the same one she wore on Monday. But this time there's no belt, and it hangs loose on her frame like an old lady's muumuu. It's like she's saying *Don't even think about it, Derek*. Fine. I won't. But then again, there's no harm in it.

She looks over her shoulder and blinks. "I didn't think you'd come," she says.

I look down at my phone. I'm eight minutes early.

"I still have time to leave if you want."

She ignores me. Drops of water fall from her high ponytail and onto the wooden railing, leaving dark, wet splashes. She smells sweet, like she's just taken a shower, and I find myself leaning in just a little closer.

"You do that a lot," she says.

I stiffen up, stuff my hands into my pockets. "Do what?"

"You take off your hat. Run your fingers through your hair three times. Exactly three times."

"Huh." I shrug. "Habit, I guess. Don't even notice it anymore. Keeps my hands busy."

"Why? Are you handsy?" There's something teasing in her voice, like for a second she forgot to hate me.

I bite my lip, try not to smile.

Her expression clouds over. She turns away and leans against the railing. "Anyway. Thanks for buying me lunch this week."

"You already thanked me."

"Well, I'm thanking you again. It was a nice thing to do. Seems out of the norm for you. To be honest."

Something in me prickles. "The norm? What do you even know about me?"

"Not much."

I swallow, try to bury the irritation, try not to think about all the things she doesn't know. "You should probably talk less about things you have no idea about. To be honest."

She narrows her eyes. "Things like you?"

"Like me."

"Fine. Not even curious." She turns her back to me, hands on hips, and studies a wooden post with such intensity, you'd think she was an architect.

"What do you think about the venue?" I ask, trying to move on to a neutral topic. She turns to face me, and God, she's nice to look at.

"It's definitely much better than the school gym," she says with a clip in her voice. She walks thoughtfully around the rows of back-to-back benches, stepping from shadowed canopy to open light, and looks up at the wooden roof. She shifts her weight on the boards as if testing their sturdiness.

"Are you expecting elephants?" I ask.

She suddenly laughs, and dimples burrow beneath her high cheekbones. It makes something inside me buzz. I stare at her hair, the tiny droplets of water leaving dark spots around her feet. A slight breeze carries her floral scent and I take a step closer.

"Derek, I like it," she says simply. She looks toward the water in the distance and nods. "It's great, actually. We're outside, we have cover for bad weather, there's sand, ocean, trees. I think it's great."

A family dressed in swimsuits waves at us as they take the walkway around the pavilion toward the beach. The teenage son carries a giant unicorn floatie while a small girl scampers after him in tears. "Lemme hold it!" she wails. Jae and I share an amused glance.

When they pass, Jae leans against a beam with her arms crossed under her chest. I try to focus on her eyes.

"Why did you even agree to help me?" she asks. "You didn't seem too happy about joining the club. Like somebody made you go."

"It was either the poetry club or community service. Someone tipped my decision."

There's a question in her eyes, but then she shakes her head like her brain is an Etch A Sketch.

"Do you at least like poetry?" she asks. "Like, have you ever written a poem in your life?"

I make a face.

"What? You don't like writing or you can't?" There's a little twinkle in her eyes.

"I'm not a Neanderthal. I write stuff."

"Stuff?"

"Yeah." She seems a little disappointed, so I add, "Just to get ideas out of my head."

She nods. "See, that's why I love poetry. When my head's spinning with thoughts I can't work out, I start writing and it all makes sense. Or starts to, anyway."

"You show them to other people?"

She frowns. "Not usually. But I've entered a few contests. And I kept a poetry blog for a while."

"But why bother sharing your thoughts like that? I don't think people really care how others feel. Not really. They care how people's feelings affect them."

She cocks her head and nods slowly. "Maybe. But what if you had the power to make people care? I think that's what poetry does. It tells your truth in a way that helps other people understand it."

"Well, I think I'd be shitty at it. Especially this free verse stuff. In my book, a poem's not a poem unless it rhymes. Otherwise, it's just a statement broken up into lines." I grin. "See what I did there?"

"Not everything has to fit into a perfect mold. *Syllable-syllable-rhyme-syllable-syllable-rhyme*. It can get boring." Her eyes are sparkling. Her hands are dancing left to right as she explains. "With free verse, you can manipulate the spaces. The rhythm. The shape of it on the page. It all adds to the meaning."

Her excitement makes me smile. But when I do, she turns away, looks to the horizon with her hand on her forehead like a visor. *Hey*, I wanna say, *don't lose your joy on my account*. It's like a constant rising and fizzling out. Like she steps away as soon as she realizes she's getting closer. I'm not used to girls doing that.

She leans against the railing, and I step up beside her, nod toward the ocean. “Hey, you wanna check it out up close?”

She hesitates. Looks at the water, then back toward the parking lot.

“I mean, we don’t have to do the open mic in the pavilion. It could be a beach thing. You know, like beach weddings. Or beach parties,” I say in a rush.

“I guess . . .” She walks past me, carrying that sweet smell with her. Her white dress moves against her body, and it’s all curves.

I sigh and follow. At the end of the boardwalk we take off our shoes and step into sand.

The ocean gets louder with each step, gentle waves rolling over themselves. When we reach the shore, she drops her shoes and steps to the edge of the water. She’s looking straight down, as if she’s trying to see her reflection. “I’m seriously a walking stereotype. I’m scared of water.” She turns her head and looks at me, eyes shadowed by embarrassment.

“Plenty of people are scared of water,” I say. “That doesn’t make you a stereotype. Have you ever been to the beach?”

“I’ve never been outside Atlanta.”

“Oh.” I can’t imagine what it’d be like to stay in one place my whole life. To not have summer memories dispersed in other cities and countries. You’d think it would make you more secure, being from one place, knowing where you’re from. But Jae says this thing about Atlanta like she’s ashamed.

“That’s not a bad thing,” I say, glancing up at her as I bend over to roll my pants up to my knees. “Don’t judge me, either. This isn’t a style I’d normally go for.”

Then I step into the Atlantic Ocean like I’m stepping into the past. It’s a moment captured in our family album: me, pint-sized, water up to my shins, wearing bright yellow shorts with pockets inside out, holding a red bucket full of cheap treasures. I'm alone in this picture, but somewhere under the same sun is Mom, a red-haired Ariel lounging with a book and a drink, and Dad, a phone camera up to his face.

"Come on," I say, turning back to Jae.

"No way." She shakes her head. "I don't know how to swim."

"You don't have to. Just wade out a little."

Jae stands there, a look on her face I can't read. And the longer she looks at me, the more I think she can't see me. Her eyes are soft and unfocused, the spark gone. She blinks slowly, steps into the water, and holds out her hand like she's looking for mine.

I reach out, take a step. "Come on."

Suddenly, she turns and runs back to shore.

"Okay, that's a start," I say, walking back to her. "You were in the water for, like, point oh-oh-oh-three seconds."

She won't look at me and collapses onto the ground, dusting sand off her feet.

"You stand there long enough, you feel like the water's a part of you," I say. "You didn't get the full experience."

She shrugs. "It's . . . it's cold. The water."

"Felt warm to me."

"Well," she says. "I like the pavilion." And then, "I guess I should get going."

"Yeah. Me too. I should get going."

But neither of us moves. She's hunched, hugging her knees, staring blankly at her feet, and I'm wondering what she's not telling me. Wondering why she's talking like she doesn't have enough words.

"Why are you scared of water?" I ask, feeling like she's still tethered to that moment.

"It's like you said. If you're in there long enough, it becomes a part of you."

It sounds like something Jae would say, being a poetry lover and all that, because what she's saying is not what she means. I'm about to ask more questions when nearby, a man shouts, *Hey, kids, enjoying the beach?* as he launches a kayak. The way his dark brown hair parts at the side and swoops over his ears, the way his eyes crinkle gently in the corners as he smiles and waves at us, reminds me of Dad. If I believed in reincarnation like Mom does, it *would* be Dad. My heart sinks. Like the sun, everything good fades, and I decide to leave before it gets too dark, before the sadness gets too heavy.

As Jae waves and watches him drift out to deeper water, I roll my pants down and walk over to my shoes.

"I'm gonna go," I say, pointing vaguely over my shoulder.

I'm not sure if she hears me. She's watching a group of people set up drums on the beach a ways down. "They're going to play," she says.

We watch as a gray-haired white guy with dreadlocks the size of sausages sits down and adjusts a large drum between his legs. He and a Lenny Kravitz look-alike with a feather in his Afro tap out a rhythm. Three others join in, a not entirely synchronized harmony of drums.

Then a woman with a tambourine walks to the center of the drum circle, bounces her hips here and there, and calls for everyone who passes to join them. Some people stay curious, standing far away, but the drum circle grows. A mother laughs nervously as her son pulls her in, and together they swing their arms and kick up sand with their feet. An older couple enters the circle. A few high school students.

Suddenly, alarm bells go off in my head. Anyone could be here. I scan the small crowd for a familiar face, a Bellwood student. Worst-case scenario, Miguel and Henry.

How would I explain this? Hanging out on the beach with the bathroom girl? They're sure something went on between us and they won't let up. Won't quit asking questions there's no answer to: *Is she good?* Me dancing with her on the beach would be all the evidence they need that something really did happen between us.

I mean, I wish something *had* happened, not gonna lie. You don't meet a girl like that and not fantasize about it. But that's the dumb part of me. The smarter Derek appreciates the reality, what *actually* happened: I had a moment of relief. Like when a boxer is getting pounded relentlessly and suddenly breaks free. That moment. He can breathe. He can find his bearings. He's not gonna fall. That's what it felt like. Someone for one second cared, gave me a moment to breathe, and it wasn't my friends.

My mind wanders to Tillman, and I feel bad that I scared him, feel bad that Jae was there for that. Fear will make you do dumb things.

Jae grabs my arm and tries to pull me toward the group. I stay planted. "I'm not dancing," I say.

"Why not?"

I survey the growing crowd and don't see anyone I know. But still, dancing doesn't sound enticing. Besides the social risk, I'm more of a head-banging fist-pumper than a dancer. In one of my spontaneous moments, I danced along with Madhuri Dixit in *Devdas*, just to make Mom and Dad laugh. But that doesn't count. The only time I've ever *really* danced was in middle school. Suit and tie. Both hands on the girl's hips as we slid side to side. That kind of dance.

"You want me to dance with a bunch of strangers on the beach?" I ask flatly, trying to show my lack of enthusiasm.

"Not with strangers. With me," she says, and my heart does a quick *thud-thud*. Her eyes are big, her lips pouty, and I'm thinking, *Damn*. I remember her teasing voice at the pavilion. It's like a cat that brushes against you while it slinks by and then pretends not to care you're there. No, there's something in Jae's voice, and it makes me tingle. And after what just happened at the water, seeing her sad and deflated, I can't say no. If I'm a sucker for anything, it's those freaking dimples.

All resistance is gone and she drags me to the group, leaving our shoes behind in the sand.

The drums are pounding, the tambourine is shaking, and Jae is smiling like she's found the lost city of Atlantis.

"This is so cool!" She giggles, winding her shoulders.

"Dancing?"

"The drum circle. I saw it on YouTube. I wanted to know as much as I could about Delray before I moved here. This looked like the most fun."

"Really?" I laugh. It's easy to see why she's happy. She's a great dancer.

"Loosen up, Derek," she says, and I try.

Everyone's moving differently, like they're hearing different rhythms. So I follow my own, move my hips to the *ta-tara-TA ta-tara-TA* of the bongos and djembes. Jae's doing a sidestep, right foot out, then left, hips and arms flowing like water. Soon the drummers give a final *ta-ta-ta ta-ta-ta TA*, and the crowd applauds and cheers. People start milling around, and Jae stares at me with her head cocked, hands on hips.

"Derek, you can actually move!"

I chuckle. "I'll take your word for it."

"No, seriously. Once you forgot about people watching you."

"I didn't forget."

She grabs my arm and shakes. "Wasn't that fun, though?"

She lets go, but the feeling of her touch lingers. "Yeah," I answer, but I don't elaborate. It was fun watching *her*, seeing how confident she is in her body when it's in rhythm. Like she's infatuated with her shoulders, her hips, her feet. It's hard not to get lost in that.

The musicians are brushing their fingers against their drums like they're ready to start up again when a guy in a Hozier tour tee and three nose piercings saunters up to us. He has sun-kissed ringlets and magical blue eyes and looks like he just stepped out of *GQ Teen Edition*. He reaches for Jae's hand and pulls her to a small group of his friends, and his eyes are glued on her. He's practically drooling. She looks back apologetically and calls me over.

"Naw, I'm good!" I say, and walk to the outside of the circle, where I sit cross-legged in the sand and watch. It's annoying. This guy is incredibly smooth, leaning close into her ear, finding any reason to touch her hand or her waist. I pull out my phone to mindlessly scroll, and three dances later, Jae comes bouncing back.

"Are you sure you don't wanna dance? Brad and his friends are so nice."

"*Brad*?" I huff. "No, I'm gonna go. Super hungry."

"Wait, what time is it?" she asks, panic-stricken as she pulls her phone out of her pocket. "Seven ten? *Seven*?" She stuffs her phone back, runs to pick up her shoes, and waves at Brad's crew as he tries to holler for her number. “Sorry!” she yells, and glances over her shoulder at me as I grab my shoes and catch up to her. “Why didn’t you say something?” she says.

“And interrupt Brad?” I laugh. “No. When Brad has his mind set on something, no one can stand in his way.”

She tsks. “You seem a little bothered by him.”

“By Brad? No, everybody loves Brad.”

Both our feet are sinking into sand, and she starts to get out of breath. “Light, shadow, rain, sun, breathe deep, carry on,” she repeats.

“What is that?”

“Oh,” she says, like she forgot I was there. “It’s an affirmation.” We pass a blue-and-white lifeguard tower, and then she adds, panting, “It reminds me to . . . just keep breathing.” It’s the way she says it that lets me know there’s more to it. Like water becoming a part of her. There are things she’s not saying. But I’ve got my own things, so I nod.

“Who’s your favorite poet?” I ask, just as we pass through the pavilion, because poetry is the one thing that can make her words spill out.

“Right now, it’s Lucille Clifton. Sometimes I read ‘won’t you celebrate with me’ before I sleep. I think one day I’ll have something to celebrate too.”

“But not now?” I ask.

She blinks up at me. “Do you?”

We’re both quiet until we get close to the main entrance. The sky now is dimmer, a faint pink bleeding into the clouds. She stops walking, faces me with hands on hips. “We danced when the sun set,” she says.

“Huh?”

“It’s a poem. You do the next line. We danced when the sun set.”

"I think I've done enough embarrassing things for today," I say, stuffing my hands into my pockets. "Enough to last a lifetime."

"What, are you really that terrible at poetry? You suck *that* much?" There's a small glint in her eyes and I know she's teasing. I take the bait.

"Fine, start again," I say.

"We danced when the sun set."

I lick my lips and stare up at the meandering clouds, searching for words. "Um . . . We danced when the sun set. It's not something we planned."

"The sun must have left its magic."

"It might never rise again."

She shakes her head and smiles. "And you say you can't write poetry. If you keep this up, you could be famous. On-the-couch-with-Oprah famous." Her stomach growls, and she looks down at it in shock. "Wow," she laughs, and starts walking again, faster.

We reach the bike racks at the entrance, and I bend down to unlock mine, shiny dented silver.

"How're you getting home?" I ask.

"Walking. I like walking."

"I mean . . ." I look up and down A1A, cars passing. "It's gonna get dark. I'll walk with you."

"You don't have to."

I shrug. It's not like anyone's waiting for me at home.

We start down the sidewalk, which is partially shadowed by trees, and she starts naming them. Then she suddenly says, "You can't walk me all the way. My uncle can't see you."

I laugh. "Come on, I'm sure he'd love me."

"Not a chance in hell."

I gasp, clutch my heart. "Because I'm not *Brad*?"

"Because you have a Y chromosome."

We're quiet most of the way, and I can almost hear her, under her breath, stepping to the rhythm of those words, *Breathe deep, carry on, breathe deep, carry on*. It's like she's in a trance. But it's funny, I'm in my own, stuck on Jae dancing on the beach. With Brad. I think, *She'd look good with a guy like that.* And when my stomach sinks a little, I stop wheeling my bike so fast, it clips me in the leg. *Wait. Why the fuck do I care?*

"Hey!" I shout at her back. "I'll see you later!" And then I jump on my bike, try to ignore her voice calling me, and pedal as fast as I can in the other direction.

CHAPTER FOURTEEN

Jae

Everyone's already there when I get to the grove Tuesday after school. Derek's sitting on a stump with his ankle resting on his knee as he plays with his shoelaces. When he looks up, he gives me the teeniest of smiles, which makes my insides flip-flop. *Don't do that*, I tell my body, as if my body has ever listened to me before. The skin around his eyes looks slightly gray, like he didn't sleep at all last night.

I didn't sleep either. Being at the beach with Derek took my mind somewhere else for a while. I can't remember the last time I laughed like that. But then I came home again—to Uncle Rowan's house—and it was like all the lights in a dark room were turned on at the same time. The glaring reality of where I was and why. The laughter, the dancing on the beach, all that felt shortsighted and ridiculous. Uncle Rowan had expectations, and I had resolutions. I wouldn't lose myself in another boy, in another trouble.

I couldn't sleep without waking up to thoughts of June. Worries. I wondered what it would have been like if I had kept her—if I *should* have kept her. I wondered how she would do in school later, being born in June and being so small. I wondered if teachers would want to love her as much as I did. Or if they would see her shiny brown skin and see trouble. I dreamed and I worried and I made myself forget about the beach and that small sliver of joy I felt.

Until now.

I don't look at Derek as I take the last stump, right beside him.

"Pssst." He leans toward me. I pretend not to hear.

Mrs. Aldana's sitting on the fallen log, hugging her gold shawl tightly around herself. "William, do we have any business to get to before we get started?"

William stands up and redoes his ponytail, smoothing down the blond edges. "All right. We decided last meeting that Derek and Jae would look for a venue for the open mic. Do we have any updates on that?"

I nod. "On Friday we went to the pavilion at Atlantic Dunes Park. There's lots of standing and sitting space, plus covering for bad weather. And it's nice with the ocean and everything."

Swan, sitting cross-legged on the blanket beside CJ, fluffs up her dark hair, which today looks curled and hair-sprayed. "Hey, not a bad idea. Good job, newbies. Would be nice to have a few more options, though."

"But it's perfect," I say.

"What if it's already reserved? Or we need something else last minute? Anything can happen." She sighs. "Can you just give us a few more options?"

I exhale slowly and nod. I sneak a glance at Derek and he's staring at me, so intensely I can see the honey flecks in his dark eyes.

"Well, that's all the business we have for today," William says. "Unless someone has something else to add."

We all shake our heads. William sits down, and we turn our eyes to Mrs. Aldana.

She stands up and walks slowly around the fire pit. She looks almost mythical, like she should cast a spell or start chanting or offer up prayers to the goddess earth.

"Today for our five-minute poem," she says, "I'd like you to write to someone you need to forgive."

I suppress a sigh, but Derek doesn't. He's staring at the ground and letting out a slow breath through inflated cheeks. He suddenly looks up at her. "Why? Can't we write about rainbows and stuff like that?"

She smiles. "I don't think *rainbows and stuff like that* could make you feel what you're feeling now. This is your mission, if you choose to accept it." She watches Derek shift uneasily on his tree stump. "Do you wish to accept it?"

He crosses his arms over his chest. "I dunno. Maybe."

"Maybe the first person who comes to mind is the person you need to forgive the most," Mrs. Aldana says to all of us.

I drop my eyes so she can't see through me to the woman who smells like gardenias. The one who slipped away from me, not once but twice, like I wasn't worth fighting for. Who, on most days, was red-eyed and barely there.

It was during the holidays, a week before Christmas. Dad was away on his yearly trip "back home" to Ghana. I found a picture tucked inside the cover of his physics textbook and beneath a pile of student exams that needed grading. A woman the color of milk chocolate with red lips and a shiny, tapered wig. Her hands rested on two kids, one barely up to her hip, the other reaching her shoulder. And Dad's hand was on her waist, and he smiled like he belonged there. With them.

There wasn't enough money to take us all, he'd said before he left. But I understood, even though I was just a knobby-kneed six-year-old holding that photo, that Dad didn't take us to Ghana because there was already an *us* there.

When he came back, the house trembled constantly, like we were planted on train tracks and a train was forever approaching. Plates broke. Brooms broke. Mirrors broke. And then it was quiet.

His leaving was sudden, like a sky that pours down rain, giving you no time to find shelter. And when he left us, Mom left me.

There was no more humming in the kitchen. The leaves on the Guiana chestnut started to yellow. Her flesh, her voice, her eyes lost their softness. To the world, she was the same Paula, but at home she sat motionless, like the world didn't exist. And I knew every time she looked at me that her sadness was the most real thing, and that I would never be enough.

But that first leaving was a long time ago.

When June Baby was growing inside me, making me bigger and bigger, Mom was making me smaller. Her eyes cut across the room at me when I got up from the couch. Her tongue clacked when I cried from sadness. Her head shook when I doubled over from nausea. Every down moment since I got pregnant was an opportunity to point out my failure. She wasn't there for me to lean on until after June Baby was gone, like that was the condition of her love.

So when Mom called last night, I didn't pick up. When she called Uncle Rowan trying to reach me, and when he came to my room with his phone, I pretended to be asleep. I told myself I'd call her later, but I won't. Mom is back home in Atlanta where I need her to be, and I'm here, trying to forget.

I can't share all this with the club. This pain is mine. So I write two poems again. And when Mrs. Aldana calls my name, I read:

you remind me of Uncle Phil
from The Fresh Prince of Bel-Air
you got that look
like nothing in the world
could please you
so why even try? why even care?
when you're just Uncle Phil
from The Fresh Prince of Bel-Air

Swan's poem is a visual poem, words hidden among words, and can't be read out loud. So she passes around her notebook, showing the meticulous swirl of purple calligraphy filling the entire page. "we're not supposed to be strangers," it's called. "Have you ever looked for me?" it asks.

William shares a poem about his cat, Meow-Meow, who goes for blood, and CJ reads a simple line: *I still can't talk about you.*

When it's Derek's turn, he winces. "I wrote something. I tried. But I don't wanna read it."

I can't help but think about our poem on the beach and how he surprised both of us. *Just read it*, I wanna tell him. *You're a writer.*

But then Mrs. Aldana praises his progress and moves on with the meeting. She hands out copies of last year's anthology and we discuss possible themes for this year's. We talk about using the open mic as a fundraiser so we can print anthologies in color. And then we critique poems we've written during the week. Again, Derek doesn't read, and

I don't know why it bothers me. Maybe I'm curious about him, but maybe I just think he's better than he gives himself credit for.

When the meeting ends, Derek is the first one to get up. He's walking, head bent over his phone, and a tree branch smacks him in his face. His hat falls to the ground.

"Shit!" he says, and turns around when we laugh. Sheepish, he picks up his hat and runs his fingers through his wavy black hair. He pushes his hat back on, and he's wearing a smile that looks far from embarrassed now. He's pleased. Like he's a court jester who met his first success.

I pick up Lucille and follow him. "You shouldn't text and walk," I say.

"Apparently."

"Can we talk about the open mic? What do you think about having a title? Like 'Moonbeams: A Poetry Open Mic.'"

"I mean, sure. Or we could just call it 'Bellwood's Poetry Open Mic.' You know? Keep it simple."

I shrug. "Yeah. Okay. But hey, Derek. You're not bad at poetry. I heard you last week. Why didn't you read?"

He smirks. "Why didn't *you*?"

"I did."

"Oh, come on." He stops walking and turns to face me. "You're holding out, Jae. You wrote two poems. I wasn't trying to look, by the way, I just saw. You wrote two poems in five minutes. Like some kind of savant. The first one, you finished super fast. And then you sat there like a tortured poet and wrote the other one. I think the one you read was the easy one."

I bite my lip. How did he figure all that out? "Well, if you weren't so busy spying on me, maybe you could have written a poem you were proud of."

He chuckles. "All right."

"All right," I say.

He holds my gaze for a moment longer than necessary, until I'm thinking about that moment in the bathroom, his midnight eyes in the mirror's reflection. And that moment after, his shirt pulled up to dry his face. His bare skin, smooth.

He starts walking again, his gait slow, like he wants me to follow. *Go home*, a voice inside me says. But it's like he's pulling me through the trees, and I trace his steps, his light depressions in the grass, and leap over a fallen tree entombed in vines. A small red bird hopscotches along its length.

I'm quietly watching him, the way he walks with the straightest back, the slightest swing of his head, his tanned calves in bleached white sneakers. I shouldn't enjoy watching him this much.

"Have any other ideas for venues?" I ask, giving myself a reason to be there. "Swan wants more options."

"The school gym is still available," he says, stopping to look over his shoulder.

I frown and he laughs, his teeth annoyingly perfect.

"If you can come up with a couple more options," I say, "I'll look into catering." We're standing close, under a clear patch of sun with no shadows.

"Cool," he says.

"Cool?"

He shrugs. "Yeah." He grabs the straps of his backpack at his shoulder and looks down at me. I should leave him now. I should leave now.

And then he says with a small squint, "You live with your uncle. How come?" And I wonder how long he's been thinking about these things, the words we said on the beach.

My mouth is clumsy, uncommitted to intelligible sounds, until I can finally say, “I just needed something new.”

“But if it sucks so bad with him, why stay?”

“He’s really not all that bad. He just has a narrow idea of how I should live my life, and somehow I’m doing a terrible job at it.”

“Sounds like every adult in history.”

“Right? Like my mom is—” I snap my mouth shut. I can’t go there. I can’t go back there to Atlanta. I can’t talk about Before, especially with Derek. “Anyway, my uncle’s who I have now. I mean, there’s family on my dad’s side, but I don’t really know them. Most of them still live in Ghana. I think there’s a bunch of them in Canada and Germany, too, but I’ve never met them.”

“Wait. You’re African?”

“Half Ghanaian. Who knows what else. We never did one of those ancestry DNA tests or anything. And anyway, it’s hard to say I’m Ghanaian when I don’t know anything about the country. It was like my dad was too busy being Ghanaian to show me how to be.”

“Maybe he just took it for granted. I know my dad did. My mom was the one who tried to make me feel connected to the Indian culture. You should see her cookbook collection, it’s obscene. She dragged us to Indian festivals and planned our Bollywood movie nights. Those were *looong* nights. But I couldn’t even pretend to hate them.”

“So, do you actually feel connected to Indian culture?” I ask.

He purses his lips. “My dad is Gujarati. But honestly, nothing about me feels distinctly Gujarati. I think . . . I might always feel like there’s something missing. I’ll never be as Indian as some people think I should be, and I’ll never be as American.” He shrugs. “But it’s whatever. Too much or not enough, it is what it is. I am what I am.”

"Right?" I say, grabbing his arm before I can stop myself. "That feeling that you're too many things and nothing at the same time? I've never met anyone else who gets it."

"Mm." He nods, blinking slowly at me, and then he looks down at my hand on his skin. I drop it and step back, and he looks at me quizzically, like there's a million thoughts he's trying to parse. His quiet is unnerving. He wears it easily, like he could sit with it all day, wrapped around him, content to think. It's not what I expected, and I hear him say again, *I am what I am.*

But who is he really?

"What I don't get," I say, "is how sometimes you're like this, and then sometimes . . ." I stumble for words. "Sometimes you're not a good person."

His eyes widen and his thick eyebrows furrow. "Why am I not a good person?"

"Besides letting your friends bully me?"

He closes his eyes and takes a deep breath. His hat casts a dark shadow over his face.

I cross my arms over my chest. "CJ. He's Tillman. I found out. Christopher James Tillman."

"Okay?" He scrunches his face in confusion. Then his gaze wavers and he looks at the ground. "Oh." He turns away from me, starts walking ahead with wide steps.

"So, why'd you do it?" I ask, following, legs moving double-time. "Why'd you rough him up? He's obviously still scared of you. Every time you talk, he starts folding paper like he has to keep his hands busy."

"I didn't rough him up."

"No? I must have misunderstood the body slamming into the wall. I didn't realize *you'll regret the day you met me* was just friendly talk. I come from Atlanta, so I'm not used to small-town lingo."

"Stop, Jae."

"I just want to know. What did he do to deserve that?"

"Nothing."

"Then why'd you do it?"

His jaw tenses. "Let's just stick to planning the open mic. Okay?"

"Just tell me—"

"No. You tell *me*. What did your other poem say? Tell me why you stop yourself when you're about to mention your mom. Why are you so scared of water? And why do you have to remind yourself to keep breathing?"

I step back, mouth agape.

"So. Let's just stick to the open mic. Okay?" He talks slowly now, not taking his piercing eyes off mine. "Unless you have other things you want to share."

I'm glowering, sending waves of indignation his way. Did Derek Patel just call me out? Did he chastise me? Was I just *chastised?* If I weren't so annoyed I'd be impressed. He notices everything.

"Fine," I snap.

"Good." His mouth is crooked. Sheepish. "I need your number."

"What?"

"I need your number."

"Why?"

"For planning. Or we could communicate solely in person like cavemen."

I want to say *No* just for the heck of it. For the chastisement. But we still have to do this project together and I won't be the one to slow us down.

He saves my number, then turns around, waves his phone in the air like he's saying goodbye. It's like this with him, I realize. Wanting to be close, and wanting to be at a safe distance. Like needing fire, needing water, but never too much. Too much, and it becomes a part of you. You stop existing.

The poem on the right:

The Art of Leaving

When you leave a daughter behind
To chase a memory that was a lie,
Make sure you leave the photos
Misaligned,
Collecting dust.

Keep the fridge bare
And the stove on,
Sink into darkness till you are
Impossible to find.

Teach her that love is leaving
Without a goodbye,
To fill yourself
With memories,
Until you forget to eat and sleep,
Until you're someone you never hoped to be.
Until you leave
And
Leave
And
Leave.

When you leave a daughter behind,
Don't make it subtle.
Leave a hole
Where home used to be.

CHAPTER FIFTEEN

Jae

I'm about to step out of the grove when I hear someone call my name. I look back into the trees. The sun beams onto the forest floor through the open windows of the canopy. A bird is perched inside the hollow of an oak tree, and its head jerks sharply as it sings. But there's no one.

A loud whistle pierces the air. "Jae!"

I step back in, walk past elegant palms and lazy oaks. I jump over a newly planted dwarf bottlebrush and scare off a hummingbird.

The voices get louder until I'm finally face-to-face with a banyan tree. The thick branches shoot out and up, hiding everyone inside like an open palm with curved fingers. It's like a colony of trees weeping together, roots melting into branches with beginning and end indeterminable.

Mom and I had planned to visit the largest banyan tree in the world one day, all the way in India. It's about two hundred fifty years old, covers four acres of land, and has three thousand aerial shoots. It looks like a small forest, but it's a single tree.

I don't know what happens to our plans now.

William calls down, "Don't just stand there!"

I walk around the stalks of the tree, which look like a tangle of silly string. A thick rope ladder hangs from one of its branches, and I pull myself up until I see them all, sitting, hanging, lounging around like a primate family.

"What are you guys," I say, out of breath, "doing here?"

CJ's climbing up higher, standing on one of the tree arms and reaching for another. His rectangular glasses are slipping precariously down his sharp nose. He wipes his hands on his jeans and grabs the branch, then heaves his legs over it and lets his hands go. He's upside down, letting his arms swing, and his shirt has fallen over his face, revealing a soft and pale stomach.

William leans back on one of the limbs like it's a reclining beach chair. "We hang around sometimes after the meeting," he says. "Climb on up."

I pause. I'm quite content this far off the ground. The last time I climbed a tree—I mean climbed up really high—Mom had to call the firefighters to carry me down.

I'm about to decline, and then I remember: *See? I told you she wouldn't come*. That's what my friends back home said when I stopped going to parties with them, because I was too busy noticing my growing bump to notice how *gorgeous* Paul Sutton looked, or how *Tamera never says hi to us anymore*.

I clench my teeth and stuff my bag into a hollow dip in the tree. I reach for the branch Swan's standing on and let out a loud grunt as I pull myself up until I'm standing next to her, face-to-face. She blinks and her bright red eye shadow flashes. We're so close I can smell whatever tart candy she's sucking on, and her perfume smells like money.

I lean against one of the thick shoots perpendicular to the ground. The ground. I'm probably twelve feet above the ground, and it feels like a hundred.

Just then, my bag tips slowly and falls with a thump into the tree's hollow below. The contents spill out. Textbook. Phone. Pen. Lip gloss. Notebook. Letter. Photo.

It's June Baby, lying on her back with her arms outstretched. I lurch, ready to climb down and rescue her, but I realize no one's paying attention to my bag, and if I climb down to hide the picture, I'll draw attention to it. So I stay put, trying not to stare down at the smiling dark face.

"Why didn't you guys call for Derek, too?" I ask.

"CJ's frightened," William says.

CJ pulls his shirt away from his face and tucks it into his jeans. "Oh, Derek coming up for a friendly chitchat sounds plausible." He rolls his eyes. "He'd probably gut me and stuff my internal cavity with leaves and turn me into a punching bag."

I can't help laughing. "He wouldn't do that."

"No?" CJ asks. "You know what he eats for breakfast? Fresh hearts."

"I think . . ." I start slowly, because I don't know how much I should say about Derek when he's not here. "I think he's afraid to let people see his soft side."

Swan looks up at me with a cocked eyebrow. "*Soft side*? What do you know about his *soft side*? How soft are we talking?" She reaches into her pocket and pulls out a roll of candy, which she holds out to me.

I shake my head and clamp my mouth shut and she returns the candy to her pocket. I think it's better to keep the beach dancing and Bollywood movie nights to myself.

"I'm surprised he even wrote a poem today," William says.

"*I* almost didn't write one," Swan says. "I have a long list of people who've screwed me over. It was hard to choose one. But writing about my Korea mom made the most sense."

"Who's harder to forgive?" CJ asks. "A person you don't even remember, or a person who offed themselves?"

Shocked, I stutter, "Wh-who . . ."

"His brother," William says quietly.

Swan stares at CJ for a while, then shuffles over to his branch. She wraps her knees over the tree and lets herself fall over, hanging upside down beside him. She pokes his pale stomach. "I don't know, Ceej," she says. "It's hard to forgive someone who says in the cruelest way possible, *You're not enough for me to stick around.* I think whatever they're dealing with just gets so big it consumes them. They can't think of anything else."

"Yeah," he says.

"We can talk about Gary if you want," she says.

He shakes his head. "You wanna share, Swan? About your birth mom?"

At the words *birth mom*, my heart does a thing, a sinking, wrenching thing. Everything I hear now is filtered through the sound of blood pounding in my ears.

Swan shrugs. "I mean. There's not much to share, right? I have no idea who she was. She obviously didn't think I was worth sticking around for. She could have been a librarian. Or a spy. Or maybe I got in the way of her trot singing career. I mean, who knows. But if she could have kept me and she didn't, that's just unforgivable."

Unforgivable. That's not true. It can't be. I made the right choice. It wasn't the right time for June and me, and I did the right thing by placing her with another family. Didn't I?

"Who's that in your picture?" Swan asks, as if she can read my thoughts. She's looking at me, upside down, waiting for an answer.

My lips move around invisible words and nothing comes out.

She points below at the items scattered on the tree. "The baby. Who is she? She's cute."

My surprise suddenly turns into something else. Something bigger, redder. "Why do you care?" I snap.

Swan's eyes widen. "Wait, are you serious? It's a simple question."

My face burns hot and I'm thankful they can't see it beneath my dark skin. I lower myself slowly from the branch, reaching with my toes for the one below. I can feel everyone's eyes on me. William's telling Swan to let it go.

"I'm not trying to be an asshole," she says, "I just asked a simple question. She never shares anything real about herself."

CJ's saying something I can't hear because the blood is rushing too hard in my ears. I'm remembering all the reasons I *don't* share anything about myself. I'm tired of being judged.

Unforgivable.

I finally jump down to pick up the fallen items and tuck the photo into my notebook. I stuff everything else into my bag. Rung by rung, I lower myself toward the ground, the words repeating in my head. *Unforgivable. She never shares anything real about herself. Unforgivable.* I jump to the forest floor. I wince at the sharp pain that runs from my feet up my legs. I wait for the pain to dissipate. And then I run, the words thundering beneath my feet.

Don't tell them anything.

Don't tell them.

Don't tell.

Don't!

CHAPTER SIXTEEN

Jae

That night, for the first time, I walk up the driveway and continue along the path to the backyard. I can see it from my window every morning, the swaying palm fronds, the blushing pentas, the bold gerberas, the portulacas round like bursting suns. And at night I see their muted colors surrounded by garden lights. I go there, past the pool and to a soft stretch of grass. I sit on a beautiful rustic garden bench where there are flowers near my feet and a towering hedge at my side.

I realize now why I haven't spent any time in Uncle Rowan's backyard. Gardens were Mom's place, *our* place, and I'm still angry.

Am I unforgivable? Is she? Did she forgive Dad? Did she forgive me?

A cloud of memories hovers over me. Mom on the couch, licking cinnamon roll icing off her fingers. Me walking in holding the pregnancy stick. She shook her head and said, "Nope. I want nothing to do with that."

I started to cry. I felt defeated. I stammered through words that didn't make sense, even to myself.

"Who's going to take care of that baby?" she asked.

"I will."

"Oh? Because you're so grown?" she scoffed. "We taught you better. *I* taught you better. What are you going to do now, Janelle? You're gonna drop out of school?"

"I'm not dropping out. There are lots of single mothers that make it work."

"Well, I'm a single mother now, and it's no cakewalk."

"I made a mistake, Mom. Okay? I made a *mistake*. And now I need you. I need your support."

"You need my support? I wasn't there when you made that baby, was I? What business do you have getting pregnant when you can't even take care of yourself?"

As the days passed and my belly grew larger, the anxiety grew too. Austin avoided me and students whispered as I walked down the hallway. I started to wonder if someone would try to hurt me, to push me into the lockers or push me down the stairs like I'd heard happened at other schools. And then one day the vice principal called me into her office.

"You'll need to withdraw from your honors classes, Jae." She blinked at me through bejeweled horn-rimmed glasses.

My heart plummeted to the floor. "Why? I'm doing well in all my classes."

"Honors classes are not the place for pregnant students. You can continue your studies in regular classes."

"Is that a policy somewhere? Is it written down somewhere that I can't be in honors classes with a big belly?"

"It's more than that, and you know it."

"Is it a policy?" I pressed.

"It is now. It's been decided, Jae. I've already spoken with your teachers."

My shoulders fell, my body deflated. For a few weeks, I had noticed my teachers watching me in a new way. Eyeing my belly sideways as I walked into class. Refusing to call on me when I raised my hand. Docking points on my tests that shouldn't have been. And all the while they had that look in their eyes that said *We knew you'd fit the stereotype somehow.*

"Is there anything I can do? I like my classes," I said, my voice wavering.

"No. You leave honors or you leave school."

That's when I started researching P-schools, or pregnancy schools, schools that offer childcare and health services and counseling. But most of them were already shut down because they had subpar education. The good ones that were left were out of state, which meant that even if the school provided childcare during the day, I'd have to work to afford a place to live on my own. And I couldn't work enough hours to cover childcare, housing, and my school tuition.

I felt guilty that I couldn't do what other women seemed able to do. Without any support, I couldn't make the puzzle pieces fit. Hopeless, I called a free hotline. A woman with a chocolatey-smooth Macy Gray rasp introduced herself, and I felt immediate calm.

"What do you need to have to take care of this baby?" she asked me.

"Help. I need help. I need my mom," I choked.

"And you don't have her support."

"Not at all."

"And what do you want the most for yourself? Not for anyone else. For yourself. What's important to you?"

"To finish school. I don't want to drop out."

"Then, Jae, sweetheart, I think it's time we talk about adoption. Would you like me to refer you to an agency?"

"You mean just give my baby away?"

"No, I mean find amazing parents to take care of your baby so that you can finish school. What do you think? I can at least give you some information to think through."

I didn't have to think much. I knew it was the right choice. June Baby couldn't stay with me. Ms. Rosette was right about that. Mothers have to leave sometimes. But it doesn't mean it's easy to forgive ourselves.

Raise your right hand for me. Do you understand that once you sign, you will have given up all your rights to your child, and that you can never change your mind? Do you understand that this decision is irrevocable?

But I didn't understand. There was no way to understand.

So hearing that word *unforgivable* from Swan—a birth child to a birth mother—brought the past and the future together into a painful point. Is that where my baby will be one day? Hanging upside down in a banyan tree, saying how much she hates the woman who left her?

Unforgivable. Swan dug that word up from the darkest corner of my heart where I'd tucked it away.

They might know the truth already, that the baby in the picture is mine. Did I ruin my chance at friendship with Swan? With all of them?

A light turns on in the upstairs bedroom and I see Ms. Rosette's shadow moving behind the curtains. I stand up and brush away the wetness from my cheeks and bend down to cup the glowing face of a portulaca.

Milk stains on clean tees
Like bursting honeysuckle
For small lips

Don't cry
        over
                spilt
                        milk

CHAPTER SEVENTEEN

Jae

Mom: Jae. When are you going to talk to me?

Me: Just been super busy.

Mom: Doing what?

Me: Sitting in a banyan tree

Mom: A banyan tree

Mom: It's lunchtime. Aren't you supposed to be at school?

Me: You could say that

Mom: Well then why aren't you?

☽

Unknown: hey, it's Derek

Me: Hey

Derek: got a new venue idea, super cool. wanna meet tomorrow?

Me: Have to ask uncle

Me: Don't hold your breath

Derek: 7pm atlantic avenue at gulf stream

CHAPTER EIGHTEEN

Wednesday evening. The sky is fading. Lamps around the water glow like engorged fireflies. Everyone's stepping around me to board the yacht and I'm staring at the palm trees lining the street. Waiting for Jae to materialize.

What if she doesn't come? What if her uncle doesn't let her? I look down at the two tickets in my hand, the prices stamped big and bold in the center.

A slow breeze passes, and something tells me to look up. When I see Jae, my heart skips.

Shit. My heart *skips*.

She's walking up the sidewalk in a long yellow dress that hugs her body when she moves. She's wearing a small cardigan that covers her up, but not really. It's nothing fancy, but it's not a muumuu, and on her, it looks like a million bucks.

I don't know what to do with my hands. I stuff them into my pockets.

She looks over my shoulder at the giant body of the yacht and looks up at the deck, where people are already standing and pointing out across the city. Her eyebrows shoot up. "A boat? We're getting on the water?"

"Your first water experience was a major disappointment. Remember?" I imitate her jumping around like a deer and she laughs. "This is a two-hour ride. What do you think?"

"You want an open mic here?"

I shrug. "You wanted unique."

She nods slowly. "Yeah . . . That would be kinda awesome, wouldn't it?" Then she smiles. Big and dimply. And I'm trying, *I'm trying*, not to notice how my body reacts.

"You're not scared?" I ask.

"As long as we don't sink like the *Titanic*."

"Don't worry. You could always dump me in the ocean and keep the floatie to yourself."

She laughs. "Not helping."

I lead the way onto the boat. "So how did you make it out of the house? What did you tell your uncle?"

"The truth. I said I was looking at a venue with someone from the club."

"And he was cool with that?"

"Uncle Rowan and *cool* don't belong in the same sentence. He let me leave after a long-ass sermon, full of warnings and admonitions."

We pass a dining room paneled in polished wood and go up a winding staircase to the upper deck, where there are six or seven other passengers. I'm trying not to stare at Jae walking in front of me. I'm trying.

Let's just stick to planning the open mic, I say again, but this time to myself.

When we're standing side by side, there's a quiver and the yacht roars to life. Jae grabs the railing and looks up at me, her eyes the size of Jupiter. Then we're pushing through the Intracoastal Waterway, our version of Venice. Mansions pass on either side, giant yachts parked in front like cars. Most of the houses are unoccupied, waiting for their humans to return. Empty hot tubs, empty lounge chairs under shadowy arches, doormats that won't be stepped on for months. Every so often we see someone, and we get a glance, a wave, a shout hello.

There's excited chatter as everyone walks across the deck to take in Delray from this higher vantage point. For a long time, Jae and I don't talk, and it doesn't feel like we need to.

A waitress walks around carrying a tray of drinks, with nonalcoholic punch for us. For the first time, I look around and realize we're the youngest people here. A Japanese couple is taking turns with a digital Polaroid camera. Then the guy walks toward us, the camera hanging around his neck, and waves us together with his hands.

"One picture," he says.

It's awkward, but Jae and I take a step toward each other.

"More, more," he says, with more hand-waving. He motions for me to put my arm around her shoulder.

I don't know what happened between dancing on the beach and now, but I'm scared to touch her. I let my hand hover a millimeter above her shoulder, and she looks up at me with a look that says *Don't be dumb,* and we start laughing. Short nervous chuckles, and then we can't stop. In the middle of it, the camera flashes.

The guy gives us a thumbs-up and the picture rolls out of the camera. As he waves it around, I drop my hand from Jae's shoulders and we ease into another silence, watching the mansions pass.

"So what do you think?" I ask. "This versus the pavilion."

"It's definitely unique. It might be a little distracting, though, don't you think? I mean, it's a gorgeous view, all these houses passing."

I nod. "We could consider the dining room downstairs."

"Yeah, I could see that. At least Swan can't say it's unoriginal." She pauses. "So, we're only talking about club stuff, right?" she asks.

"Yeah."

"Okay. What kind of stuff do you write? You didn't say."

"That's not club stuff."

"Loosely related."

I don't want to go there. To life inside the pink bungalow. It's a minefield of miseries in there. I want to stay here where there's something to smile about. But Jae's looking at me now with intense interest and I'm feeling greedy.

"I had this shoebox full of my grandpa's old baseball cards. They were worth thousands. Anyways, my mom sold them. All of them."

"Without telling you?"

I nod. "I hardly see my grandparents—on either side, actually—and I don't have much to remember them by. So I kept the box and now I fill it with scripts. Screenplays. Sometimes just the bare bones. Enough so I don't forget the premise, you know?"

"Wait. You want to make movies? I would never have guessed."

"I dunno. It's just for fun, I guess. I can't really say what I want to do for sure, you know? There's soccer. I'm pretty good at that. Aren't you supposed to do what you're good at?"

She looks like she just bit into a lemon. "But you don't sound *excited* about soccer. You sound excited about writing. That's the fuel, don't you think? If you're excited about it, you'll probably keep going. You'll get better anyway."

I pause. It's the first time I've really thought about it. That maybe I would rather write a script than play soccer. But the idea of me becoming a professional screenwriter is too far from what I've always thought I'd do, becoming the next Messi, Mbappé, Cristiano Ronaldo. I shake my head. "I dunno. I guess if I could make a difference in Hollywood, that would be cool. I'd love to see more Indian superheroes. I mean, Krrish was something, but . . ."

"Huh?" Just then a bird whizzes past her shoulder. She screams and ducks, grabbing her heart. We both laugh. "So . . . what is Krrish?" she asks, still clutching her chest.

"Well . . . it's kind of . . . so . . . okay." I take a breath. "*Koi . . . Mil Gaya* was the first movie in the franchise—okay?—where this guy gets a brain injury as a baby and then this little alien Jadoo magically heals him. *Krrish* and *Krrish 3* are the sequels about his son named Krrish—of course—who inherited superpowers."

I snap my mouth shut. I realize I'm talking with my hands, and Jae's looking at me like I'm the little alien myself.

She shakes her head. "I'm confused. It went from *Krrish* to *Krrish 3?* What happened to *Krrish 2*?"

I laugh so hard I'm grabbing the railing, and Jae chuckles, watching my face. "You're not the only one asking that question," I say finally.

"You laugh a lot," she says, amused. "I mean, more than I thought you would."

"I get it from my dad," I say, and leave it at that.

The camera guy taps my shoulder and holds out the developed photo. "Beautiful couple," he says. "Beautiful couple."

"We're—" Jae starts.

"Thanks," I say, reaching for it, and he walks back to the waiting woman. I shrug at Jae. "Who cares. We're never gonna see him again. You want it?" I hand the picture to her.

She looks down at it for a while, touching the corners, running her finger down the sides. I've never seen anyone so enthralled by a Polaroid before. "No, you keep it," she says, almost shoving it back into my hands.

"Geez. Do I look like Shrek or something?"

"No," she says quietly. "You look good."

The corner of my lip is just itching to smile. I tuck the photo in my back pocket and lean against the railing. The sun is setting, sending broad strokes of paint across the sky. The night air is crisp. I nudge closer to Jae, let our arms touch. She doesn't move away.

"So how did you end up in the club?" she asks.

"We're supposed to stick to poetry," I say.

"No, we agreed to club stuff. This is relevant."

I almost tell her to forget it. I'm not ready for her big doe eyes of disapproval. But hey, she knows about Tillman and she's still here. And anyway, not even the guys know what really happened. It might be nice to tell *someone*. To not have to keep everything locked inside like Fort Knox.

I wince a little, ease myself into the truth like wading into a pool of piranhas. "I got into a pinch of trouble."

"A pinch? A pinch gets you community service?"

"Yeah. A pinch."

"Okay, what'd you do?"

I cock my head to the side, glance at her through the corner of my eyes. "I don't want you to think poorly of me."

"I couldn't think any more poorly of you."

"Well, in that case. I'm a serial sand thief."

She laughs and rolls her eyes.

"Naw, I'm a professional license plate blocker."

She tsks. "Whatever, Derek."

"Okay, for real, though. I shave cats without their owners' permission."

She bursts out laughing. "Where do you get this stuff?"

"The news."

We both get quiet as we pass a house where a family is having a backyard barbecue. Two men stand around a grill with beers in their hands, laughing as a gentle smoke trails into the night. Two women sit at a table and clink their champagne flutes together. A boy and a girl sit in the pool splashing water on each other. There's something eerie about the picture. Two men, two women, two children. A barbecue, champagne, a pool. It's too perfect, too normal. I wonder what will happen when the two families go their separate ways. I wonder if the mother will pop pills tonight, if the father will sneak off to see his mistress, if their son or daughter will lie in bed wide awake, knowing something isn't right.

"I broke into Mrs. Aldana's house," I say, and Jae makes a sound between a gasp and a scream. She clutches my arm.

"No," she says.

"Yeah."

"No!"

"You have gum in your ears, Jae?"

"Why the hell would you break into Mrs. Aldana's house? Of all people. She's . . . I mean . . . There's Mr. Cuomo. Did you consider Mr. Cuomo? The creep stares at our boobs in class. What the hell, Derek? How'd you even get in?"

"I knew the trick to the door."

She gasps again.

"I know, I know. But you asked."

Jae's saying something, but my heart is doing jumping jacks. There's a familiar dark yellow house along the waterway. Miguel and Henry are outside on the smooth black patio. Miguel wasn't supposed to be home. It's arcade night. And after arcade night there's always drinking in the grove behind the school.

Henry is breakdancing in slow motion, showing Miguel how to get into a windmill. Then he pops back up to his feet and looks over his shoulder at the yacht. I drop down to the floor, my eyes level with Jae's knees.

"What are you doing?" she hisses. I'm sure she hasn't seen them yet, or she'd be down here with me.

I reach for her hand and nudge her to sit down.

Her eyes burrow into my head. "Why are you being so weird?"

I am. I'm being weird. I'm being the biggest coward. I just don't wanna deal with these guys today.

"Is that . . ." Jae's voice fades. "No."

"*Hey!*" I hear Miguel yell. "Is that Easy?"

I groan. Stand up. Take off my hat and brush my hair aside, buying time.

"Derek!" shouts Henry, hands cupped around his mouth like a megaphone. "What the hell's going on, man?"

"Ignore them," I say to Jae's mortified face.

Miguel's voice strains to be heard as we float farther away. *"You taking her to the boom-boom room?"*

My face burns. I turn around and lean against the railing, too embarrassed to look at anyone else on the boat. I seethe and take in a deep breath through clenched teeth. I wish I could just laugh it off, but the look on Jae's face is killing me. "They're idiots," I say.

"You don't have to say anything." She crosses her arms. Her eyebrows are so furrowed they almost fuse together.

I don't blame her for being upset. Me hiding from the guys is epic-level douchery. But she doesn't know them like I do. They're all about appearances. Jae is fun and cute, but absolutely not what you'd call cool. And the poetry club is so far from cool you couldn't see it with the Hubble.

Before, I never had to think about fitting in with the guys, about losing them as friends. I had all the right shit. Now I don't, and I'm still pretending I do. Something about that feels . . . shitty. Especially now, with Jae standing next to me, daggers for eyes. *Shit shit shit.*

I try to talk to her, but it's one-word answers until we dock again. Then it's *goodbye.*

You can't blame her. But at the same time, she could never really understand.

CHAPTER NINETEEN

Jae

I wind my way through the tables in the cafeteria with my plate of lasagna, crisp around the edges. In my periphery is Derek's table, the Who's Who of Bellwood High. *Is that her?* someone whispers. The kind of whisper that wants to be heard. A loud snicker follows. I clench my teeth, remembering Derek on the floor of the yacht, hiding from his friends.

Is it that hard for people to stand with me?

I keep my gaze forward and head toward the Free Verse table, wondering if I'll have a seat there today or if I've been cast off the island. Maybe I ruined the best chance at friendship I had.

I revise Tuesday's scene in my head: me and Swan at the banyan tree. *Who is that?* she asks. *My cousin*, I answer. But I know this better than anyone else: That lie could never roll off my tongue. June is my baby. My daughter. Mine.

CJ, William, and Swan look up as I set my tray down. Almost down. It hovers millimeters above the surface. "Can I sit here?" I ask.

"Why would you even ask?" William says. "Of course you can."

I expect that from William, so I glance at CJ and Swan. CJ nods vigorously and *mm-hmms* around a full mouth. Swan nods, avoiding my eyes.

I sigh into my seat. My tray thunks onto the table. "So. How are you all doing?" I ask, fiddling with my carton of chocolate milk.

"We're doing quite well. How are you, Jae?" Swan asks.

"Fine," I say weakly, and lean over my food.

Swan is unusually quiet, content to write in her poetry notebook in silence, and I feel a niggling guilt. Was I wrong for running off?

And then comes a rush of righteous indignation. It was an uncomfortable situation because Swan made it that way. How could I tell her the truth after what she said about her birth mother?

"He keeps staring at you," William says, interrupting my thoughts.

My heart jumps. Derek? I take a quick peek just as he looks away. He's sitting at the end of the jock table, leaning back with arms crossed. Too cool to do anything, including eat.

"Did you put a spell on him?" William asks.

"Me?" I guffaw. "A spell? Right. Like I could do that."

Just then, Valeria sashays over to Derek, leans forward in her low-cut shirt, and shows him a picture on her phone. He chuckles, then goes back to sitting cool. And *she*!—she just stands there, manicured hand on his shoulder, bum so close to his cheek that if he turned his head he'd be kissing it.

"How is he?" CJ asks.

"Huh?"

"He's helping you with the planning and all that?"

I nod. "He's come up with two great ideas already. It's just . . . he's confusing."

"Confusing or confused?" CJ says, pushing a piece of notebook paper toward me. I scribble on it—*Nature never did betray the heart that loved her. —William Wordsworth*—and slide it back to him. He starts folding.

William cuts into his lasagna with flimsy knife and fork and takes a hungry bite. "You won't have to worry about him for much longer. So take heart."

Unfortunately, I actually *like* spending time with Derek. He's smart and funny and I keep discovering things that soften his edge. But his friends are the element that completely sours the milk.

"You could just *not* have us plan the open mic together," I say.

"It's tradition," Swan counters, like that ends the conversation. Like being a senior gives her all the power.

I make my voice light. "He found an amazing venue. A yacht. Isn't that cool? We went yesterday. It was actually a lot of fun at first. We just stuck to topics around the poetry club, nothing too deep."

"Surprise, surprise," Swan mutters, not even looking up. CJ raises his eyebrows, and William gives a dramatic shrug, two hands in the air like he's carrying platters. I decide to ignore her.

"But anyway," I continue, "when the yacht got close to his friend's house, he hid. But it was too late. They saw us."

"He ran off?" William asks, incredulous. CJ snorts and shakes his head.

"No, he dropped to the yacht floor," I explain. "Dropped like a hot potato."

"Why does that bother you?" Swan asks. "You're good at hiding too."

"Swan." William shakes his head.

She sighs and closes her notebook. "Well. We kinda knew what we were getting into with him, right? Can't expect someone with his social clout to just give it up. Especially when he's trying that hard to keep up an image. I just think we should lower our expectations. Derek's going to show up at the meetings because he obviously has to, and that's it." She pauses. "And I'm lowering my expectations for you, too, Jae. I really thought we could be friends."

"Wh-what?" I stammer. It's like she slammed a door right in my face. I didn't join Free Verse just to write poetry. I joined for friends.

"You ran off without saying anything," she says. "I still don't know why my question was so offensive."

"It wasn't your question. It was . . . You . . . You can't just say anything without consequences. Sometimes your words affect people."

"What did I say?"

I wince. *Unforgivable*. How can I explain that without saying the truth?

"See, Jae?" she says. "You can't even tell me what was wrong with what I asked." She sighs, closes her eyes. "Look, I'm sorry for giving you a hard time. I just don't take rejection well."

"I didn't reject you."

"It felt like it."

I press my lips shut and take a breath. "I . . . I'm sorry. It's nothing. Really. Don't worry about it."

"Okay," she says. "You're entitled to your secrets, and I'm sorry if I offended you. But it might happen again because I still don't know what I did wrong." She shrugs. "But hey, Ceej, I got a star poem for you."

I stare at my food. Stab my milk carton with the straw over and over again. Rewrite all the moments that have gone wrong since I set foot in Bellwood High. Starting with Miguel. Starting with Derek.

For the rest of lunch, Swan is normal. Almost. She talks to me, but it's as if she's craning her head over a giant wall to do it.

CHAPTER TWENTY

Jae

Today at Free Verse when Mrs. Aldana asks Derek to read, he leans his elbows on his knees and stares at the pages of his poetry notebook.

He reads.

Let's rewind
You say, Are you okay?
And I say, No
I grab your hand, because I like how it feels,
Not because I'm trying to hide
Let's rewind
Back in time
I'm not supposed to rhyme, am I?
So it's like . . .

We're in a different dimension
A different place in space-time

That's what I'm thinking about sitting on this dead tree
Surrounded by book dweebs—but
I'm one of them now, F me
What would it feel like if we could just rewind
If I could just unwind
If I could just be me

Derek closes his notebook and looks right at me and I don't think I'm breathing yet. I don't think I can hear anyone else's voice yet. He read his poem out loud for the first time, and he's definitely not Langston Hughes, but he read his poem! I'm so proud of him I forget to be mad. And it was about *me*. I'm sure everyone knows this by now, with the way he's looking at me, eyes so dark but clear beneath the visor of his cap. How do you feel normal under a gaze like that? How do you stop your whole body from glowing, from feeling warm and tingly?

If we could just rewind. If I could just be me. I think about the small glimpses I've seen. His sobs in the bathroom the first day we met. His scriptwriting and love for Bollywood movies. Him trying to get me into the water. Dancing on the beach. Laughing on the yacht.

Do all those moments cancel out the negative ones?

I'm next, and I read my poem, distracted. Then I listen to CJ and Swan, distracted. Nothing seems to hold the same weight as Derek's words. Until William reads.

He stands up. He never stands up to read, but today he does, and he stuffs one hand into the pocket of his baggy jeans and holds his notebook with the other. It's the way he's standing that makes me pay attention. And I hear every searing word.

<u>*Strike-a-match*</u>

Six foot three
From Washington, DC
Likes the smell of fresh coffee
French toast on weekends
And road trips to find winter snow
Name is easy: Arnie Ainsley
Stepdad #3

When
He didn't like the groan of the radiator
Or the sunlight on his hairy toes
Or I asked for more food than I should have
Or Meow-Meow meowed too loud
When
Mom's dress was too tight or too loose
Or too red or too blue or
Something.
Anything.
His fists found a reason
For everything.

And then, because we can't ask questions about our five-minute poems, we all sit quiet for a while, and the birds are the only ones talking. Then Mrs. Aldana tells William to see her after the meeting. And we're all filled up like pitchers with words that mean too much.

CHAPTER TWENTY-ONE

Jae

After the meeting, Mrs. Aldana pulls William aside. CJ and Swan head to the banyan tree and Derek stands over me. He's shifting his feet, nervous white sneakers in bright green grass.

"Hey," he says.

"Hey," I say.

"Umm . . . you heard my poem?"

"I was there."

"So, what do you think?"

I'm quiet, letting him shift uneasily as he waits. *Rewind.* Does he mean erase? As in, forget about everything that happened and start with a blank slate? Does he deserve a blank slate when I don't get one?

"I don't know, Derek," I say.

He breathes in deep. "I wanna try again."

I sling Lucille over my shoulder and stand up, my forehead nearly touching his chin. He takes a step back. "Try what again?"

"Meet me? This Sunday at the Sundy House."

He's clamping his bottom lip between his teeth, waiting for an answer. And I don't know. I'm pulled to him—it's hard not to be. But at the same time, my memories pull me back. Tell me to tread lightly. Tell me to run.

I breathe in slowly. "Is this about the club? Or something else?"

His eyes flick around the grove, landing on William and Mrs. Aldana, who've stopped talking. William heads toward the banyan tree and Mrs. Aldana toward the school. She waves at us, gives a radiant smile.

"The Sundy House is a good venue," he says. "But I . . . I really wanna take you there. I think you'd like it." He takes off his hat and runs his fingers through his hair. Then he looks resigned, embarrassed, like he expects me to say no.

"That sounds like a date," I say.

"Maybe it is?" The teeniest crooked smile.

My heart. It drops or it jumps or it malfunctions completely for a second, and I lean away from him. "Your friends."

"I don't wanna talk about them now," he says.

"You can't just keep hiding from them. And pulling me down with you."

"Okay. I get it. There's a lot of stuff to tell you. I *want* to tell you, but . . . not now. Sunday?" he asks, hopeful. "How about eleven?"

Scouting venues on the weekend means Uncle Rowan will have more time to be nosy, more time to wonder what I'm really up to. But I guess I'm going to take the risk because I want to hear what Derek has to say. And if I'm honest, I want to see him more, date or no date. "I'll try," I say. His shoulders drop like he's been tense this whole time.

"I'm going to the banyan tree. Are you coming?" I ask, pointing over my shoulder.

"Maybe next time," he says, a shine in his eyes.

"All right." I bite my lip to keep my smile from growing too big, then wave and walk away, down the path leading to the banyan tree. But when I look over my shoulder expecting to see the back of him, his eyes are watching me, and I could melt. Right there.

☽

I feel light, like I should be able to skip the rope ladder altogether, float up and settle soft on a limb. But I pull myself up, rung by rung, until CJ's scuffed-up Keds are dangling above my head.

"Hey, Jae," they all say together, and laugh.

William's hanging upside down today, legs wrapped around a branch like a sloth. "Is Derek coming?" he asks.

"He said maybe next time."

"Ooooh," Swan croons. "Maybe next time."

CJ chuckles. "How does it feel to have a poem written about you, Jae?"

Swan waves her hand in the air, all thespian. "How do I love thee? Let me count the ways."

"Shall I compare thee to a summer's day?" William adds, arms swinging.

"Rapunzel, Rapunzel, let down your hair," CJ adds.

I try not to laugh. "Whatever, guys," I say.

Swan laughs too. Then he frowns and looks at William. "Your poem was a bit . . . heavy. Are you doing okay?"

"Yeah," he says. "Mom's getting married again next month. Brought back some bad memories. But I'm all right."

"How long was Stepdad Number Three around?" CJ asks.

"Two years, five months, and seventeen days," William says, righting himself on the branch. "I used to not talk about him. I felt super embarrassed."

"Even though it wasn't your fault?" I ask. I understand shame, but shame for someone else hurting you? That I can't understand.

"I felt like it *was* my fault," he says, pulling his hair out of the ponytail and winding the band through his fingers. His hair falls across his face as he looks down toward the ground. "But Arnie could make you believe rain in April was your fault. Anyway, I can write about it easier than I can talk about it. But yeah. I can talk about it now. With the right people."

"That part." Swan nods and places a hand over her chest. "Well, I love you, William Shakespeare, and I'm honored to know you. This club would be nothing without you, you know that? And I hope Arnie Ainsley rots."

William chuckles, but his blue eyes are dull when he finally looks up at us. "I love that you guys know me better than anyone else in this school."

Swan nods. "Me too. Frankly, William, a lot of them don't deserve us. Like Jane Keen! She had the nerve to ask me if I could teach her Korean, after she said I smelled like kimchi!"

I gasp. "She said that?"

"I eat danmuji with literally everything and it drives my mom nuts. So, kimchi where? Like, no, Miss Jane. You can rot in ignorance."

"Why would she even ask for your help?" I say. "That's like throwing pearls before swine."

"Huh?"

"It's in the Bible. Don't cast your pearls before swine. Like, don't give the things you value to people who'll just trample over them."

"Aaah . . ." Swan nods. "So, in *your* case, we're the swine? Because we're not worth sharing things with?"

My mouth falls open. "No. That's not what I meant."

"Okay." She shrugs.

"Swan . . ." I let my words drift off. There's no way to gather them in a way that makes sense to her. I can keep my secrets and she'll tolerate me like she does now. Or I can tell her the truth and she'll hate me.

As much as I want to smooth things over with her, I remember my friends not calling me, my teachers ignoring me, Uncle Rowan and his constant judgment. And Mom, so disappointed she couldn't love me.

I'll keep my secrets. The truth does not set you free.

CHAPTER TWENTY-TWO

Jae

The Sundy House is a six-minute drive from home, but more than a forty-minute walk. Instead of ordering a rideshare for me, Uncle Rowan insists on driving me himself.

Sitting beside him in his pristine Cadillac, I remember how nervous I was riding with him to Delray. Right now, he's tapping a long finger on the steering wheel, peering straight ahead at the road. He's deep in thought, because his brow furrows and releases, over and over again. He clears his throat.

"This friend from the poetry club," he starts, and he pauses for so long I wonder if he'll ever complete his thought.

This friend from the poetry club. Derek. The boy I wish I could stop thinking about but can't. The boy with the softest smile, the darkest eyes, a heart that gets sweeter the more I see of it.

"This friend," Uncle Rowan continues, "is a boy?"

"Yup," I say lightly. I pick up my bag from the floor and dig around inside to find something invisible.

"Is that why you're dressed like that?" He scans my dress, knee-length with blue and white stripes. "This doesn't seem like a school thing to me."

I don't want to lie. Not completely. "He said it's a possible poetry venue."

"Okay. This . . . *boy* who took you to the pavilion—in search of a proper venue, of course—is this the same boy who you met last week?"

The words stick like glue in my mouth. I want to tell Uncle Rowan to let me live, to let me be a teenager and meet a cute boy for brunch, but I can't give him lip if I want to stay in Delray.

"Yes," I say.

"And now he's meeting you again. On a weekend. This sounds like a date to me, Janelle."

"He told me to dress nice because it's a nice place. We didn't decide to work on this project together, Uncle Rowan. Swan and William chose us because we're new to the club. And who knows, maybe if we put on a great event, I'll get to be an officer in the club next year." I look at him out of the corners of my eyes. "To be honest, it's just really nice to have friends here. It wasn't too easy at my last school."

"And you know why." His voice is rough and suddenly makes me want to crawl inside myself. He speaks again, this time softer. "I know how hard it is to be a teenager. I also know how easy it is to mess up your life." He gives me a knowing look. "I push you. But I don't do it to make you feel small. I want you to be hungry for better. That's all I want."

I nod.

"There's greatness in you, and you can't even see it."

My face warms and I look down at my feet. I don't remember the last kind thing Uncle Rowan said about me. And now he's saying there's greatness in me. In *me*. It's not that I don't believe in myself. It's just, when the people who are supposed to love you only point out your flaws, you start to forget there's anything else.

"The poetry club," he says. "I pressed you about that club and you folded." He pulls up to a red light and looks at me. I avoid his eyes. "I used to tell your mama all the time, if you want to become a diamond, you have to get pressed."

I look at him, surprised that the words Mom always said to me first came from him.

"You know what I wanted to hear from you, Janelle? *I'm going to be the best damn poet this world has ever seen and that club is going to be my training ground.*" He punctuates his words with his palm hitting the steering wheel. "The more confidence you have in your own decisions, the more confidence I'll have in you. Easy as that. I'll keep pushing you until you figure out who you are. But until then," he says, pointing a finger at me, "I *will* tell you what you *won't* be."

I shift in my seat as the light turns green and he revs up the engine.

"You will not be a teen mom for a second time. You will not be a high school dropout. I refuse to let you accept less than the best because you don't know what better looks like. So you be careful with this boy," he says, tapping my knee. "If you can't make the right decisions, I'll make them for you."

I sink lower in my seat and turn away to look out my window. Uncle Rowan's words linger like must in fine clothes. There's greatness in me, he says. But only if I do what he wants.

He pulls into the driveway of a quaint yellow house and stops the car. I peer out the window.

"That's it." He leans over the steering wheel to look up at the house. "It's the oldest house in Delray. Been here since the early 1900s. Built by Delray's first mayor, Jim or John or Jack Sundy." He waves his hand. "Name starts with a *J*. Doesn't look like much on the outside, huh?"

No, it doesn't. It looks cozy, and I imagine inside there's a floral sofa somewhere and a table with a doily on it. But I can't see anything so special about it that Derek would want to come here.

I open the car door to step outside.

"What's his name?" Uncle Rowan's voice stops me.

"Huh?"

"His name."

I lick my lips, buying time. "Derek Patel."

He blinks quickly and frowns. "I'm going to be on an important call for the next couple of hours. Can you order a ride back to the house? I'll add you to the family account."

I nod and close the door and watch him pull away from the curb. I take my phone out of my purse. It's ten minutes to eleven. I check my text messages to see if Derek's already here, but there are no messages and no missed calls.

A high-pitched birdsong makes me turn, to see a red finch peeking out from the lower branches of a flowering tree. Its head whips left and right, and then it freezes when it sees me. It sings, its black beak brilliant in the sun, *For the second time. For the second time. For the second time.*

CHAPTER TWENTY-THREE

Jae

I hear my name and turn to see him, a shadow in the doorway of the yellow house. His hands are stuffed into the pockets of dark slacks, and his baseball cap shades his eyes. It's strange how different, how new he looks, how darkness can shine. He walks toward me and his eyes don't leave mine. He stops. Full mouth. Icy mint wafting from smiling lips. His irises are gradients of lights and shadows. He runs a cool hand down my bare arm until our fingers intertwine. It's the most breathtaking hello I've ever felt.

"You made it." His smile crinkles the edge of his eyes.

"I made it."

He runs his thumb along mine, slowly, stopping to rub my knuckles in gentle circles. I laugh to stop the shivers running bone-deep.

He clasps my hand tight now and leads me slowly toward the side of the house, past a friendly valet, under palms, to a small wooden bridge. The boards thump hollow as we walk over them, over a pond encased with leaves and flowers.

He suddenly stops and pulls me closer to him. "Careful. Alligator."

I see it, mouth ajar, and I jump away from the railing, expecting it to lunge at us with its iron teeth. But it's frozen. Lifeless. Statuesque.

I kiss my teeth and lightly push Derek's shoulder.

He laughs, grabs my hand with both of his, and leads me across the bridge. We walk past tables of people eating eggs and French toast with sugary red berry sauce.

"We have time to kill before our table's ready," Derek says. "Let me give you the VIP tour first."

We walk through one of the most beautiful botanical gardens I've ever seen. Tall bamboo shoots like wild spears. Trees spreading leaves like verdant wings and their canopies fluttering with the movement of chirping birds. I wonder if Derek feels how small we are.

"My mom and I used to visit gardens every Sunday," I say. "We loved wisteria, looked for them everywhere, especially the purple ones. We stopped doing that some years ago, but . . . this is amazing."

"Amazing enough for a poetry venue?"

"Definitely. It's going to be a tough choice."

He leads me to a large pool surrounded by trees, where small yellow fish glimmering like glass flit through the water. He steps out of his shoes and pulls his socks off.

"What are you doing?" I ask.

"Come on," he says, sitting down at the pool's edge. He pulls the bottoms of his pants up and sticks his feet into the water. The fish swarm his feet. "Try it."

"No way."

"Come on. You only live once. It's not as cold as the ocean."

I don't blame him for coaxing me. He doesn't know my history with fish, that I can hardly eat fish, let alone touch them when they're alive. He doesn't know that I had nightmares of Dad's mounted bass coming down from the wall and eating me. He doesn't know that I drowned and nearly died because I thought being an ugly fish was better than being me.

But Derek looks over his shoulder and reaches for my hand and I take it. I slowly sit down and lower my feet into the water next to his. Tan and dark brown, shimmering in liquid sunlight. Within seconds, I feel soft nibbling. My feet jerk out of the water.

He laughs. "Give in to it. It's just a hundred tiny kisses, that's all."

I lower my feet again and close my eyes and try to feel the hundred tiny kisses and then all I can do is laugh. I laugh, and he laughs, and then we laugh because we can't stop.

This feels good. It feels *too* good. He doesn't know anything about me. What if he found out why I moved here? What would he say?

I push the intruding thoughts away. Today, I feel the sun. Today, the air is singing. There is no room to place my secrets.

Not here. Not today. This is good.

But Derek's eyes are suddenly dark and he's furrowing his thick brows.

"What's wrong?" I ask, pulling my feet up to the warm stones.

He takes in a deep breath, looks at me sideways, dark eyes brooding, and then looks up at the canopy. "My dad died right before freshman year. Car accident. I dunno. I just thought of him and . . . Things can be totally fine, and then I laugh, and then I remember his laugh, and then it suddenly becomes . . . too much."

"I'm sorry" is what I say, even though those words are just two grains in a sandcastle of emotions. *I'm sorry your dad's gone. I'm sorry you're sad. I'm sorry you know what it feels like to be left.*

"Thanks." He hunches over cross-legged on the wet stones, fiddles with his shoes and plucks the laces. He presses his eyes hard like you'd press a wound to stop the bleeding. Then he opens them again, lets more words out, but his voice is taut. "Losing him was shitty enough. He was my best friend. Back then, things were good. There's almost nothing left of that now. The good things."

"How about your mom?"

His jaw tenses and he shakes his head. "Mom is Mom." Then he snickers. "That's not even true, but whatever."

I don't understand and I don't push it. I know more than anyone that some doors are better left closed.

"Here," he says, lifting up the tail of his button-up to show his poetry notebook rolled up in his pocket. He pulls it out, flips to a page, and passes it to me. "I wrote it for him. What do you think?"

So I sit quiet as the faint sounds of conversations from the brunch tables, and the birds, and the whispering water fountains all fade into the background. I only hear Derek's words.

your song

here comes the sun
dancing in the moonlight,
boogie shoes
tangled up in blue

i'll be there
summer nights
i've had the time of my life

don't fear the reaper
kiss and say goodbye
go your own way
across the universe
the long and winding road

i'll be there
summer nights
i've had the time of my life

"Every line is a song title," he explains. "Dad loved seventies music."

"Wow," I say.

"We went on these long highway drives together, blasted Meat Loaf and Chicago on the radio like we were characters in some movie." He closes his eyes and with the most dramatic face, starts singing, "You're the Inspiration."

I join in, both of us over-the-top vocalists for Chicago. "Holy cow, Derek. I mean, this is so creative. It's . . . I don't know. I can't even . . ." I pass the notebook back to him. "He would *love* it."

He grimaces and tucks the notebook back in his pocket. "Thanks." He clears the rasp from this throat and asks, "Ready to eat?"

We put on our shoes, then he holds out his hands and pulls me to my feet. He places his hand on the small of my back. Warm.

I feel it. All over.

CHAPTER TWENTY-FOUR

Derek

Heliconias. Jae's sitting across from me at our table, pointing to these brilliant red-and-yellow flowers that hang over a small statue. They look like a vertical row of flamingos. I'm amazed at how she remembers all these plant names. But maybe it's like knowing that Leo's brightest star is Regulus. Maybe it's like knowing the constellations on her face, the tiny birthmark above her left eyebrow, right at the arch, and a darker mark about two inches away on her left cheekbone.

"What?" she asks, brushing a hand across her face, self-conscious.

I smile. Shake my head. "Nothing."

A waiter takes our order, and as soon as he leaves, Jae leans in across the table.

"Doesn't he look like Steve Urkel?" she whispers.

"Who?"

"Jaleel White."

"No idea what you're talking about."

"*Family Matters*."

"Nope."

She leans back, gives me a suspicious look. "*The Bernie Mac Show*?"

"Who?"

She drops her head onto the table. She groans. Then she looks up and whispers, "*The Cosby Show*?"

"Can't blame me for not watching that."

She sits up. "No, I can. The Huxtables were everything." She sighs. "Okay, so what *have* you seen?"

"Black shows? *Black Panther. Luke Cage*."

She groans. "Marvel. Okay."

"Is there some law against enjoying Marvel? Okay, what Indian shows have *you* seen?"

She cocks her head, looks up at the sky. "Well . . ."

"I'll make it easier. Bollywood actors. Go."

She lights up. "Priyanka Chopra."

"No crossovers."

"What's wrong with crossovers?"

"What's wrong with Marvel?"

She throws up her hands. "Fine. Okay. If you had to recommend one show, what would it be?"

"To watch with me?" I ask, heart feeling warmer by the second.

She grins. "Sure."

I look down at the table and peruse my inner catalog of movies, from superhype *Dhoom* to ubercute *Kuch Kuch Hota Hai*. What do I want to watch with her sitting beside me? A movie where darkness fades into light. A movie about unexpected encounters and how they can change your life. "*Jab We Met*," I answer.

"*Jab We Met*. What does that mean?"

"When we met."

"Ah," she says quietly, and I know she's thinking about it too. That day I looked up in the mirror and saw her face. *Are you okay?*

"Sounds like a romance to me," Jae says, coal-dark eyes blinking. She runs her fingers slowly along her water cup dripping with condensation. Drops roll down and dampen the tablecloth.

"It is," I say.

Her eyebrows spring up. "Oh. Okay. Maybe . . . yeah. Okay. Sounds good."

Something about this makes my heart do a cartwheel. She looks nervous. I'm making her nervous. That means . . . Does Jae actually like me? I look away, trying not to be smug, but wanting to bask in the joy of *maybe*. "What would *you* recommend?" I ask, throwing her a lifesaver, because she's obviously drowning in nerves.

She sighs in relief and stirs the ice in her cup with her straw. *Clink clink clink*. "*Girlfriends*," she says.

I laugh. "Sounds promising."

"Don't be a chauvinist." She wags a shiny nail at me. "Those aunties are hilarious *and* fine. I would kill to have Jill Marie Jones's lips. *Kill*."

I shake my head. "I wouldn't change your lips for anything," I say. They look soft. A reddish orange tint today. Wet from water or from licking them, I don't know.

"Okay, okay," she says in a rush, and I realize I'm staring. She tucks her bottom lip into her mouth, averting her gaze, and it sends my insides swirling and shifting and tightening. What I would do to just . . . I shake my head, dislodging the thought.

The waiter stands over us and places our dishes on the table. French toast and berry compote, waffles, eggs, perfectly roasted potatoes, and tall glasses of freshly squeezed juice.

And then I don't know why I say this, except, I shared Dad with her, and it felt good. It felt like she belonged there in the memories of him. So I say, "My dad swore up and down that food tastes better with your hands. Something about the heightened sensory experience. Well. He was talking specifically about Indian food, but . . . whatever."

Jae's jaw drops. "My dad said the same thing. Except it had nothing to do with the senses. Just . . . the magic of the hands, I guess." She laughs. "I thought it was an African thing."

I lean back, really look at her, take her in. She fits. We fit. Jae and I both rip off a piece of a waffle. She holds it up.

"Cheers," she says.

"Cheers." Our waffles touch and we laugh, then proceed to stuff our faces.

The phone in my pocket buzzes. And buzzes. And buzzes. I shun the pretense and lick my fingers—we're eating with our hands, why use a napkin?—and then pull out my phone with "Sorry, one sec," to Jae.

help come home

I'm confused for a moment, like I'm high in a plane and looking down, and not deciphering the splotches of color, the miniatures below. Then my heart beats faster as I start to understand. I push my chair back from the table, like I need this distance between Jae and Mom.

Mom what happened?

I stare at the phone, waiting for a response. Nothing.

Nothing.

Nothing.

I stand up, let my eyes flick to Jae's concerned face as I excuse myself, hurry past the pink flamingos—*heliconias*—and stand over the wooden bridge in front of the alligator's mouth. I call Mom's number and it rings till it goes to voicemail.

Did Peter finally snap?

I text her again, but nothing.

Nothing.

Nothing.

I sigh, defeated. My gut is being wrung out like a shirt holding seawater.

She fits. Jae fits. But only in some parallel universe where I'm allowed to hold on to happiness, where it's not wrung out of me by tight fists. It's not *my* universe, and it's not today.

"What's going on?" Jae asks when I get back to our table. My face must be glowing red hot from embarrassment and I can hardly look at her.

"I'm sorry. I really have to go. I'll pay the bill, don't worry."

"No, that doesn't matter. What—"

"Do you have a ride home?"

I finally meet her eyes, silent black moons.

"Jae, do you have a ride home?"

She nods.

I nod.

And then I'm gone.

When I told Mom I was meeting Jae at the Sundy House, she got that crazy look in her eyes and clapped her hands and said, "Torticas de morón!" which are Cuban sugar cookies she learned how to bake from Mrs. Montero. And I said, "It doesn't make sense to take food to brunch. I'll give them to her later." She shooed me away like a gnat and started pulling out ingredients I didn't even know we had. I tried to ignore her sudden change in mood, tried not to think about what it meant that she seemed so happy, because today wasn't about her.

"Is this a *date*?" she asked. "You haven't brought a girlfriend around since Valeria."

"That doesn't count. That was middle school."

"Exactly! Are you gonna let me meet this girl?"

"No way. I'd rather get alien probed."

"What does that even mean?"

I didn't get very far in my explanation before she sent me a death glare. "*De*-rek."

But now, when I open the front door, Mom's in the kitchen, doubled over, grasping the counter. The tray of cookies sits inside the open oven door. She looks up at me, and everything in her face says she's scared.

I hurry to close the oven and feel the heat hit my face. I pat her back and her shirt is drenched with sweat. I lean over her and put my hands on her shoulders and feel their rise and fall as she struggles for air. "You're okay, Mom. You're hyperventilating. Just breathe slow." I pause. "Is it Peter?"

Her hand shakes as she brings it up to her head and I know she's dizzy.

I put my arm around her shoulders and lead her to the orange sofa in the living room. The curtains are parted slightly and I can see our neighbor Mr. Hall standing on his back porch surveying his lawn.

Mom makes a choking sound. "It's a heart attack this time, I promise. I can't breathe."

The first time Mom had a panic attack, we were both sure she was dying. I called an ambulance. But then it happened again. And again. And again. When the nurses asked how often she drank alcohol, she said, "Not a drop since my husband died." And when they asked her what medications she was on, she stumbled through an incoherent explanation full of *onlys*. Only when she needed them. Only a few. Only when the pain was too much to handle.

"It's a panic attack." I try to keep the irritation out of my voice. "It's a feedback loop, that's all. You get stressed and start hyperventilating, then you feel dizzy and your heart starts pounding like crazy. You start to panic, and then you panic because you're panicking. Just breathe easy. In—one, two, three, four. Out—one, two, three, four, five, six. Come on. You gotta do it with me." I brush a bright strand of hair away from her forehead.

It takes a few minutes, but soon she's breathing in rhythm and her hand stops shaking. She drops her head back against the sofa and looks up at the ceiling. A small tear flows down toward her ear. She wipes the sleeve of her shirt across her nose, which has started to run, and across the sweat on her forehead.

"I'll never get over it," she says.

I don't have to ask what she means. It's Dad not being here. It's him sleeping beneath an ordinary headstone with an ordinary inscription. IN LOVING MEMORY OF ASHWIN PATEL. BELOVED HUSBAND AND FATHER. I think about the rows of carefully plotted tombstones in the cemetery. The mountains of granite that keep the bodies down. Rows and rows of birth dates and last days. Flowers that smell like the living.

How could we ever get over it when there are days like this? When I have the smallest glimpse of happiness and she tramples on it? I try to keep my voice neutral, try to keep the anger out. Try not to think about Jae sitting there, wounded, as I walked out on her. Anytime I try to pull away, Mom sucks me back into her orbit, and I don't know how to get out, how to let her deal with the damage she's done. I comfort her, I lie for her, I pick up the pieces of her broken glass, hoping that tomorrow, she'll put the vase back together. Tomorrow, we'll have something beautiful again. But it never happens.

"I think you need help," I say, as gently as I can. "I think you should see someone. Gina said there's an emotional and psychological component to addiction. She said you need coping skills to help with losing Dad. I think you should see someone."

Her green eyes are dull and uninterested. "Tell Gina to mind her own business."

"Mom—"

"Don't." She gives me a warning look and pushes herself off the couch. I notice again how thin she is, the smallest version of Mom I've ever seen. She hurries out of the living room and there's the rattling sound of a pill bottle being emptied out. I know she's standing at the bathroom mirror, counting them, worried there won't be enough. I follow her to the bathroom, where she's sipping tap water from her hand. The hair at her nape is matted.

"You're running out of pills a lot faster," I say. "You're changing doctors—"

"Dr. Dao had no idea what she was doing."

"I know. She didn't know anything. Dr. Shetty didn't know anything. Dr. Burke didn't know anything. The only person who knows something is you."

"Okay." Mom holds up a hand and turns around. "You're not going to talk to me like that. Not in my own house." She shuffles to her bedroom and I follow.

"I don't want to fight with you, Mom. But please. Get some help."

"*You* get some help," she snaps. "You think your delinquent behavior helps me in any way? Breaking into a teacher's house. Supergluing lockers shut. Oh! Condoms. Yes. Condoms on the flagpole. That's *beautiful*. You're a stellar example of a responsible son. Exactly what I need in my life right now."

The truth in her words hits me, and I'm silent.

She looks at me, eyebrows raised, keen green eyes. She almost whispers when she says, "If you're not making my life better, Derek, then I don't even know why you're here. Your dad should be the one who's here."

"What?" I've had the thought a million times. Dad should be here. But that's not what she's saying. My eyes sting.

She's violently opening and closing her dresser drawers, scraping her fingers along the cracks, feeling through each and every pocket of her clothes. "All you remember about that accident is that your father died. You don't seem to remember me flying through the windshield and having three back surgeries. And now I have to deal with you and everyone else calling me an addict."

I catch the glimmer of light on her wedding band and suddenly wish I could crawl into a corner and cry. I try not to hear the words again, repeating in my mind. *I don't even know why you're here. Your dad should be the one who's here. I don't even know why you're here.*

I put my hand up to my chest. No knife. But I feel it.

"You think this is a good life?" I ask her, my voice shaking. "You don't care about anything anymore, you don't care about me!" Something brief, like shame, flashes in her eyes, and I seize it. "Look, there's that rehab center. It's not far. I'll go with you. I'll take you right now."

"I don't need *help*. I need doctors to do their job."

"Mom, no doctor in their right mind would give you more meds. You're not happy without them. You need more and more. We can fix this, but you have to want help."

"Well, I don't want it," she says slowly, shaking her head, exasperated. Like I'm the problem. Like her life would just be better if I disappeared. *Your dad should be the one who's here.*

She stands quiet, lips in a thin line, an old painting of a sunrise behind her like a nimbus. Then she grabs her purse from the water-stained nightstand and pushes me aside as she leaves the room. "I've had enough," she says.

Just then, the smoke alarm screams, sending my heart racing.

I run into the kitchen and fight to open the rusty old window. The cream curtains flutter like smoke as fresh air wafts in. I open the oven and pull out the black disks of sugar cookies and slam the oven door shut. The pan clatters on the stovetop.

Every blink sends a trail of fresh tears down my cheeks, and I swipe at them desperately. They keep falling, like the hurt doesn't want to stay inside—there's no room left.

I hear Mom hurry past me, turn to see her rush out the door.

And I can't move. I can't move my feet.

CHAPTER TWENTY-FIVE

Jae

Today the cafeteria is swarming as I wind my way to the Free Verse table. I steal a glance toward the jocks, where there's an empty chair beside Miguel, as conspicuous as a missing tooth in a row of veneers.

Worry shrouds my layers and layers of disappointment. I'm wondering why he didn't answer my texts and where he is now. Our moment together, turned into a question.

When I get to our table, Swan's in the middle of telling a story about her imo Janet, her mother's younger sister, who visits from LA every few months.

"She literally jumped out of the hot tub and threw a stone at his window—hey, Jae—and then she yelled, *Now you can get better look!* Seriously, I'd be embarrassed, but the Peeping Tom deserved it."

I slump into a seat, let my tray clatter on the table.

"Last time"—she pauses to take a bite of her sandwich, then continues, cheeks stuffed with grilled cheese—"this unfortunate soul at the pub asked her, *No, where are you really from?* And Imo lost her shit and poured cranberry gin all over her head. Ha! They see a little Asian lady and they think, *She's harmless. Maybe she's confused.* But Imo will cut a bitch."

Chocolate milk shoots out of CJ's nose just as William arrives and sets his tray down. He asks no questions, just pushes paper napkins CJ's way, and Swan continues, unfazed.

"I respect her, but damn. I dodged those genes. One point for being adopted."

I don't bother telling Swan she's just like her imo.

William says, "Jae, you look awfully sullen today. The grotesquely greasy grilled cheese doesn't whet your appetite?"

"*Grotesque* and *grilled cheese* don't belong in the same sentence," CJ says, revealing the orange cheddar on his braces. "That's blasphemy."

Derek's voice echoes in my head. *Get the hell out of here. Go eat your freaking cheese sandwich.* That Derek is so different from the one who makes my heart flutter.

I'm caught again in worries. Him running out on me, no explanation, no answers to my texts. There has to be a good reason. Right?

Before I can answer William, a pair of hands slap our table. We all look up to see Valeria Montero. I bristle, just like every other time I see her walking into English class and sitting behind me, or wrapping herself around Derek like another layer of skin. I don't know what's going on between them but I'm too embarrassed to ask. He never reciprocates, though. That's something. Right?

"Hey, guys," she says, all business. "So, we got an invite to this super-freakin'-amazing Halloween party and I'm extending the invitation to you all." She drops a flyer on the table.

"Oh, Valeria, thank you!" Swan says, flipping her wavy black hair to one side with the flair of Tina Turner. "Freaks. You forgot to say, to you-all *freaks*."

Valeria rolls her eyes. "Can we get past what happened in middle school, Swan? Like, for real. I'm trying to be nice here."

Swan sighs and bites into her sandwich.

CJ sets his food down. "A party with all the cool kids? Why are you telling *us*?"

Valeria's jaw drops. "This whole table needs a healthy dose of self-esteem. Seriously! Look. Derek's going, okay?" Her eyes flick to me. "We'll be going together."

My heart drops.

"It's not a lack of self-esteem, Valeria. It's a lack of trust," William says.

"You know what? This is going to be the Halloween party of the century, and I thought you might want to be part of it. So there! And Swan. For the last time, I didn't smash your Easter eggs on purpose. Okay? Please get over it."

Valeria walks away, swishing her hippy hips in yoga pants, and Swan smirks. "She totally did, guys. She totally did."

William laughs under his breath. "So, are we going?"

"Hell yeah," Swan says.

"Really?" CJ says, his voice high. "Why'd you make a big deal out of it, then?"

Swan's eyebrows wiggle. "Because she's super hot when she's angry. I mean, that'll fuel my dreams for the next month."

William groans, turns to me with an eye roll. "Swan had a gargantuan crush on Valeria last year."

"Sounds like she still does," I say.

Swan frowns thoughtfully, then nods. "Hm."

I clamp down on my lip, wince from the embarrassment. But I have to ask. "Are they dating?"

"Who?" Swan asks.

"Derek and Valeria. She said she's going with him."

She shakes her head. "She says she going with him because she thinks she owns him. They had the shortest relationship I've ever seen in my life. Even by his standards, she was insufferable. Derek, do this. Derek, do that. Derek, Derek, Derek."

A small wave of relief washes over me as I glance at Valeria's table. "Well, he's not here today," I say.

"Huh?" CJ looks over. "He was in class, though. Wonder where he is."

I shrug. "Where he is, where he went, where he was, where he's been, where he's gonna go . . ." They all look at me in confusion. "So, we found a third venue yesterday," I start. "The Sundy House on South Swinton."

Swan sits back in her chair. "That's freaking *brilliant*. Yeah, I can see that. Cool. So we have three good options."

"Yeah . . ." I say.

"What?"

"We were about to have brunch and—"

"Brunch?" CJ sputters. "Brunch? You were having *brunch*?"

"Sounds like things are getting personal," William says.

"Kind of?" I admit.

The three of them *oooooh*.

"I mean, we're not dating. There are just moments where I think there maybe could kinda be a chance for more."

"So what's the problem?" Swan asks.

"He ran out on me. Right when the food came."

CJ gasps.

"It wasn't on purpose. He got a text or something. Then left like his pants were on fire. He paid for it all. So . . . I dunno." Everyone's quiet, and I sigh. "He is so confusing. So not boyfriend material."

"I could have told you that," Swan said. "Derek Patel of yesteryear, maybe. Derek Patel of now, not boyfriend material."

"Because of his dad, though?" I ask.

I want to tell them it's not an excuse. I lost my dad too. It makes everything hurt, even happy moments. It's all noise and quiet at the same time. It's loneliness that walks with you. It's a question that hangs over everything you know.

But it doesn't make you an ass.

"Weeell." Swan draws it out, rocking her head side to side. "Not *really* because of his dad. Like, not *really*. It was more—"

CJ clears his throat, cutting her a look. Then he has a face of reverence. "It was a drunk driver. Head-on collision. Only Mrs. Patel made it out."

We're all quiet for a moment, then Swan continues. "Everyone loved Dr. Patel. Remember, CJ? When he brought in a human brain to middle school?"

CJ nods, biting into his sandwich. "And brain-shaped cupcakes that squirted blood. Or jam."

"Their house was one of the nicest on Ocean. No one even knew Derek moved out until recently. Right, CJ?"

It's obvious that Swan is prodding him, poking at him. CJ doesn't answer and his silence screams loud. I sit up straight.

"Wait. Is that the secret Derek made you keep?" I ask.

"Huh?" William frowns. "What secret?"

CJ sighs. "Maybe. Can't say any more. I want to keep my teeth."

I sink back down. *You keep your teeth, I keep my heart*, I think, eyes pointed at my food. I decide that Derek Patel, however beautiful he might be under all that dust, is a hope a heart should not have, a flashing yellow light, a reflective CAUTION sign in the dark. DETOUR. DEAD END.

"Mrs. Aldana lives in their house now," Swan says.

I almost laugh, but not because it's funny. "So that's how he knew the trick to the door."

"Huh?" She looks at me confused.

I explain, hands moving to show the logical sequence of events. "Derek told me he had to join the club because he broke into Mrs. Aldana's house. He knew the trick to the door because he used to live there."

I pick up my sandwich, then slap it back down on the plate. Not hungry. I'm worried about him. But at the same time, I'm tired of finding more and more layers of dust!

Then I sit there, trying to puzzle Derek out while the rest of them chitchat and write poetry on origami. The boy who bullies someone in the bathroom, then cries about it; who dances on the beach and writes poems for his dad; who makes me laugh and feel impossible things, and then leaves me hanging.

The bell rings to end lunch and everyone scurries off like mice to their next class. I drag myself along, stuck somewhere in our conversation, feeling heartbroken for Derek, but wondering if he could ever be the person my heart wants him to be.

CHAPTER TWENTY-SIX

Derek

On my bed. In the cosmos. In a pink bungalow.

My history book is open to a World War II timeline full of dates I have to memorize. But I can't focus for shit. Why?

Besides the fact that I'm trying not to think about Jae every second, or the date that ended in disaster, or the guilt I feel for not knowing how to respond to her what happened? texts, and thus avoiding her at school, making me the biggest, douchiest coward at Bellwood—besides all that, the TV in the living room is turned up high, and Mom is yelling at Paro to let Devdas go. I always wonder how she can't see herself in these tragic, dysfunctional Bollywood relationships.

I use my finger to scan the page to help me focus. V-J Day. Victory over Japan Day.

As soon as I read the small black words, they disappear from memory. Frustrated, I'm about to close the book when my eyes settle on a black-and-white photo of a sailor in a dark suit kissing a nurse in a white dress. His arm is tight around her neck, dipping her back, and her arm hangs at her side. His lips are locked so tight against hers, you can't even see her face.

The caption reads: *"The Kiss," the famous photo taken in Times Square, August 14, 1945.* I'm suddenly curious about the two of them. Did their love survive decades of marriage? Did they have a bundle of kids? Maybe they ended up strangers who resented each other. Maybe he died in a tragic car accident.

I do a quick search on my phone. The couple, an article reads, were not actually a couple at all. They didn't even know each other at the moment of that kiss. Excited about the end of the war, the sailor had some drinks and then grabbed the first nurse he saw and planted his lips against hers. Except, it turned out, she wasn't a nurse but a dental assistant. *There was nothing romantic about the kiss*, she told reporters.

"Well, damn." I turn off my phone.

I flip to the front of the history book, where I keep the picture of Jae and me standing on the deck of the yacht. And I wonder, if I ever got a chance to kiss Jae, who would we be when it happened? And if I was still hiding stuff about myself—all the shitty stuff that matters a whole shitty lot—would the kiss even be real? And if I *didn't* hide the truth, would the kiss even happen? Isn't it just easier to stop wanting anything with Jae at all?

A loud engine rumbles outside and dies. I part the curtains to see Peter stepping out of his truck and slamming the door. The buttons on his shirt are done up wrong, so that one side hangs lower than the other. His gold chain sits like it always does in the middle of his burly chest. My stomach does a flip-flop and my heartbeat quickens. It's the way he's walking, running every two steps, like he wants to slow down but his body won't let him. It's the flushed red of his face, the vein running like a swollen river across his forehead.

I close the history book and jump off my bed. I'm about to call Mom, to ask her if she knew Peter was coming, when the front door opens and slams. The house quivers.

"Mom?" I call, opening my door.

I step into the hall just as Peter walks past, not even glancing my way. I follow him into the living room.

From the TV screen, Paro screams *Devdaaaas!* as she runs toward her dying sweetheart while the drumbeats swell louder and more urgent. Mom turns down the volume. "Hi, honey," she says to Peter.

"Don't honey me." He breathes in deep and the sound of mucus rattles in his throat. A tuft of brown hair lies wet above his eyes. "You went to Becca's shop." He paces the floor, wiping his hands on the front of his jeans, flexing his fists. He's trying to stay calm, so I try to stay calm too.

"What are you talking about?" Mom nervously plays with the sash of her robe. Behind her concerned face, the TV screen flashes. "I didn't go to Becca's shop."

"You did," he growls, his eyes cutting into her. "She was crying all night, wouldn't tell me what the hell was the matter. 'Why you crying, Becca?' I say. 'Tell me what's eatin' you.' She says nothing! The whole goddamn night, the whole goddamn morning, the whole goddamn evening. Then she says, 'Peter, are you cheating on me? Peter, do you have a mistress?' And I'm standing there like an idiot 'cause I don't know what the hell she knows. Then she says you called her yesterday. That you went to the flower shop and harassed her, told her I was going to leave her." He takes a moment to wipe the sweat off his forehead. "You went to my wife's flower shop, Nancy? My *wife*!"

Mom stands up now, stumbles a little, and steadies her hand on the sofa armrest. "No, I didn't call Becca—"

"Don't call her that."

"Well, I didn't. I don't even know where her shop is, to be honest." She runs her hand over the hair at her nape. "I—I don't think I went there. I wouldn't do that."

"You don't *think*?"

"No, no. I'm sure. I didn't go." She takes a step toward him and reaches for his shoulder. He swats it away.

I step into the living room. "I think you should go," I tell him.

"Stay out of this, Derek," Mom says. She stumbles back to the couch and digs between the cushions. Her hands are shaking, and she says over and over again, "I didn't call her. I didn't go there. I didn't."

"You're a junkie," he scoffs. "You wouldn't remember sitting on a tack."

"Don't you dare call me that!" Mom screams, looking over her shoulder. "I didn't call her." She pulls out her phone from behind a seat cushion and starts searching through it, hands still shaking. She freezes and stares at the screen for what seems like hours. "It's . . . Okay . . ."

"Okay what?"

"I don't recognize this number. I—"

Peter grabs the phone and looks down at it. He stabs a fat finger at the screen. "That's my wife's flower shop. See it? Becca's number?" He grabs Mom's chin and holds the phone up to her face. The light shines into her green eyes, glassy and wet and full of confusion.

"Let her go." I hurry toward them and grab Peter's arm. It's dense with muscle and it won't budge.

"That's her number," he says again, pushing the phone up to her nose.

"She can see it!" I yell. "Let her go."

I might as well be yelling into a vacuum because neither of them looks at me. But Mom's eyes are running with tears now, and she's saying, "I'm sorry, I don't remember," and Peter's hand is tightening on her face, pressing into her cheeks. I drop my hand from his arm and flex my fist. I could punch him, but I'm a hundred percent sure he'd punch me back and maybe Mom, too.

I pull my phone from my pocket. "I'm calling the police."

Peter pushes Mom's face, throws her into the sofa like she's a rag doll, and she lies there clutching pieces of her robe like she's trying to gather herself. His chest rises and falls. He spits on the carpet, then steps over her spindly legs and walks past me.

An ugly sound escapes Mom's mouth. She mumbles apologies so fast I can hardly understand her. She races after him and grabs his wrist. "I shouldn't have gone to her shop. I don't know why I did it. I don't even remember it."

"Let go," he says, and I see this flash in his eyes: He's at the end of his rope. I hurry over, grab Mom's shoulder and try to pull her away.

"Don't go," she says to him, ignoring me. "Please."

He wrestles with her desperate grasp and finally pulls his hand free, swinging his arm around. *Thwack!* My lip.

I stagger. Stunned. Taste the blood before I see it on my fingers.

Peter steps away from both of us. "Nancy, don't call me."

His footsteps leave. The front door slams. It's not until his car engine roars away that Mom comes to life again. She lunges for my phone and throws it against the wall.

"I told you to stay out of this." She points toward the kitchen, her voice getting louder. "You made him leave! How will I get my pills now?"

I feel like I've been hit by a meteor. So that's what she saw in Peter. More drugs.

"Don't look at me like that," she snaps.

"I can't take this anymore." My voice is shaking. "You should be glad he's gone." I touch my lip again, then reach for my phone. Blood smears across the cracked screen. The backlight wavers, turns pink, and flashes. I throw the phone back on the floor.

I run to my room and grab my sweatshirt, my keys, my backpack. Mom is still yelling at me, but anger is pooling inside me and I don't hear a word. Her voice follows me as I walk toward the kitchen.

Throwing open the front door, I look back at her. "See this?" I point to my lip. "You're supposed to be my mom. You're supposed to care."

I'm too angry to unlock my bike. Too angry to figure out where I'm going. All I want to do is walk until I'm nowhere close to the pink bungalow where everything falls to pieces.

CHAPTER TWENTY-SEVEN

Jae

The night is black and calm. A sailboat cuts through still water, spreading ripples like silver hairs through the darkness. There's movement in the grass at the edge of the sand, but my eyes can't make anything out. I take a final breath of the crisp air and close the window.

Downstairs, Ms. Rosette is singing "Toboli," a beautiful *Eve* lullaby, in her yearning, warbling voice. On nights like this, when Uncle Rowan's out having dinner with colleagues, she moves around the house like air, unfettered. I sit at the edge of my bed and listen to her song and imagine Anne singing to June Baby.

I suddenly miss Mom. I miss the voice that comforted me during my six-hour delivery. I miss her chicken noodle soup and her *You'll be all right. It doesn't hurt forever.* The cream she rubbed into my skin to help me heal when I didn't want to lift a finger to help myself. I miss that Mom.

But there's the other Mom that intrudes on my thoughts. The one who only saw my mistakes.

Something like sand trickles against the window. There's not enough wind to whip up sand tonight, so I walk over and look out across the coastline, then at the place where the grass waved, and then at the dark figure standing beneath the window.

I scream, then quickly clasp my mouth when Derek steps into a stream of light by the pool.

"What is happening?" Ms. Rosette calls from downstairs.

"Nothing!" I call back.

I open the window and stick my head outside. "What are you doing here?" I half whisper, half yell. "How did you know this was my room?"

"I didn't," he says. "But no one came to the other window, so I figured I'd try this one."

My mouth falls open. "You're lucky my uncle's not here to kill *both* of us. What are you doing? Where have you been? What happened at the Sundy House?"

Even from far away, I can see the hesitation in his eyes. His mouth opens, but nothing comes out. That's when I notice the gash in his lip, the dried blood on the corner of his mouth.

I gasp and lean a little farther out the window. "What happened?"

When he doesn't answer, I feel something horrible sink deep into my stomach. I hold up my hand for him to wait there and run downstairs to the main floor, where Ms. Rosette is organizing a pile of magazines in a rack.

"What is going on?" she asks with a slight glance my way. "I know something is happening. I have three daughters. Remember that."

"I have a guest," I say quickly. "He's going to come upstairs for a while—"

"*He?* Wooo, Yesu!" Ms. Rosette shakes her head and walks away from me, her hand waving frantically over her ears. "I don't hear *a-ny-thing*! I am playing my music, okay? I don't hear *anything-o*."

I let out a long sigh. "Thank you."

"For what? What are you talking about?" She busies herself with rearranging the pillows, avoiding my eyes.

I fly through the back door, run around the side of the house, and smack right into him.

"Whoa," he says.

My eyes sweep up from his thick sweatshirt to his face, the red gash through his bottom lip. "What happened to you?"

"I'm fine," he says.

But he's not. Just like the first day I met him, I can see it written all over his face.

I grab his hand and lead him toward the back door, away from the driveway, where Uncle Rowan could pull up any second. I scrunch my nose. "I hate to say this, but you smell like smoke. Uncle Rowan will smell it a mile away."

He groans. "Shit. Sorry. Look . . . I can . . ." He stops walking, ready to leave. I pull him back.

We pass under the lamps and light splashes across his face. I'm almost breathless at how real he looks. I've missed him, I realize. I've missed seeing him so close. Your mind can never re-create the flesh and the colors of a person. His eyes are more piercing, speckled with yellow, his skin is more textured, his eyebrows are darker. And his full lips are red, red, red.

Inside, Ms. Rosette has disappeared somewhere and we make our way upstairs. In my room, he lets out a heavy sigh and swings his backpack off his shoulders. "I'm sorry," he says again, washing his hands over his face. "I—I don't wanna get you in trouble."

"Then you're gonna have to change," I say.

"What?"

"I'm serious." I run to my garbage bin and pull out a few fresh plastic bags and hand them to him. "Your clothes. In there." Then I run to my dresser and pull out the biggest shirt I have, Mom's Bernie Mac tee. "And put this on."

Then I grab my favorite body spritz from my table and spray like I'm attacking the plague. Derek coughs into his sleeve.

"It's better than smoke, believe me," I say. He looks at the T-shirt warily.

"Does this outfit come with pants or do I walk around swinging?" he asks.

"You're not walking around and you're not swingin' nothin', okay?" I hear the sound of a car engine approaching and freeze. Then it passes and I snap my fingers at Derek. "Seriously, Derek. Like yesterday. Change. Now."

Both hands, he lifts his hoodie and shirt and hat off with one swoop, and I swear I could have—would have—melted in place if the fear of Uncle Rowan showing up weren't so strong. But dear God, it isn't fair. He looks *good*. And he knows it. He chuckles and unbuttons his jeans, lets them fall off his hips. Green boxers. Green boxers against a tanned torso. He steps out of his jeans, and shrugs as if to say, *Good now?*

We are so good.

I'm not supposed to feel this way. Not now. Not my insides all tight and wound up. So I clear my throat. Hurry and pick up his clothes and hat from the floor, my head inches away from his carved muscles.

"Let me do that," he says.

"Just put the shirt on. Please," I say, nodding at Bernie Mac. I bag his clothes myself, just to give my hands something to do. I hurry to the closet, stuff his clothes into the corner, and shut the door.

I turn around and plant my hands on my hips. "We'll have to be quieter when Uncle Rowan comes home."

"I'm sorry," he says again, softly. He's wearing that same expression I saw when I first met him, when I saw his wet eyes looking at me in the bathroom mirror. He looks embarrassed. Alone.

"Stop saying sorry," I say. "Seriously. It's fine. You're staying, right? For the night? We'll figure it out."

He nods. "Thanks."

I make my way toward the bed and sit down. But he moves slowly around the room, stopping to look at the books lining the shelf. Then he moves to the desk against the wall and settles into my chair.

"You can sit with me," I say.

He shakes his head. "I'll stay here. It's safer." He chuckles. He leans forward with his elbows on his knees and stares down at the floor. A wisp of wavy black hair falls over his forehead. "I'm sorry. I shouldn't have come here with your uncle and all that. I just didn't feel like seeing anyone else."

Thump. My heartbeat is loud. Heavy. Did he hear it?

"It's fine," I say again.

His eyes rove the room, avoiding my gaze.

"Can you come here? Please?" I say. "So it's not so awkward? Just talk to me. Like we're . . . we're at the fish pond. Just a hundred tiny kisses, right?"

One corner of his mouth tips up. Then he walks toward the bed and the closer he gets, the closer I want to get, like he has his own gravitational pull. He sits on the edge and I swing my legs up and lean against the pillow, giving us both more space.

"So, are you finally going to tell me how you got that split lip?" I nudge. "It's not from soccer."

He grimaces. Looks toward the door like he's thinking of leaving. Finally, he says, "My mom doesn't . . . she . . . she has this boyfriend." He stops. Looks down at the floor and sighs heavily like he's a hundred years old and so tired. "I shouldn't even be here. I shouldn't be telling you all this. Look at this room," he says, pointing to the walls, the curtains. "It's pink."

"So?"

He looks at me and smiles. "You're like a sweet princess and I'm a frog."

"Hey, I've never met a frog I didn't like," I say. "And you're sincere. If you're a frog, you're a sincere frog."

A half smile. "A sincere frog, huh?" He lets out a short laugh and looks down at his bare feet.

I lean forward and poke his shoulder and he looks at me sideways, his eyes big, making him look years younger.

"So? Tell me?"

I can hear him swallow. He licks his lips. The red crater.

"Mom dates this guy. Peter. Parasitic alien life-form. He has a temper, but he's never put his hands on her before. Well . . . he got mad at her for . . . well, that doesn't matter. He was grabbing her face. Hard. So I was gonna call the police. Then he decided to leave and Mom tried to stop him, grabs his hand, he pulls his arm free, and . . . well. Crack. My lip." He points to it. "It wasn't on purpose, but it hurts. Or maybe it hurts 'cause . . . Mom didn't really care?" His voice is taut. His Adam's apple bobs. He's trying to keep himself from breaking.

"I'm sorry," I say.

He shakes his head. "Jae. I'm trying not to scare you off. I've been trying this whole time. But I'm doing a really shitty job of it. I kinda like you."

For a second, I lose my breath. I smile. "Kinda?"

"God. See? You're just so f—" He censors his words. "So cute. I *really* like you." He looks at the window, shakes his head, and clicks his tongue.

"Wait, are you annoyed?" I laugh, holding the pillow against my chest.

"Yeah. Yeah. I am. 'Cause you're sitting there all . . . you know . . . and I'm sitting here in my freaking boxers and . . . dammit . . . Hey. Pass me a pillow, 'kay?"

I bury my face in it so he can't see me laugh. Then I throw it to him and try my darnedest not to look. He places it on his lap and takes a deep breath and stares at the books on my bookshelf.

"One. Two. Three. Four. Five."

"Are you counting my books?" I ask.

"*Shhhh.*"

"Derek. Let's just talk."

"Don't say my name." He mutters on and on to himself, and I sit there like I'm watching the unraveling of a sane mind.

"*Okaaay*. Patel? Can I say Patel? Or does that make you hot too?"

He huffs. "Does that make me . . ." He sucks in air through his teeth, looks up at the ceiling and laughs. "Does that make me hot. She asked if that makes me hot."

"Derek! Come on! I just wanna—"

And he's up. The pillow falls to the floor and before I can blink, he's hovering over me, so close I can feel his breath, so close I see faint freckles on his nose. When he speaks, it's rough like gravel. "It's your fucking voice, do you know that? It's . . . Jesus. What, Jae? You want what? What do you want?"

Nothing, I try to say, but it's barely a whisper I can even hear.

His eyes are a dark whirlpool. I could get lost in them. I could disappear in them. I want to disappear in them. My breaths are shallow and he sees it, looks down at the small rise and fall of my chest, and his eyes spark like flint. His head drops closer, his nose brushing my collarbone, his warm breath on my skin, and then he lets out a groan and pushes away, collapsing onto the bed with his eyes on the ceiling.

"I . . ." He sucks in a breath and breathes out slowly.

I sit up, make my way toward him, savoring the question, the glint, the fire in his eyes. I brush thick waves of hair from his forehead. Rake my hands through it. It slips through my fingers, falls back over his eyes, a dark curtain covering darkness.

"God, Jae. What do you want?" he asks, his voice strained. I bring my head close enough to feel his breath whispering against my cheek. My neck. My ear. "You're killing me."

"*Shhh*," I say, and he sinks into the bed, eyes swimming.

It's like magic, the way his body responds to mine. I touch his sharp jaw, and it clenches. I brush his chin, and his mouth falls open, waiting. I take my time, letting my hands feel how real he is. The grooves around his abdominals, the indentations on his pelvis that lead down. He groans at my touch, sits up on his elbows to watch my hands, and I'm drunk off the feeling that someone so beautiful is melting beneath me.

I straddle him, right at the base of his abs, plant my hands on his rising chest. He shifts against my thighs and everything is electric.

He's watching me through narrow eyes, through eyes like a night sky, teasing me with how they dance, how they scan me from my lips to my chest.

I wonder how his lips would feel everywhere. I wonder how long my breath would catch and how good it would feel for the world to end at the tip of our tongues. I lean in to his mouth, waiting for him to flinch, but he doesn't. My mouth meets the corner of his, and I let it rest there, so light it feels like air. Feeling his chest rise against mine, hearing his breath come faster, I press my lips harder. My heart races as my lips explore the shadows of his face, gently seeking the places that are red and swollen and hurt, trying to tell him with my skin on his that he is so good. That no matter how bruised he is, he is beautiful to me.

CHAPTER TWENTY-EIGHT

Derek

That day she wore the yellow dress, I wondered what she felt like, all those curves and arches. But now she moves over me as close and as soft as water and I almost can't take it. I'm straining to keep myself together. Is this real? Our lips memorize each other. My fingers memorize the way her limbs flow. How soft and careful she is. How sure she is in her quiet. Everything she does is another star in her constellation and I could look at her forever. I want to keep her with me, my own moon.

At the thought, I gently lift her off me.

She giggles at first, and then she grabs my face, worried. "Did I hurt you?"

I take her hand and place it on my chest, like somehow this will stop the feelings from moving around so hard and so fast. "Jae. Everything in my life gets screwed up. Okay? I don't want this to . . . Everything breaks. Everything breaks."

She leans in and kisses me right underneath my lip. Soft. Then rolls onto her back with her arms open. I let myself in, rest my head against her shoulder, my mouth against her chest. I feel her breath in my hair, and I almost cry because the last time I felt that, it was Dad hugging me. *You beautiful boy*. I miss him. I miss him.

I don't cry. My tears knot up in my throat. But soon, the knot is gone. And I settle into something that feels like rest.

☽

The house is quiet. The room is dark, except for the sliver of moonlight cutting through the parted curtains.

"Jae. What time is it?"

She leaps off the bed and grabs her phone. "He should definitely be home by now."

The house creaks and our eyes flick to the door. Nothing.

She hurries to her closet and pulls out a couple of blankets from the top shelf. She lays them out on the floor in the space between her bed and the window. "It's time to hide now, little frog," she says.

I lie down on the floor and sit up on my elbows so I can see her move around the room. A pillow comes flying at me. I catch it, lie down. I cross my arms behind my head and stare at the ceiling.

"Stars. You need stars," I whisper as she pushes a laundry basket to block the blankets from view.

"Stars for what?"

"To count. To make wishes on."

"I don't think wishing on plastic stars counts."

"You never know."

I hear the creak of her bed and then her head suddenly peeks over the edge. Her hair hangs over and hovers above my face. She smiles as I reach for it and wrap it slowly around my finger. She is moonlight and dimples.

"So, you never told me what happened," she whispers.

"When?" I whisper back.

"When you left. Brunch."

I close my eyes. How do I talk about this and where do I stop? "I'm sorry," I say. "My mom was having a panic attack. It happens sometimes. She thinks she's dying but . . ." I shake my head. "I wonder sometimes if it's her way of keeping me close, you know? But I'm sorry. I'm sorry I ran out and I'm sorry I didn't tell you why. I felt . . ." But I'm not sure which word to pull out of this alphabet soup of emotions.

"What?" she asks.

"Hopeless?" I pause. "Ashamed? I mean, that's what I'm scared of with you. I feel like I'll always be apologizing for something. 'Cause things are just . . . not good."

She reaches for my hand. I drop her hair and get entwined in her fingers instead.

"You could have told me," she says. "I would have understood. I promise. I want you to tell me things."

I'm getting choked up again. I blink away tears. Tell her things? Like my mom's an addict? "Yeah," I say. If anything could put out the light between us, it's those words. There's no redemption in them. And now I'm crying for real, the only words that make sense to her and me. Jae's not scared of my tears. But the truth? I don't know.

"Hey." She squeezes my hand. "You okay?"

I finally meet her eyes. I finally tell her what's true. "No."

She climbs down from the bed, throws her arm across my chest, and nuzzles against my neck. I wrap my other arm around her.

She fills up the empty space that's been here for so long, but she is weightless, and I could hold her forever.

"I can't wait to move out," I say. "Start over."

"Yeah . . ." she says. Her voice is full of unsaid things, like her poems.

"Your turn," I say. "I want you to tell me things too."

Her breath stops blowing on my neck. One. Two. Three. Four. Her breath rushes out.

"My mom and I aren't really talking right now. It's one of the reasons I came here."

"What happened?"

She's quiet for a long time. "She . . . it feels like . . . she's never there for me when I need her the most. Like when my dad left, she kind of disappeared. She just couldn't see past her own hurt, you know? And I was hurting too, but it was like that didn't matter. I had to patch myself up, take care of myself."

"That sounds familiar."

"Yeah? Maybe our moms loved our dads so much they couldn't see us," she says.

"I see you." Her breath tickles my skin. I lift her chin up, touch her lips to mine. I let my tongue taste her a little, just to get away from the sadness, to feel my insides spark up with light. We go deeper, and then, softer. "I see you," I say again.

"And I see you," she says.

I smile and she suddenly looks bashful.

"I think my parents were soul mates," I say.

"That's beautiful," she sighs. "Hm. I wonder if my dad left us because that woman was his soul mate. I never thought of that before. Hm. Then again, maybe soul mates don't exist. Maybe we just make choices. Maybe that's even more romantic."

"Maybe. Have you seen him since? Talked to him?"

She shakes her head. "No. He hasn't tried and I don't think I'd talk to him anyway. He railed against absent fathers and then he became one. He made me a statistic."

"There's more to you than that," I say.

She looks up at me, gives me a weak smile, then wiggles out from under my arm. She hops up onto the bed and this time I can't see her. She says nothing.

"There's more to you than that, Jae," I say again, because I know she needs to hear it.

She shifts on her bed. A sniffle. A quiet *Thanks*. Then, after a long pause, she says, "I know."

"What?" I ask.

"There's more to me than that."

"That's a good thing."

"Yeah," she whispers.

Then, like we're a pair of lungs in a giant aching chest, we breathe out loudly at the same time. And then we laugh.

"Thanks for letting me stay," I say.

"Yeah. Yeah, of course. Um . . . we should sleep. You'll have to leave before Uncle Rowan wakes up tomorrow."

"Okay."

"I'll wake you up at five."

"Okay. Night, Jae."

"Good night."

I know I won't sleep. Not here. Not where every touch of space is filled up with her. My mind sees her walking toward the closet, sitting back against her bed, nuzzling against my chest. I smell her body spritz, still, clinging to every molecule of air, and I know

I'll never forget that scent, like flowers in rain, or something that beautiful.

When I think she's asleep I tiptoe to my bag and pull out my poetry notebook. I lower myself slowly into her desk chair and turn on a small reading light. She stirs, then settles into her blankets again. I write.

Destiny

Don't tell me what you see in the stars
I can read the sky and tell my own story

She is radically beautiful
Cosmically impossible
The wonder in everything
Like a single drop of water
That reflects the whole rainbow

She is my destiny

There's no way I'm wrong
I've seen the universe in her smile

I tiptoe across the room. I open the window and look up at the moon. A waxing gibbous. Almost full. Almost complete.

The view from Jae's bedroom feels familiar. The moon, the ocean. A slender boat cutting into the moonlit reflection. Sand and reeds. A man.

A man.

He stops walking. Looks up at the window. We stare at each other. He points at me, holding me beneath his finger. He walks away, opens a door, and slams it.

The house shakes.

CHAPTER TWENTY-NINE

Derek

He says two things when he throws the bedroom door open and turns on the blinding light:

"Janelle, pack your bags," and "You, come with me."

Jae sits up in bed and blinks in confusion. Then she's muffling a scream with her hand and her eyes dart between me and her uncle.

She nearly falls out of bed, throwing the covers. "Uncle Rowan. Wait—"

He holds up his hand. *Stop*. Then stands frozen in the doorway with his arms crossed like Mr. Clean. A steady heat seems to be rising from his skin, like steam. Like he could grab me by the throat and sear me.

"He needed a place to stay," Jae says, hurrying toward him. "He had—"

The way her uncle looks at her. She snaps her mouth shut. I hear the clamp of her teeth.

My heart is twisting, my chest tight, my breath shallow. "I . . ." I shake my head. "I wanted to see the moon." A laugh escapes me. How stupid could I be?

I avoid Jae's eyes, walk over to the closet, and take out my bagged clothes. I pull on my jeans, flushing red as I look down at my green boxers. Not wanting to strip down any more, I throw my hoodie over Jae's shirt.

"Sir. We didn't . . . you know. We didn't," I say.

He ignores me. Points at Jae and says, "Pack your bags."

He turns to go and I look at Jae, and she's crying. Her lips trembling. I step toward her, and she shakes her head. *Just go*, she mouths.

"Hey!" Her uncle's voice booms from the hallway, making me jump. I grab my bag and race after him.

He doesn't ask me where I live, and I don't ask where he's going. I already know. He's gonna throw me to the gators. They'll never find my body. He stares straight ahead, fisting the steering wheel. The streetlights glow against his dark skin.

Green light. Tires screech. My head slams against the headrest.

Red light. I fly forward against the taut seat belt. I hang on to the door, too scared to reach for the handle at the roof in case he might sense my fear.

He cracks all the windows, and I know he smells the smoke clinging to my clothes. How much more could this man hate me?

"Please don't make her leave, sir," I finally manage to say. "It was my fault. I should have gone somewhere else. It was my fault."

He grunts loud, like a boar, and I shut my mouth.

Every so often he breathes in through his nose loud, like he's trying to put out a fire inside. And then I'm surprised when he pulls into my neighborhood and stops at the rickety chain-link fence.

"How . . ." I mutter, and he steps out of the car and slams the door. His large shadow thunders through the dark yard and I don't know what I'm more scared of, him or what he'll find inside the house.

He turns around now, and I shake off the fear and open the car door. How dumb am I? To end up in the same place I was only a few hours ago. Except now it's worse. Now I've ruined everything for me and for Jae.

He waits at the door, towering over me as I climb up the creaky porch and fumble for my key.

"Um . . ." I say when I finally put my key in the lock. "Thanks for driving me home?"

"What do you think this was, door-to-door service?" he asks in a voice octaves lower than mine. "I want to talk to your mother."

"But how do you even know—"

"I know who you are. You think I don't know who you are? I know who you are, Derek Patel." His eyes bore deep into mine. "Open the door."

I'm not in the business of letting people in who demand entry. But considering I was just in *his* house, and he found me undressed in *his* niece's room. Well. I have to make an exception. I open the door. It feels like the darkest corner of space in here. It doesn't smell like his house, that cinnamon-spice stuff people sprinkle on everything in the fall. Here it's the gentle waft of alcohol souring in the carpet, the overpowering notes of cigarette smoke, the je-ne-sais-quoi of spoiled food you can't identify.

I turn on the light, hurry to throw away an old dinner container on the counter.

Jae's uncle steps in. "Where's your mother?"

I suck in a breath. "Listen. My mom's not doing good, okay. I don't think it's a good idea. I know you really wanna talk to her, but sir, please. She's not doing good."

He squints behind glasses that reflect the yellow kitchen light. His eyes stay on me for a while before he steps into the hall, his retreating footsteps quiet against the carpet. I lean over the counter, bury my head in my arms, pound the cold surface with my fist.

I turn around when I hear his footsteps come back. His eyes have lost some of their hellfire blaze.

"There's a whole lot of bottles on the table. Painkillers and scotch."

I don't say anything.

"Hers or yours?" he asks.

"Definitely not mine."

He shakes his head. "I thought as much. And your lip?"

"An accident."

He purses his lips. "If you ever need help, you come to me, you hear? To *me*." He reaches into his pocket and pulls out a black-and-gold business card. ROWAN OAKLAND, CORPORATE ATTORNEY. "And you know where I live." He says this last thing stiffly.

I stuff the card into my jeans and he leans against the counter, crosses one foot over the other, and runs a hand over his goatee.

He sighs. "Let's get to it, Derek. All right? Now, you got a woman in there"—he stretches his hand down the hall toward the living room where he just came from—"a little on the thin side, to put it mildly, passed out on the couch. I'd think she was dead but she's snoring like the Tasmanian devil. Now, something tells me she's taking more than the recommended dose."

My eyes flick down the hall, but I don't want to go there. I don't want to be here.

He takes off his glasses and slowly cleans them on his shirt. "Your dad passed away, is that right? I'm sorry to hear that. I didn't have a father around. Father figures are important." He slides his glasses back on his nose and squints at me. "Janelle hasn't had a father around for a long time. She's had a lot of heartbreak. Trauma. Now. How are *you*, how is *your* situation going to help her in any way?" He looks around the kitchen, taking in every square inch of it, and then shakes his head again. "This isn't the kind of place I want her to be. And you're not the kind of boy I want her to be with."

Thwack. It couldn't have hurt more if he'd punched me. I stuff my hands into my pockets and clench my fists, trying to ignore that shrinking feeling, that feeling that I'll eventually disappear.

"You were in her room. In her room. In *my* house, under *my* roof, half naked in your goddamned boxers." He takes a step toward me, like his anger has found new fuel.

"Sir. It wasn't what it looked like."

"Are you gonna tell me you didn't touch that girl? You gonna tell me that?" His eyes are daring me to lie. I look away, and he scoffs. "I wasn't born yesterday. I'm doing all I can to keep that girl in line, and you come along. What's so great about you, huh? What do you have that's worth her losing everything for?"

I swallow a lump in my throat.

He takes a deep breath, arms up in half surrender, and steps back to lean against the counter again. "Look. I was a boy once. I know how it is. You take it where you can get it—"

"No." Now my anger flashes and I stand up straight. "That's not me. You can say what you want about me not being good enough. Fine. Whatever. Maybe I'm not. But I would never just . . . I wasn't taking advantage of her. I wouldn't do that."

He nods slowly and rubs his goatee. "She was talking about that poetry club. All you kids in there. She said something about you. You're a good athlete. You're smart. You have a lot of potential. But I can't sugarcoat what I see." He breathes in deep and shakes his head. "She doesn't need any more loss or unstable relationships. I'm what she needs right now. You understand? Stability. Support. Someone who will always be there for her. You'll just bring her a lot of tears and trouble, whether you mean to or not. And I don't think you mean to, son. But she deserves better than that."

His eyes flick to my lip and I instinctively tuck it inside my mouth. I find my head nodding. He's right. Jae deserves better.

"Now, if what Janelle says is true," he continues, "if you have that potential, I want to help you out." He reaches into his pocket and pulls out a checkbook. He flips it open and walks over to the kitchen counter. I hear the click of a pen and I see the back of his tall body, his hand scribbling something on the paper. "Your mom won't be able to help you much with college, but I can."

I almost laugh from shock. He's going to give me money. Enough money that I won't have to work at Old-Timer every week and during the summer. My stomach turns. My throat feels thick.

"I don't want it," I say, my voice tight. The words come out before I can stop them, but once they're out, I know they're right.

"What did you say?" He turns around, his hand still poised over the check.

"I don't want your money." My voice is clear this time. "I'll get a scholarship or I won't go to college at all, but I won't take your money."

I want him gone. My eyes scan the kitchen counter for my cigarettes, and the fact that I can't remember where I last put them makes me want to punch something.

Jae's uncle stands still, watching me. Watching my chest rise high as I control my breathing. Watching my hands flex into fists at my side. Watching my feet plant themselves wide. "Please get out. Sir."

I hear the click of the pen, and then he's putting the checkbook back in his pocket, still watching me. "Don't be too proud to accept help, Derek. Are you sure?"

"I have nothing, right? I don't even have parents I can count on. But at least I have my pride."

He blinks a few times and gives a perfunctory, closed-mouth smile before he walks out the door.

CHAPTER THIRTY

Jae

I'm leaning out the window, taking big gulps of air. My suitcase is open on my bed. Empty. I can't leave. I can't go back to Atlanta. Back to what? A new school where people might know about me, the chick who got knocked up as a dare? Back to Mom, who made an already difficult pregnancy the biggest heartbreak of my life? What do I have back there?

I half-heartedly pull out clothes from my drawer and throw them on the comforter. My phone dings with a notification. Flight Confirmation.

Flight confirmation. Uncle Rowan already booked my flight. He booked a flight. It's real. He's done. He wants me gone. I leave in a few hours. I leave Delray. I leave Free Verse. William and CJ and Swan. I leave Derek.

I'm on the floor now, melting into tears. How did the night turn so bad? I went from feeling safe, wrapped up in arms, to being completely alone. Where is Derek now? What is Uncle Rowan saying to him?

I wipe away tears and dig through my bag for June Baby's picture. Something to hold, to make me smile. But looking at her only deepens the sadness. I'm going back to Atlanta, and she won't be there. She's gone.

I put the picture away and head to the desk to gather my things. But there sits Derek's blue-and-yellow poetry notebook, open to a poem, dated today. *Destiny.*

The front door slams. I shut the notebook, toss it into my suitcase.

Uncle Rowan doesn't waste any time coming up the stairs and throwing my bedroom door open.

"Ready?" he says. Not a question. He glances at my suitcase. "Just throw it all in. We're not missing this flight."

"But how you could just"—I stand up, blurry-eyed—"just send me away like that?"

He takes a deep breath in and crosses his thick arms over his chest. "Here with me or there with your mother? Doesn't matter. You're going to do what you're going to do."

"Do what I'm going to . . . what are you saying? Like, I'm a whore? Like I can't keep my legs shut?"

"Hey," he says in a warning voice.

"He needed help!" I say desperately. "His mother's boyfriend hit him in the face. Didn't you see his lip?"

His face darkens. "Is he being abused? Tell me the truth."

"He said it was an accident. But he didn't want to be home with all that chaos. He needed a place to stay. For one night. And I knew you would never say yes if I asked."

He frowns, shakes his head. "You don't know that. You don't know that at all. But look what I came home to. A half-naked boy sleeping in your room. Dammit, I didn't think you had the nerve! I thought you might be sneaking around with him, doing more than that poetry project, but I didn't think you'd have him here under my roof without my knowledge. I'm happy to see you kept *your* clothes on," he says, waving me up and down.

"Uncle Rowan, I didn't *do* that with him. I didn't go that far."

"That far? How far, then, Janelle? How far?" He holds up his hand to keep me quiet. "You know, I don't want to hear it. It went far enough. This has all gone far enough. Let's get going. I'm tired."

"Let me stay. Please let me stay."

"Ticket's been paid for."

"I promise I won't sneak around. I promise I'll be responsible and decent and I'll come home right after school and if I have Free Verse I'll come home right after that. No more scouting for venues."

He grunts. "This ain't about the poetry club. It's about the boy." He pauses. Leans against the doorframe. "No more Derek Patel."

My mouth freezes. "But—"

"The club isn't big enough for the two of you. One of you has to go." His black eyes bore into mine. "That's my rule, Janelle. You want to stay here, you stay away from that boy. That's my rule. Will you obey it?"

Fresh tears prickle my eyes.

"Ja-*nelle*!" His voice reaches to the ceiling now. *"Will. You. Obey it?"*

CHAPTER THIRTY-ONE

Jae

At school, I hear Derek's voice everywhere, sometimes calling my name. I take hallways I never go down. I walk double-time, making up for my short strides. I become a master of elusion and soon, he stops calling.

The school day ends, and it feels like my heart is punching against the walls of my chest.

I walk through the grove and see the top of his white hat. My foot snaps a fallen branch and the noise makes everyone look up. But Derek's head barely rises. I'm thankful. I miss looking into his eyes. Miss the soft swirl of black hair against his ears. I miss him.

"Hey." I hold out his poetry notebook, and his eyes snap up to meet mine. He reaches for it slowly, quietly, and for a moment, we're both hanging on. Fingers inches apart.

"I can't be in the club with you," I say quietly. "If you want to stay, I can't."

One side of his mouth slips into a smile, and I notice that the cut in his lip is now a faint purple line. "Hey, don't look so chewed up about it," he says. "I was trying to get out of here, remember?

Your uncle's doing me a favor." Something passes in his eyes and his smile widens. "I'll talk to Mrs. Aldana. No worries."

"I'm sorry." I let go of the notebook. Let go of all the words inside about destiny, about the stars telling our story. I walk away from my usual stump beside him and sit on the edge of CJ and Swan's blanket, hugging my knees. They're talking about the Halloween party, only weeks away, and I'm lost in my own thoughts, my nerves pulled tight.

Derek stands up and picks up his backpack, tells Mrs. Aldana he has to go and will see her later, waves at everyone, and walks off. He walks through the trees, head bowed, and I hug my legs harder, press my face into my knees so no one knows my heart is wringing.

When Mrs. Aldana asks us to write our five-minute poem, I write one. Only one.

Afenyo

My last name means
Home is good
But home has always been the place where
People come to leave
So how could home be
Anything but

Empty

CHAPTER THIRTY-TWO

Derek

Next day, the final bell rings. People run out of doors like bulls at a rodeo. I'm not in such a hurry. I change into my soccer jersey. Head to Mrs. Aldana's classroom.

When I walk in, her eyebrows shoot up and her face brightens. A book is open on the desk in front of her, and she closes it firmly, giving me her full attention.

"Derek! What a beautiful surprise on a Wednesday afternoon. Don't be shy. Come in! It's just you and me and the Muses. What can I do for you?"

I shift my backpack and slowly step in. "Can I talk to you?"

"Please do!"

She sits down in one of the student desks in the front row and pulls one close beside her. I slide into the seat, trying to avoid her intense gaze.

"I can't come to the club anymore," I say, giving her a quick sideways glance. "I know I'm supposed to 'cause I got into trouble. But I got into even bigger trouble and I gotta quit."

She leans back slowly. "Quit? Can you tell me what happened?"

I don't think any talking I've done in the past week has helped any. If anything, it gives me a false sense of comfort, of resolution. "No. Not really," I answer.

"Would you feel better if you did?"

I pause. "I mean . . ."

She nods like she's coaxing a scared kitten to a bowl of milk. The stakes are low here, I guess. The worst has already happened.

"Jae's uncle thinks I'm a piece of shit," I say, "wants her to stay away from me. He *did* find me in her room, in my boxers, at night, when he wasn't home. But he thought it was more than it was."

Mrs. Aldana takes a deep breath, and for the first time ever, I think she's out of words. "Okay," she sighs out, and leans in slightly. "And there's more? Tell me."

"More? Yeah. Lots more." Hot anger and frustration rise. I press my fingers into my palms, somehow feeling less helpless with my hands balled up. "Maybe if I still lived in a nice house and I had two parents at home and I didn't fucking smoke and . . . if my life weren't so messed up. But that's how things are, you know." And then, holy shit, I'm crying because Mrs. Aldana is rubbing my back like I wish Mom would do. "Things are just . . ." My voice catches. "It's not even my fault! I wish it were. I wish it were my fault. 'Cause then I'd deserve this. But I don't. And it's not fair."

"My," Mrs. Aldana says. She squeezes my shoulder. "Oh my. Derek."

"And Mrs. Aldana, this poetry stuff isn't half bad. It's actually fun, if I'm being honest. And those nerds are all right. I might actually miss them. But I can't go anymore. If I stay, Jae has to go. And she needs this. It's her special place. I don't wanna take that from her. I'm not just making excuses to quit, for real. I'm actually . . . It's . . ." I choke up.

"Okay," she says quietly. She takes a deep breath in and out, as if she's meditating, looking for answers. "You like Jae, but her uncle does not like you because of your home situation?"

I nod.

"That's a lot for anyone to hear. That you aren't good enough for the love you want."

My face glows fire hot and she gives me a knowing look. "You know that's not true. Those external things don't make you good enough or not good enough."

I shrug. "It doesn't matter what I think."

"It matters *most* what you think." She pauses. "Do you want to tell me more about home? How is your mother doing?"

I turn away, look at the bulletin board covered with student reports. "Just ready to get the hell out of there." I laugh, but it sounds hollow.

"If you ever need a place to go, our door is open. But you already know that." She winks. "My husband won't mind. You can use the backyard whenever you want, Derek, even if we're not home."

"You mean I can just come over? For real?"

"For real. I know how much you loved that house." She pauses. "And about quitting the club. You don't have to come to the meetings, but I still want you to write your poems and submit them to me every week."

"That's it?"

"And of course, you'll be there for the open mic," she says.

I inhale deeply and let out a long sigh. Everything is shot to hell. But still, there's a tiny fire somewhere in the deepest, darkest part of me that refuses to be trampled out. *You'll be there*. Those words are like oxygen bringing the fire to life. I'll be there, even if I can't talk to Jae or touch her or hold her. She'll be in my orbit again, at least for that one night.

"Okay," I say. "And Mrs. Aldana? Since I can't work with Jae on the planning—"

"Don't worry about it," she says. "We'll take care of it."

The locker room is empty when I get there. I hear the shrill whistle outside and Coach's voice shouting orders. A part of me is itching to race onto the field and let go of everything. Dribble the ball from foot to foot and let my lungs ache. I want to smell the grass, feel the sweat dripping down my face. Anything to tell me I'm still Derek, the star player, and I'm going to be okay.

But I can't move. I sit on the bench in front of the lockers. Open my backpack and pull out my history book. I flip open to the inside cover, to the picture of us on the yacht. Jae in that yellow dress. Me, laughing.

I lick my bottom lip, which doesn't hurt anymore. I know that's how it's supposed to work. You get hurt and then the pain goes away. I won't always feel like this when I think about Jae, like there's a knife sticking into my chest. But I wonder how long it'll take to feel normal again.

The locker room door swings open and Henry strides in, already pulling his jersey up over his head. I snap the history book shut and stuff it into my bag.

He turns on the light switch. "What are you doing, man? Missing practice again? You realize you're sitting in the dark, right?" He walks past me. His Mohawk is still perfectly spiked up and I'm convinced he mixes his gel with concrete.

He opens his locker, which has a smiling poop emoji on the door. "You okay, man?" he asks, pulling out a towel and wiping his sweaty face.

"I'm good," I say. "Leaving early?"

He wipes the towel over the rest of his body and throws it back in the locker. "My mom called. Grandpa's in the hospital." He steps out of his cleats and his shorts and grabs clean clothes.

"Sorry to hear that. Text me later. Let me know how he's doing," I say.

Henry's hand pauses on the way to grabbing his bag. "Really?"

I shrug. "Sure." I take off my hat and run my fingers through my hair. "Don't act so surprised."

Henry grabs his bag and slams the locker shut. "Well. We've always been, you know. Just cool with each other. Nothing more."

"I know."

"But why?" He leans against the locker.

My face feels warm. Maybe a part of me wanted him to notice my distance. Now that he's pointing it out, I want to crawl away. But it's been a day full of confessions, so why stop now?

I take a breath. "When my dad died, I thought I could deal with it 'cause at least I had my best friend. And then all of a sudden . . . I didn't."

Henry's face falls. "Man."

"It's not your fault," I add quickly. "It's just what it is. You were the cool new friend without issues, you know?"

Henry nods. He reaches into his pocket and passes me his vape. It looks like something out of a sci-fi movie, a shiny silver with a glowing blue light at the bottom.

"Berry-gasmic Explosion?" I ask, turning it over in my hands.

"Huh?"

"The flavor."

"No, dude, it's like cherry or something."

I hand it back to him. "No thanks."

Henry stuffs it into his pocket and shakes his head. "Everybody's got issues, Derek. My mom smothers me." He pulls out his phone from his pocket and sighs. "Gotta go." He stops halfway out the door. "You sure you're okay?"

I nod.

He nods.

The door shuts behind him and the locker room is quiet again except for the steady drip from a leaky faucet.

CHAPTER THIRTY-THREE

Jae

As Halloween approaches, the lone pumpkins on front steps turn into families of jack-o'-lanterns. Skeletons perch on stone walls. Witches peek through iron gates.

But the biggest change that autumn brings is no Derek. I don't see him anymore, except for those brief moments when I'm walking to Free Verse and he's running across the field with the soccer team. I let my eyes linger for longer than they should. Watching him run across the field, watching the ball move like it's under his spell, makes my stomach twist in knots.

At the first meeting without him, Mrs. Aldana is careful with her words. "Derek won't be joining us. At least for now." I wonder how much he told her. I wonder if he has someone to talk to.

Uncle Rowan's hard edges soften. He doesn't nag me at dinner as much, but he sends watchful glances my way between sips of wine. He clears his throat like he wants to say something, but when he does, it's something that doesn't matter to either of us. *It's a lot warmer this fall than I've ever seen here. That house down the street finally sold.*

Today after dinner, which Ms. Rosette made with vegan ground beef, I head up to my room and sit on the edge of my bed. The curtains are open, and I'm looking past the yard and to that stretch of brush lining the sand. It's still and no one is there.

Getting ready?

It's a text from CJ. They're all excited about the Halloween party and I haven't even gotten a costume. Time moves so slow, I thought I had more of it.

No costume, I text back.

Just be a sexy pirate. Wear a patch or something. Text me when ur ready. Will pick you up.

I have nothing that looks like a patch, and I'm not in the mood to put something together. I throw on a dark pair of jeans, a black tee, and a black hat. At least the colors work.

Uncle Rowan is downstairs, standing in front of the bay window, his hands folded behind his back, the light from above making his brown head glow. I adjust the purse on my shoulder.

"Uncle Rowan, the poetry kids are getting together tonight. Is it okay if I go?" I pause and then add, "It's Halloween."

He's quiet for a long time and I suppress a sigh. I'm turning to head upstairs when he says, "Used to be my favorite holiday."

I stop and stare. Something about Uncle Rowan and candy doesn't mix.

He talks over his shoulder. "It was the only time I appreciated your mama's nosy nature. She knew exactly which houses were handing out Bible tracts and laying on hands." He chuckles and turns to me. "You don't want to stay home and hand out candy? Ms. Rosette bought some."

"I'd just really like to see my friends."

"And Derek?" His gaze is unwavering.

"He quit the club. I haven't seen him in so long." My voice hitches and I swallow all the emotions down, try not to sound angry. "We don't talk. So I don't know where he's going to be or when. We don't talk."

He turns back to the window and watches a yacht race past. "Be careful," he says. "Be back by midnight or you'll turn into a pumpkin."

It's the closest thing to a joke I've heard him make since I moved in. I hurry out of the room before he can change his mind.

I text CJ once I get outside, and minutes later, he pulls up in his silver Honda, pizza sign on the roof. William leans over to open the back door for me and I slide in beside him, the smell inside as strong as stepping into a pizza shop.

William's wearing a Robin Hood costume, his blond hair gathered into a shiny black ribbon. A bow and a quiver full of arrows sit on his lap.

"Why do those look real?" I ask, pointing to the arrows.

"Could turn Hunger Games in there. Or the Purge," he says. "Someone has to protect us." He laughs at my expression. "They're not real."

CJ turns around in the driver's seat. "Hey," he says, and I laugh at the thin circle of brown hair at the edge of his wrinkled bald cap.

"Friar Tuck?" I ask.

"That's right."

"So you and William coordinated?"

"Yeah. And you were there," Swan says from the passenger seat, where a tall black hat touches the car roof. She throws a bag to me. "Thought you might need a costume, since you've been in la-la land lately. You're Maid Marian."

"Hey, thanks," I say. "How about you, Swan? You don't seem dressed to the theme."

She turns around and screeches so loud, I fall back against my seat. Her lips are a deep purple, fading into black. "I'm a witch," she cackles. "A witch! A *wiiiitch*!"

"Yes. She's a witch," William mutters. "Every year."

"Hey, let me help you, Jae," Swan says, her voice back to normal as she grabs a blanket at her feet. She and William hold it up and I manage to wiggle modestly out of my clothes and into the costume. CJ blasts Rockwell's "Somebody's Watching Me." We sing along while my stomach quivers at the thought of maybe seeing Derek and what I'll say and if I should say anything at all. I remember Valeria's directed gaze. *We'll be going together.* My stomach fills will new dread.

Even with our music blaring, we hear the party before we see it. A cast of decapitated characters are vaping on the front steps of a cream-colored mansion. Two girls in booty shorts and heels pass the car and catwalk to the front door. The boys outside nearly break their necks watching them pass.

"Fairies." Swan stares out the window after them. "Oh, yeah. We're warding off evil with wings and lots of skin."

"I for one appreciate the effort," CJ says as they step outside. "Very, very much." He throws the pizza sign on his seat and slams the door shut.

I step onto the sidewalk and look down at my bloodred medieval dress. I swish the hem around my ankles, then suddenly look up toward the house, feeling eyes on me. Is it possible that our bodies are still connected, even from a distance?

I shake my head. It doesn't matter. Derek and I were never together. Not in a way that could last. We were standing on a bridge together, never crossing over to the other side where there was something solid to stand on.

"Maid Marian?" William is in front of me, holding his elbow out. I close the car door and link my arm through his. CJ and Swan are already miles away, on the trail of fairy wings.

"I didn't know Robin Hood was such a gentleman," I say in an accent that doesn't exist anywhere on earth.

"Well, he wasn't. He owned no property. He had nothing to offer a lady like Maid Marian. Well, depending on what version of the story you like. She was a mere shepherdess in some iterations. Anyway, all Robin Hood had to give was his heart. And his arm."

I smile. "How romantic."

"It is Halloween, the most romantic day of the year." He wiggles his eyebrows and squeezes my hand gently in the crook of his arm. When we pass the bludgeoned and decapitated smokers, we stand with CJ and Swan in front of the crossed scythes of two grim reapers blocking the way to the door.

"What's up, guys," one of them says from the shadow of his black hood.

Swan leans in toward him. "What's up? The moon, a cauldron bright, of wishes, dreams, and terror, fright. But 'morrow brings a golden light when dawn becomes the day."

"Did you just make that up?" CJ nearly wails, his voice high in disbelief as the black hood leans away from her.

"Freestyle." Swan shrugs. "Maybe I was a rapper in my past life."

The scythes separate and the other grim reaper rushes to open the front door for us. "Have fun, guys," he says in the most nasally voice. "Happy Halloween."

Inside, the room is a steam oven, and EDM is blaring from speakers in the ceiling. A small group is bouncing their heads and various body parts in some sort of rhythm. I try not to judge because how does one dance to EDM anyway? But then I see a flash of white, and someone dressed as the creepy girl from *The Ring* is shuffling so fast, I can barely catch their feet. They must be gliding on ice.

"Whoa." I nod along, lost in their flow, until Swan tugs on my hand and pulls me down the hall.

In the kitchen, William, his quiver slung onto his back, is playing eeny-meeny-miny-mo with three kegs, settling on one that empties out a dark red liquid. He smells the drink and flinches, scrunching his nose. "When in Rome," he says, holding his nose and tipping the cup back.

CJ reaches for a box of orange juice and pours a cup for himself. "One of us has to be responsible," he says.

"Not me!" Swan opens the fridge and pulls out a bottle of vodka.

"I didn't think you guys would drink," I say.

"Because we write poetry?" Swan asks with exaggerated offense. "You should read more biographies, love. Imo gave me my first taste of soju when I was ten." She pours herself a shot. "Come, gentlemen, I hope we shall drink down all unkindness," she says, quoting Shakespeare.

"I drink to the general joy o' the whole table," William adds.

"Let my liver rather heat with wine than my heart cool with mortifying groans," Swan says.

CJ snorts. "O thou invisible spirit of wine! If thou hast no name to be known by, let us call thee devil!"

"I got in town on Monday, Tuesday rolling drunk, Wednesday morning, I pawned my trunk," I say.

They all blink back.

"Langston Hughes."

Swan cackles for real—not witchy this time—then takes a drink, winces, and clears her throat. "Wanna try?" she asks me.

"If I did, you would never see me again." I draw a finger across my throat. The last thing I need is showing up drunk to Uncle Rowan's house.

Swan nods. "Let's dance, bitches," she says, grabbing William with one hand, me with the other, and pulling us into a pack of undulating bodies.

"CJ!" I call over the ruckus, and I see the flashing strobe light beam off his plastic bald cap as he makes his way to us.

I try to relax my shoulders. I bounce around like the others, not sure if I'm doing the right moves. Or if there are any. Swan doesn't seem to care about the genre we're listening to. She bends over and twitches her hips from side to side. I guess you can twerk to anything if you really try. William is doing the funky chicken behind her.

"Join me, Maid Marian!" he shouts, his head and shoulders jutting in and out. So I give in to the funky chicken. By the time "Monster Mash" is playing, I've lost all inhibition.

Just then I see a heavily made-up Captain Jack Sparrow making his way through the crowd of unfamiliar faces. Miguel is unrecognizable except for the eyebrow ring that glimmers in the flashing lights.

"Easy!" he shouts when he sees me, and slings his arm over my shoulders. The liquid in his cup is dark brown and he slurs his words. "Nice t'see ya here. Once in a while you nerds shprise me."

I jerk my head away from his sharp breath and wiggle out from under him. "Well, Valeria invited us, so . . ."

"Vvvlaria?" he slurs. "My sister?" He laughs loud. "I told her not to do that but she loves to have fun."

I glance over my shoulder, scanning the room. CJ is watching us with a frown, superhero fists on hips. But no Valeria.

"Is Derek here?" I ask.

Miguel wiggles his eyebrows. "Derek's a little busy right now, but I'm free."

He leans his head in close and I step back. He steps close again. "Why don't you show me how you treat the guys in the boys' bathroom?" His liquor-tainted breath is hot against my cheek. His eyebrow ring winks. "Show me."

I shove my hands against his sweaty shirt. He staggers, falls into the sofa against the wall. His drink sloshes over and he curses, and then, eyes rolled back, he laughs. No one seems to notice this in all the chaos, except CJ. He grabs my hand and tries to pulls me. But the sight of Miguel, red mouth agape, eyes smudged with liner and squeezed shut in pure mirth, makes me glance at the quiver full of arrows on William's back.

"You look like you have murder on your mind," CJ says into my ear. "It's okay." He pulls hard on my hand.

"No, it's not."

"You're right, it's not. But let it go. He's not worth it."

Swan stops dancing. Her head whips around. "Everything okay?" she yells.

I nod, not wanting to ruin the night for everyone else.

But just then, the music stops and there's a communal groan. People look around, confused, shout, *Where's the music? Turn it back on!*

And then there's the strangest sound.

Wails. So out of place. So disorienting. Loud, grating wails that claw against the skin.

Valeria materializes from around the corner, and I almost laugh at her giant onesie and bonnet and bib. A pacifier the size of her arm. Her friends Cindy and Kiley, similarly dressed, follow behind, giddy and giggling. And they're walking toward the dance floor.

They're walking toward our group.

They're walking toward me.

CHAPTER THIRTY-FOUR

Jae

"Mama," Cindy says, lips trembling, eyes as wide as daisies.

"Mama," Kiley and Valeria echo.

I'm still, frozen beneath their gaze. Someone tugs on my arm. Swan maybe. I can hear her voice. But I can't stop hearing theirs. *Mama*, they pout. *Mama*, they cry, and I'm shaking my head, confused. How is this—how is *this* happening?

There's no space for a thought in this wailing and crying and the heartbeat thundering in my ears. Just confusion. And *how*?

They stop, and I will them to turn away, to take their performance somewhere else. It wasn't meant for me. They don't know. They can't. My heart is a drumbeat of fear in the quiet, and then my breath stops.

Valeria pulls out a piece of paper from her pocket, holds it up to the light. "'Dear Jae,'" she starts slowly, with a grin and a coldness on my name.

It's me. Jae. This is meant for no one else. But *how*?

"'This letter is hard to write because . . . I don't have the *words* to *thank you* for what you did for me and Jermaine,'" she says. "'We are *soooo* blessed that you chose us to take care of your *Sweet. Baby.*

Girl.'" She cocks her head more and more with each word, eyes glued to mine.

The whole room murmurs around me. Buzzes. Swarms. And I'm dizzy. Confused.

"'You will *always* be Sarah's mother.'" Valeria pauses long enough to snort, to let it sink in. "'No matter what I do for her. No matter how much of a mother I am.'"

Finally, I'm uprooted. Maybe it was her name. Sarah. June. My baby. "Stop," I say.

"'*You* brought her here. *You* gave her life. And for that, I can only *thank you*.'"

I scream now, "Stop!" and lunge for the letter. She holds it high over her head. I feel tears and I feel sharp. I reach for the closest thing and pull, a fistful of glossy curls. We stumble. We twist. I scream in her ear. But what am I saying? I don't know. How could you do this? Give it back? Or maybe it's the sound of every anguish I've recently held, finally finding a worthy target. A person I can hurt without caring if they leave. I scream like a mother who's lost her young. Who found the thing she loved cut open, hollowed out, and laid bare. I scream, and I scream, and I scream.

Valeria drops the letter. I snatch it, press it against my chest, and in that room I could only see in my worst nightmare, is Derek. A blank-faced Mad Hatter, only steps behind Valeria and Cindy and Kiley. There. Behind them. There. Mouth open. Just. There.

"You stupid bitch!" Valeria yells at me.

"She didn't have to go all psycho," someone says. "It was a joke."

"She's postpartum. Freaking nuts."

I move, finally unplanted. Lift my feet and move. I hear CJ and William and Swan calling my name. But I am alone. I shuffle through sweaty bodies, make it to the closest door, step on the hem of my dress and nearly tumble down the balcony steps into the backyard. “Whoa. Careful, princess,” someone in a group of vapers says. Soon they’ll find out what happened inside and they’ll have other names for me.

The yard glows with orange-and-red orbs. Someone shouts my name, but I’m running. I just don’t know where to. I don’t remember where I am. I don’t remember where home is.

I grab the hem of my dress and race past the side of the house. *It’s a dream*, I tell myself. *A nightmare. This didn’t happen. I’ll wake up soon*. But the tightness in my throat feels too real.

Wake up! Wake up!

I hear footsteps behind me. “Jae!” They call me over and over and finally, I look back. Of course it’s them, all three. Robin Hood, Friar Tuck, and a witch. They’ll want to know if it’s true. They’ll ask me questions. So I don’t stop. Not until I can’t see the yellow house anymore. I ignore their voices until they’re quiet again. Until they just stand there nearby, like ghosts, waiting to be summoned. I pull out my phone, request a ride, and then I wait for a stranger to take me to a place I can barely call home.

CHAPTER THIRTY-FIVE

Jae

Uncle Rowan's white leather recliner makes a swoosh sound as he settles into it and crosses one ankle over his knee. He rests his legal pad on his leg and scribbles across the pastel yellow surface.

I watch him from my supine position on the sofa, where I'm balancing my book of short stories on my chest. Not reading.

It's become a ritual of sorts: I come home to finish my homework, sit through an awkward dinner with Uncle Rowan, and then share silence with him in the family room, reading and writing in our own separate worlds. But today, there was no homework, no school. *Cramps*, I told him.

I didn't tell him the whole school knows my secret. He'd just say to face the music. He'd tell me to take responsibility for my mistakes. I wonder if responsibility means my name on the bathroom stall. Fingers pointing at me in the cafeteria. Sitting alone in the banyan tree.

He looks up at me over his glasses without raising his shiny head, sensing he's in my thoughts. I return to my book, turn an unread page.

Just then the doorbell rings. Uncle Rowan doesn't look up from his scribbling.

"Get that, will you?" he mutters.

I throw my book on the couch and get up. When I open the door, Derek's standing at the bottom of the stairs, his dark hair plastered to his forehead, his jersey clinging wet to his chest. My heart, unsure, takes flight, and then just as soon, plummets. *God, not you.*

"What are you doing here?" I ask, closing the door behind me and stepping onto the landing, the warm and grainy stone beneath my bare feet.

"I, uh . . . I took the wrong portal?" Derek says, his face partially shadowed by his cap.

I tilt my head, offer him only a blank stare. I'm angry the weeks didn't erase everything. The fluttering, the tensing, the lightness. My body won't give him up. I've missed his voice, its texture like something soft and hungry. *I want you to tell me things too.* Well, now he knows everything.

"Have you seen *Interstellar*?" he asks, stuffing his hands into his pockets.

"What?"

"Time. They talk about time. Brand says time can stretch and it can squeeze, but it can't run backward. That's all I've wanted for so long, for time to run backward so I could fix everything."

I sigh. "Why are you here?"

"I just wanted to see if you're okay," he says. "I know I'm not supposed to be here." He takes off his hat and runs his hand through black waves, squinting up at me like I'm the sun.

"Frankly, I'm surprised you're not still *there*," I answer, "standing on the dance floor."

"What?"

"Standing. You know. Not doing anything. Not sticking up for me."

"Jae—"

"You stood there." I take a shaky breath, the memory of the party back in fleshy detail, like he's the ghost of Christmas past, showing me my humiliation. "You stood there and let them mock me," I say. "And you show up here three days later like it actually means something."

He blinks up at me, eyes all deep black, and I ache. Our night together comes back, an echo of tender words and impatient sighs, of wanting more. I break the spell, send the echoes back.

"I had a baby." I let those words linger between us. The only words that matter right now. They've always been there, an invisible wedge. "I had a baby. I gave her to someone else. It was just me. No one was there for me."

"Jae."

"I had no closure, no entrustment ceremony, nothing. And they took her like . . . like my hands were meant to be empty. Like I didn't deserve her because I didn't wait long enough to have her. Nobody thinks I *need* her." I swallow. Blink away tears. My voice is hollow and tired. "You wanted to see if I'm *okay*? You know I'm not okay."

He looks down at the bottom stair and all I can see is the top of his white hat. He's shaking his head like those are words enough.

"Say something." I take a step, my right foot bearing down on a sharp stone, and I let it press into my skin, grit my teeth.

"Jae—"

"Say something!" The pain is like oxygen feeding my anger, and I run down the steps and onto the warmth of concrete, needing to be closer, wanting him to feel the fire emanating off my skin.

"I'm sorry." He stares at me, unwavering, dark eyes lined with shadows.

"Sorry?"

"I—I didn't know what to do. I froze. It was . . . a shock."

The woeful look in his eyes grates on my nerves. The confirmation in them, that I was right to hide the truth, that it was too big for him to handle. "Poor you," I say, my voice drenched with mock concern. "Poor Derek. You don't think *I* was shocked?"

He clenches his jaw, steps closer. Too close. His face, held into something stronger than anger, bends toward mine, making my insides gather and twist, flicker and flame, making his breath on my skin feel like soft fingers.

"You had no idea you had a kid either?" he says, his voice gravelly. "Was that a shock to you, too?"

"That was none of your business."

"I told you *my* business," he says, stabbing his chest. "Everything! Poured out my heart into those dumb poems."

I cross my arms. "You told me about your parents and I told you about mine. I'd say we're even."

"*Even?*" he scoffs. Turns around like he needs to get away from me, then comes back, pacing, caged. "*Even?* Are you serious?" I can hear his breath from here, the steady count of in-four out-six, and my insides shift when he stops and looks down at me with eyes so sharp they could pin me down. "I don't wanna be even with you. Not with you."

My heart catches, like my arms wrapped around my chest, my skin, muscles, bones, can't stop him from reaching inside. I raise my chin high, turn my head to a swaying palm tree, to the sound of its caressing leaves.

"How could you not tell me something so important?" he presses, stepping closer. "I had to find out—"

"Not my fault," I snap. "*Your* friends stole my stuff. And you didn't stop them, did you."

"What? You think I *knew* about it?"

"Didn't you?"

"No fucking way."

"You're lying."

"Jae." He gives me a look of disgust and starts walking down the driveway past Uncle Rowan's car, toward the gate. I run, plant myself in his path. His eyebrows gather like storm clouds.

"How did she get my letter?" I demand.

"I can't believe . . ." He growls and steps around me. I grab his jersey, damp with sweat, and pull him back. "Let go," he says.

I run around him, block his way, arms wide. "How did she get my letter?"

"I told you, I didn't know before she did it. And you called me a liar. You think I'd lie to you?"

"But you know *now*, don't you?"

"Jae, who cares! Valeria's not here. It's you and me. This is about *us*." He's frantically gesturing at the air.

I shake my head. "There is no us."

He breathes in, nostrils flared. "Yeah? She took it from your bag in English class. Made a copy. Are you happy now? Now that you know, and there's no us?" He turns around, makes it a few steps down the driveway before I block him again.

"Did you just ask if I'm *happy* now? Did you seriously ask me that? *Are you happy now?*" I mimic.

"Just forget it, okay?" He washes his hands over his face. Groans. "Forget everything. Or don't. I don't care."

"Well, you should."

"Then let me!" he yells, hitting his chest. "Stop pushing me away when I'm trying! I don't care about those guys." He points vaguely over his shoulder. "I leave school, and they don't cross my mind. But you do. All the time. I think about you, too freaking much. I sleep and I wake up and you're there!"

I step back like I've been stung. Clench my teeth against the flood of feelings.

He shakes his head, voice soft, melted. "They don't matter, Jae."

"They matter." I take another step back, take deep breaths. "Since I came here, I've had a target on my back, and your friends put it there." His eyes are pleading, but I'm tired, and I want everything said. "Do you realize what this costs me? This isn't the kind of place where kids have babies too young. I don't need to be the Black girl with baggage here, the baby mama. *Easy*." My hands shake. I ball them into fists to keep them steady. "I don't get it. Are you any different from your friends? Do *they* think so? They seem to think you fit right in."

I turn, feel the grate of stone against my heels, but he grabs my hand and pulls me back, so close I can feel his breath on my face, his nose almost touching mine. "Listen. I mean this. I'm gonna make sure they don't bother you again." He presses his fingers into my palms. His thumb brushes my skin.

"Why would things be different now? You've never been there for me."

"I'm right here!" His arms are open again, face red. "I'm here! And I didn't mean to hurt you. You're the last person I wanna hurt."

His voice is cracking, quivering. “I’m not good enough. That’s . . . that’s it. I’m not.” He sniffles, pushes his hat lower over his eyes. Looks away. “I’m supposed to stay away from you. I don’t want to. I just . . . I don’t want to.” He laughs, sad. “I know I’m not good enough, but I miss you so much.”

I look up at his face and swallow down hurt and fight off the sadness stinging my eyes. “Uncle Rowan said I don’t know what better looks like,” I say. “But I do. I deserve better.”

Derek’s shoulders fall. He blinks at the ground.

“Would someone like to tell me what’s going on?” Uncle Rowan’s voice carries. I turn around to see him standing at the door, legs spread like he’s guarding the entrance. But he is calm, waiting, and the hair on my arms stand up.

“I was just telling Derek I don’t want to talk to him again,” I say, giving Derek a final glance.

His eyes flicker with pain, dark under the shadow of his cap. I trek the warm concrete, run up the stairs and past Uncle Rowan. I don’t wait. I slam the front door so hard the picture frames on the wall clatter.

I’m tired of being burned. For once, I want to be the one who turns everything into ash.

To Him.—Jae

i wanted you to stay,

but the truth is

i'd still have good days

with or without you.

you aren't the wind that carries me,

and I'm not afraid to fly,

so I choose me,

janelle,

sixteen,

dark eyes.

To Her.—Jae

i am georgia

the spirits of lake lanier
roil in my mouth
i could spit them out and haunt you
my voice is a ring shout
a gullah geechee song

you're not meant to understand

CHAPTER THIRTY-SIX

Jae

I'm flat on my back, arms at my sides, staring at my decidedly starless ceiling. There's a knock, and Ms. Rosette with her shiny Afro puff peeks into the room. She puts a finger to her lips, steps inside, and closes the door softly behind her.

I sit up. "What is it?" I ask, looking to the hand she's hiding behind her back.

"I heard everything," she whispers, owl-eyed, her words slow and deliberate. "The window was open in the dining room."

"You were spying on me?"

She nods excitedly. "I know what the boy was talking about. Look." She pulls out a small stack of papers from behind her back. "I saw it there in his office, you know? And I thought, *Oh-oh, has mista found a mistress?* But it was not for *him*." She holds the stack out to me, but when I reach for it, she pulls back. "*You* found them, not me. You found them in his office. On his desk. Far left corner. When you looked for a pen. You understand?"

I nod.

"Maybe I am becoming American," she says, shaking her head as she slips out the door. She has just betrayed Uncle Rowan, or, the village raising the child.

I stare down at the small stack of papers wrapped in twine, with one stem of purple wisteria tucked inside, wilted. I pull out the stem, press the soft petals between my fingers, unwind the twine.

<u>Creatures</u>—Derek

It's a sleepover night

Miguel's got
A stack of comics, a flashlight, contraband candy

Valeria's got
Her stuffed corgi
(They're not allowed to have pets for real)

It's a sleepover night because
Mr. and Mrs. Montero are fighting

We hide under a big fort made of
Old worn-out sheets and boxes
And pretend
All sorts of things

We are creatures of the night
Bats, vampires, things with fangs and
Immortality
Nothing can hurt us
If we just pretend

We sneak Popsicles from the basement freezer
Blue sugar on Valeria's ribbons
Green on Miguel's tongue
Teeth glowing colors in the dark
High on sugar until

Miguel cries
"I think they're getting a divorce."

I put my arm around his shoulder
Hug him tight

We could do that back then
Say
I'm afraid

And now
We hide everything so no one knows
We cry

At some point you get too old or too cool
To say the truth
Even though
Scared is all you ever are

We are creatures and
Nothing can hurt us if we just
Pretend

<u>*Travel Light*</u>—Derek

Jingling keys.
Engine on.
Headlights shine.
Car reverse.
Swerving lights.
Dad's last night.

"You okay?"
Deep brown skin.
Not okay.
Hold it in.
Smiles at me.
Hope again.

Breaking up.
Memories.
Heavy hurt.
Gravity.
I am small.
Atom. Quark.

Can't move on.
Baggage full.
Set it down.
Standing still.
Emptied out.
Starless sky.
Say goodnight.
Say goodbye.

CHAPTER THIRTY-SEVEN

Jae

How long have I been lying here? I roll my head to the side, stare out the open curtains at a hazy sky, the faint outline of the moon behind clouds. The sky is a bright blush as the sun gives in to the ocean. Time is lost somewhere, moving on without me. I'm filled up with thoughts, and I try, as Mrs. Aldana said, to give them their proper weight.

The weightiest of them all: Do I love Derek Patel?

I'm still holding his collection of . . . everything. Poems. Scripts. A list titled "Planetary Humor." And Letters. Letters and letters.

It's me again, Jae. I wonder so much about you. What made you happy as a kid? What was your first movie? Mine was Toy Story. *I was five, I think. I watched it every single weekend for probably a whole year.*

It's me again, Jae. Mom's having a really good day, and that's scary. I haven't seen Peter since that night. So I wonder. Where is she getting her pills from now?

It's me again, Jae. I miss you. I'm sorry.

I'm remembering all our moments through a different lens. Him crying in the bathroom the first day we met. Him leaving brunch suddenly, when I'd never seen him so happy. Him lying on my bed, inexplicable pain in his eyes, saying he didn't deserve me. His mom. Everything.

And I see why Miguel and Valeria mean so much to him. How their families would spend most weekends together barbecuing and beaching and laughing. They remind him of a joy he no longer has.

I'm flat on my back, clutching everything, missing the Derek I see in these poems and letters. But then I remember Valeria and her friends at the Halloween party, him motionless in his Mad Hatter costume, and I seethe. The fact is, the Derek I was falling for didn't always show up. And that other Derek, I don't want to see.

But I know who I do want to see.

I cross my room to my desk drawer. Pull out my phone, which has been off for the last three days. I turn it on.

Notifications flood the screen. Texts. Missed calls. I sit down, open a group chat.

I need to call a meeting.

CHAPTER THIRTY-EIGHT

Jae

I sit up at the sound of feet thundering up the stairs. A rhythmic knock on my door.

"We come bearing gifts," Swan's voice calls from the other side. When I open the door, she's flanked by William and CJ, and she's holding a plate of glazed donuts. The sugar-sweet smell wafts into my nose and makes my mouth water. "Homemade apple fritters from chez Cho."

I didn't think they'd actually come. After Friday night, after ignoring them for the past three days, I was sure they'd never want to see me again.

"Little pig, little pig, let us come in?" William says.

"Oh." I step aside. "Thanks. For coming."

"Thanks for not fleeing the country," William answers, giving my neck a tight hug.

"I considered it."

CJ hands me a jar filled with origami stars in sparkling construction paper. "A stockpile of songs and quotes and poetry. All the pick-me-ups you could ever need."

"Hey, thanks, CJ." I'm afraid to say anything more, lest I get emotional.

"It's a win-win. Had to do something with my hands, you know? Anxiety in high gear." He pauses. Adjusts his glasses over thoughtful green eyes. "We missed you at school today. I was worried about you."

I apologize, but he's already throwing himself onto my plush pink rug like he's about to make a snow angel. William's tracing his fingers along my bookshelves, his usual blond ponytail in a single braid. Swan's sitting cross-legged on my bed with big hoop earrings, a high ponytail with a kente headband, a leopard-print camisole, and shredded black jeans revealing skin all the way up to her thighs. She has that same jean jacket from the first club meeting, the one covered in buttons and pins and favorite things. And to top it all off, she's wearing spicy ramen socks.

I think how cool it is to know these people who are so unafraid to be themselves. Now that everything has blown up around me, maybe I can be unafraid.

Swan nods absentmindedly as she glances around the room. "So pink."

"Uncle Rowan. He forgot that I aged nine years since he last saw me."

She props a pillow against the wall and leans back.

I grab a donut and bite. It's warm and melts against my tongue and my fingers. I must have let out a happy moan, because William whips his head around, shoving a book back in place.

"That good? Lemme have one. CJ?"

"Yes, please," he calls from the floor.

And then we're all quiet, lips smacking, glazed mouths and fingers.

"Mm!" William says once he's finished his off and popped his sugary fingers into his mouth, one by one. "So, shall we call the meeting to order?" He looks at me with a soft smile. "Jae, would you like to start?"

I bite my lip, not knowing what to say. There's so much.

Swan crosses her arms and tilts her head to the side, looking at me. "Okay. Start here. What the fuck happened?"

I sigh. Does she always have to be so . . . Swanny? "You were there," I say.

"Yet I still have no idea what happened. Like, we found out from *Valeria Montero* at a *Halloween party* that you had a *baby* and gave it up for *adoption*. At a Halloween party. From Valeria Montero." Her eyes dart around the room in confusion, exasperated arms in the air. "Like, where were *we* this whole time? Just, you know, sitting in a grove, pouring out our hearts to each other in poetry."

I sink farther into the bed, pick at a loose thread in the comforter.

"We came by, you know," CJ says from his half-comatose state on the floor. "After the party on Friday. You weren't answering your phone. I was seriously, like, worried sick."

My heart breaks a little. "I'm sorry," I say.

"I just can't believe you kept something so big to yourself," Swan adds, eyebrows stitched together. "It's not like we're owed every detail of your life. We just want to know you. And it's, like, something that you and I could have shared. I mean, we kinda knew the truth already, anyway."

"Wait. How?"

"It doesn't take a genius. The way you ran off at the banyan tree when I asked about the picture? You wouldn't have done that if she were your niece."

"Well, you know what? I might have told you. Maybe. But you hated your birth mother for not keeping you. What chance did I have of you liking me?"

"But who said I hate her?" She frowns. "I just wanted her to love me. Is that too much to ask?"

"I'm sure she does, Swan."

"She doesn't know anything about me."

"Trust me. That's not how it works." I take a deep breath through the rising tide of sadness. "Do you really think we're unforgivable? Because we didn't keep our kids?"

Swan sinks deeper into the bed, like she's melting. "No. And I'm so sorry. It had nothing to do with you, okay? That's just how I deal with my stuff. I get angry. I rage. I shake my fist at the world. The old Swan did a lot of crying and I'm just sick of crying."

"Me too," I say.

CJ pokes his red head over the side of the bed and climbs up like he's the creature from the black lagoon. He lies down on his back, hands crossed over his chest, and turns to look at me.

"Why did you call the meeting, Jae?" he asks. "Do you wanna talk? Write poetry? Go for a walk?"

"Honestly," I say, taking a deep breath, "I'm pissed. Valeria shouldn't have done that. She can't get away with it."

Everyone's quiet.

"I agree," Swan says slowly. "She shouldn't have done that. But Jae. It's done. The cat's out of the bag, so to speak. Valeria wins if you let it get to you. If you don't take control of the narrative. It would bring her so much joy to know you're hiding out in your room consumed by her."

"I agree," William says, leaning against the shelf.

“And in any case, you’ve already been avenged,” Swan says, smiling. “As soon as you got in the car, we called the police on the party. All that underage drinking. Tsk tsk. We sent their asses home.”

William nods. “It’s true. And a certain bully with a penchant for dramatic readings,” he says, pronouncing *penchant* the French way, “ended up in the back of a squad car. Apparently, throwing up on an officer is considered assault.”

My jaw drops. “Valeria? You’re kidding!”

“No.”

“Derek?” I ask with hesitation. “He got in trouble too?”

“Derek left when you did,” Swan says. One eyebrow tilts slyly as she holds my gaze.

“What?” I ask.

“You look relieved.”

“Well, yeah. Maybe. I guess I’m glad he left.”

“Look, the only reason Valeria went after you like that is because you and Derek . . . you clearly like each other. And she’s super possessive and doesn’t wanna let him go. Even though they dated, like, years ago.”

“Why’d they break up?”

“No idea, but they started dating after the Monteros got divorced, and if you ask me, Derek’s heart went all mush for her. But she’s so insufferable, it didn’t last.”

His heart went all mush for her. I bite back a tinge of jealousy, wondering what Derek felt inside when he looked at her. What about her made his heart go *mush*. Then I remember Valeria’s stuffed corgi, and the blue Popsicle on her ribbons, and their history built with forts and imagination.

"He wrote me letters, you know," I say. "Letters and poems and everything. And CJ. He told me about his mom. Her addiction."

William and Swan both lean forward. "What?"

"She's been abusing painkillers since the accident."

CJ sighs heavy. "Yeah. I get why he reacted so badly to me being at his house."

"What happened exactly?" I nudge his shoulder.

He pulls a lock of hair from its mousse-y mold and wraps it around his finger. "Someone ordered pizzas. And when I got there, his mom asked me if I had pills on me."

"Nooo," Swan groans, putting her head in her hands. "That's not good. That's not okay. You should have told us, CJ."

"Well, I didn't wanna piss him off any more."

"Does Derek know his mom did that?" I ask.

"Yeah." He nods, lips pursed. "I was trying to leave and she followed me to the car. That's when Derek showed up. He looked so embarrassed, I didn't think he'd say anything. We'd just pretend it never happened. But no. Not Derek. He wanted to *pulverize* me."

We're all quiet, taking it in, except William, who keeps repeating, "Wow. Wow."

My mind starts leafing through its own book of memories, and I'm stuck on that moment at the beach, when Derek's hard shell cracked and I saw inside, the shimmering. Him calling me into the water. Him dancing with me in the sand. His laugh.

I sigh deep. "What now?" It's a question, only two words, that contains all the uncertainty of my life.

Swan looks at me intently. "No more hiding. Life is too ruthless. We can't make it out alive if we hide from each other."

"No one makes it out alive," CJ laughs.

"You guys don't think, like . . . You don't think I'm . . ." I swallow the words.

Swan leans forward again. "What are you asking? If we think any less of you? Jae, it could happen to anyone."

"More than anything," William says, "I'm amazed at how well you've held yourself together, all things considered. Can't be easy, especially hiding it from everyone. But do you feel a little bit, the *teeniest* bit, better? Now that we know?"

Maybe it's the way William looks at me when he says it. But my eyes become pools of tears and I swipe at my face furiously to catch them. "Umm . . ." I quiver. "I feel . . . supported. I never had that."

"No? Why not?" William asks, crossing the room to bring me a tissue from my desk.

So I tell them. All of it. And I feel like a vine, wrapping myself around a well-rooted tree, tasting oxygen, holding rain, feeling sun.

And when I'm done, Swan whispers, "I don't know how you did it. You obviously love your baby. It's like you gave her up *because* you love her."

I nod. "The adoption counselor told me to say *placed*. So yeah, I placed her with another family. Because I love her."

"Do you want to see her again? I mean, I'm sure you do, but what if you, like, ran into her somewhere? How would you feel?"

I pause and stare down at the pink rug. "I'd be scared. And happy. I don't think I could ever be completely ready, but I would love to see her again."

Swan hugs her knees to her chest. "Maybe my birth mom loved me, too. It's hard to believe that sometimes. Things were so hard for me."

"Do you wanna talk about it?" I ask.

She drops her chin onto her knees and rocks slowly. "They found me alone on a train in Seoul. I was one. My first family adopted me. I mean, you could hardly call them a family. After they adopted me, Moira found out she was pregnant. With twins. So she had two kids of her own and a little foreign baby she didn't really want after all. They went to family reunions without me, can you believe it? Yeah. Gave me food and a Bible and thought that was enough. And then they sent me back to the agency when I was seven."

My mouth drops open.

"In the end, I'm glad they did, but it took me two years to get adopted again. So." Swan purses her lips and takes in a deep breath. "So it took me a while to get over the fact that nobody wanted me. And maybe I'm not totally over it. Maybe that's why I'm so . . . angry."

I bite my lip. "I'm sorry that happened to you." I think about June Baby and Anne and Jermaine, and my heart clenches a little. I tell myself that they would *never* send her away.

Swan gives a sly smile as she lifts a flap on her jean jacket. "What I'm about to show you all stays between us," she says, looking around the room dramatically.

"Oh, goody! More secrets!" William says, fingers strumming together in mock excitement.

I laugh. "Okay."

"You promise?"

"Promise," CJ adds.

She pulls something out and hides it against her chest. "Remember your vow. And don't laugh, either." She lays down what turns out to be a photo.

I cover my mouth to hide my gasp. It's Swan, but she's almost unrecognizable. Coke-bottle glasses. Bangs cut short and sharp. Missing teeth on both sides. A yellow raincoat and rain boots.

She groans. "Poor thing."

"It's cute," I insist.

"This," she says, tapping the photo, "is the earliest picture of me. I was nine. I hate looking at it, but I kind of love it too. That Swan had no idea she'd be okay. She thought she'd always be tossed away like garbage. But that wasn't true. And this Swan," she says, hands over her chest, "has the best parents in the world now. And I'm a teenager, so saying that actually means something."

"I'm so glad things worked out for you," I say.

"They'll work out for you, too. And look, I live just down the street. You can walk over anytime you want. If you wanna talk or write or watch melodramatic Korean shows."

"Really?"

"We're in that pink house with the—"

"—Tabebuia trees."

"Okay. Maybe. I was going to say the pink house with the red car in the driveway."

I nod. "Yeah. Thanks. Okay." We all sink into quiet, content with what's already been said, and I wonder what things *working out* would look like. "Hey. Could we dedicate the open mic to June Baby?" I ask.

"June Baby? How cute," Swan says.

"It's actually Sarah. That's what they named her." I sigh. Tug on a loc to feel something. "So, what do you guys think? I don't want to hijack the event—"

"I think it's brilliant!" William says.

"Awesome idea," CJ adds. "Show them you're not ashamed anymore."

Swan nods. "You know why I don't care what people think about me? Caring never made me happy. Just be Jae. I promise that's enough."

I sink into the thought, into the promise of being enough. Me, strong alone, but stronger held up, wrapped around my rooted tree. Not hiding in the bathroom stall, not running away from the party.

William gently clears his throat. "Can we also address the elephant in the room? Or, not in the room, rather? Derek. Will he be there?"

Swan nods. "Mrs. Aldana said he would be. Jae? How do you feel about that?"

I shrug. "Fine. No. Not fine. But it's okay. He deserves to be there."

"You know, he's been different since he stopped coming to club meetings," William says. "He doesn't really talk to anyone. To be honest, he looks quite lonely."

Swan nods. "Don't be offended, Jae, but we had an emergency meeting at lunch today. The three of us. To talk about, you know. *You*. And guess who was at the banyan tree?"

"Seriously?" I sit taller.

"Yeah. Reading *A Brief History of Time* by Stephen Hawking," she says dramatically, her hand flashing the title across the ceiling.

"You all talked to him?"

"Not much," she says. "It was like he was sorry for using our space without permission. We invited him to stay." She pauses. "Look. I don't believe in trying to change people, okay? But do I believe people can change? Sure. I mean, maybe he's not the person you want him to be now. But maybe he's getting there in his own time."

It's hard not to think about the boy who held me quietly in my room, who kissed me and said, *I see you*. But I can't control what Derek does or who he decides to be.

"Maybe he'll never get there," I say to Swan.

She nods. "Maybe he'll never get there. But you know what? Derek's not the only guy with a really nice ass." She gestures to William. "Take him, for example."

"Hey, hey, hey," William says in a fighting stance. "I'm not just a piece of meat you can fight over, all right? You have to get in line. Get in line!"

Swan snorts.

"What am I, chopped liver?" CJ mutters.

Swan leans over to kiss his forehead. "You've got the most beautiful eyes in Palm Beach County, and if I weren't so gay I'd snatch you up first. And then I'd get in line for William."

CJ laughs, braces glinting.

There's a knock on the door and Ms. Rosette once again sticks her head into my room. "Hello, friends. Are you staying for dinner? *Lots* of food."

The three of them exchange glances.

"Hell yeah—I mean! Thank you so much," Swan says in a rush. She bows her head theatrically and Ms. Rosette *humphs* with a look of amusement. At the sound of the door closing, Swan looks up again, blows her wavy hair out of her eyes. "Well. We called a meeting and we didn't even write poetry. Are we even poets?" She shakes her head in disapproval.

“It’s been free verse this whole time, hasn’t it?” William says absentmindedly as he pulls a book off the shelf. “Hey. Guess this book by the first line. Ready?”

Then we’re shouting, laughing, rolling, and by the time Ms. Rosette calls us down for dinner—*Come and eat NOW or I will finish everything!* she yells—my cheeks are aching.

I feel like I could look into that pool again, see the dark reflection, and love her.

CHAPTER THIRTY-NINE

Derek

The fight with Jae yesterday. I try to think about something else besides that. But it's like those arcade moles that keep popping up every time you knock them down. My thoughts are like moles on speed. Evil moles that call me names. Mrs. Aldana said to explore the thoughts that are worth our time and let go of the thoughts that aren't. But it's not that easy. Maybe the evil moles are right.

I'm on my bed, staring down at the blank lines in my poetry notebook, and I wonder what the others did today in Free Verse. If Jae wrote two poems. If she ever writes about me.

The shades are drawn, and the room swims with floating lights. I'm trying to create a mood, trying to make words materialize, but they don't. *The page is where we can re-create ourselves into who we want to be.*

But who do I want to be? *What* do I want to be? Not alone.

These days, whether I'm with the guys or not, I'm alone.

My phone vibrates beside me. It's an entry-level smartphone that cost me weeks of work to pay for. I look down at the blinking notification light, purple, which means it's from the guys' group chat. I ignore it, turn back to my poetry notebook. I still owe Mrs. Aldana two poems a week.

Explore the thoughts that are worth your time.

Something Jae said comes back to me. Something about an entrustment ceremony. About not having closure. I push aside my notebook and pull out my phone. Ignore the flashing notification and search: *entrustment ceremony*. And I get it. Why she would want something like this. Why this feels like the right way to give your kid to someone else. I go down the rabbit hole. Pictures and videos and blogs of mothers and babies and adoptive families, lighting candles, singing songs, sharing hopes.

Then I'm ready to face the blank page again.

I'm pressing my pen into a deep well in the paper—*the page is where we can re-create ourselves into who we want to be*—when the phone buzzes again. And again. And again. The notifications come at quicker intervals until finally I pick it up to check the messages.

I scroll all the way to the top, where there's a video and Miguel's caption: Easy's baby mama drama. I clench my teeth at the cruel nickname. Someone captured the scene at the Halloween party, and I think I might hurl when I see myself standing there in the background, watching everything unfold. Frozen. *Standing there.*

that's hilarious 😆

haha

shit u think she's ever coming back to school? i wouldn't

saw her today with her little gang of weirdos

Out of hiding now? She has balls

no, she just plays with them

😆😆😆

pass me a soda
come get it yourself
ugh. feeling nauseous

Seconds later, I'm on my bike, riding toward Miguel's house. I enter the gate code in the keypad, wheel my bike inside, and drop it at the foot of a palm tree. I'm walking past the house when I see Mrs. Montero waving from the kitchen window with a towel wrapped around her head. I don't wave back or smile or anything, because all I see is red.

When I round the corner, I see the Montero yacht out in the water. Henry's outside on the deck with some girl I've never seen. He's holding her waist with one hand and a can in the other.

"Derek!" He raises the can to me.

I tear off my sweatshirt and tuck my phone inside, feeling Henry's gaze. I step to the edge of the dock and he yells, "Hey, didn't you bring your trunks?"

No, I didn't think about bringing my fucking trunks. I didn't think about anything besides standing toe to toe with them.

I jump in with my jeans and swim toward the yacht. I grab the ladder and climb up. Henry reaches over to take my hand but I ignore it, pull myself up the last step.

"I thought you weren't coming," he says, patting my back.

"Don't touch me, man," I say.

"Oh my God," the girl says with a thick vocal fry.

I make my way inside the cabin, which smells of sweet cigars. I brush past Terry, a guy from the team who's started hanging around the group a lot. Right now, he and his girlfriend can't keep their tentacles off each other. Miguel is sprawled out on a red leather sofa, staring at the ceiling and blowing smoke rings. A few of Valeria's friends are lounging in chairs, glued to their phones, and Valeria's sitting on the lap of some Vanilla Ice–looking character with frosted tips. She flips her hair when she sees me.

"Hey, Derek," she says, her eyes flicking down to my bare chest. My jeans are dripping puddles of water on the floor.

Miguel jumps up and walks toward me, holding out his hand. I don't take it. Our secret handshake is too old to mean anything now. "Hey, what's up?" he says, furrowing his eyebrows. "Thought you were too busy to come today."

"I was. But not too busy for this."

"Wait. Are you mad about something?" His lip curls up.

I'm tired of the pretense. Like he doesn't know I like Jae. Like he forgot I was part of the group chat. I step forward. "You knew I'd be pissed, Miguel. You just didn't think I'd do anything about it. You guys were in the same fucking room texting each other. You couldn't just talk to each other? Did you forget how to talk?"

Miguel laughs. "Talk? Dude. It's not that serious, man. All that poetry's gone to your head, you know?" He twirls his fingers by his ears.

"You knew I liked her from the beginning. You saw it. And you went after her like a hawk."

His eyebrows shoot up and he laughs. I suddenly realize it gets on my nerves, that laugh that makes any serious moment irrelevant, that takes your emotions and ridicules them.

"A hawk? What is that, more poetry? A fucking, what, allegory?"

"God, Miguel," Valeria says. "It's a metaphor. Don't you study?"

"Whatever. Look. Sit down and have a drink or something. Chill out. Try and see the humor in this. I mean, can you imagine being a stepfather?" He looks around the room and they all laugh.

I clench my teeth, feel the muscles in my temple pulse. My jeans are hanging heavy on my hips and getting colder with each passing second, and that pisses me off even more.

"Did you actually *read* the letter, Valeria?" I turn to her. "Did any of it sink in? *None* of it landed? You didn't feel the least bit sorry for her? You know what it feels like to have your family torn apart."

"Hey, don't bring up our family," Miguel says, tipping his chin up so his eyebrow ring comes out of the shadows of his hat, glinting.

"Yeah. Don't, Derek," Valeria says, standing up now with fists on hips, stringy red bikini hanging loose.

"I can keep talking about your family. The fighting. The divorce. I can poke and poke and poke just like you keep doing with Jae."

"Fucking try me," Miguel says, stepping close.

"You fucking try me," I respond, and now we're nose to nose. "You say Jae's name one more time. You call her Easy one more fucking time. I'll make you feel it."

"Oh yeah?" Miguel snickers. "You know where Jae was at the Halloween party? Before you saw her?" His voice is taunting. "Upstairs. With me."

I step back. Crack him across the jaw.

Valeria screams and hurries to pick him up off the ground. He's grabbing the side of his face.

"What's wrong with you, man?" He looks at me in confusion.

"I warned you." The blood is pounding in my ears.

"Fuck you, Derek," he spits, and red saliva splatters onto the polished wooden floors. "You chose a girl from the dweebs' club over us. What the hell happened to you?"

I look at Miguel holding his jaw, and I have to tell myself that one punch is good enough. "No. What the hell happened to you?

You look for the easiest targets so you can beat them down and feel like a god. Do you even know you do that? Jae's the sweetest person in the world and you're not going to take advantage of that anymore."

Miguel pushes Valeria away and walks over to the sofa, where he collapses. "We're done with you, man."

I nod. "Yeah. I figured." I look around the room one last time. The place we used to laugh in. Play cards in. Family nights.

"There's nothing here," I say.

"Get the fuck out of here." Miguel scowls.

"There's just nothing here."

I climb up to the deck, brushing past Henry and his girl, who hold on to each other like I'm about to throw them overboard.

I take in a deep breath as the air hits my face, look across the water, across the houses, in the direction of Jae's house. I wonder if she would disapprove of what I did. Using my fists instead of my words and all that. Well. I might be a poet now, but I'm not a saint.

At once, the water swallows me whole. I fight my way to the surface and swim to the dock.

I don't make it far before I hear a splash in the water behind me. I turn around to see Henry making his way over with smooth, easy strokes. He pulls himself up onto solid ground and flips his wet Mohawk to one side.

"Hey," he says, shaking the water out of his ears. "Hold on."

"I'm done, Henry," I say, picking up my phone and my sweatshirt and pulling it over my head. "Done."

He steps in line with me as I turn to walk through the yard.

"You got him good," he says. "I don't blame you. But . . ."

"What?"

"You've been friends since elementary school. You're not gonna let a girl come between you guys, are you?"

I stop. Glare at him. "Elementary school? Come on. People change." I turn around, try to leave him behind. He follows. "I should have said something a long time ago, the first time he called her that stupid name. I let it go. I was tired of fighting everybody. I can hardly go a day without pissing my mom off somehow. Her boyfriend's a jackass. And then I have to worry about my friends, too? Some friends." I shake my head. "I did everything I could to stay in line with Miguel and the whole stupid group. It's bullshit."

I open the gate to the front yard and let it slam behind me. Henry scales it.

"Miguel and Valeria, they've got issues too, you know that," he says. "I'm probably the only one with a seminormal family. Except my grandpa exercises on the front lawn every morning since he got home from the hospital."

I try to smile at him. It doesn't work. Instead of feeling lighter, I feel empty.

"Look, we didn't know you cared so much about Jae. We thought it was just a thing. You know. We thought you'd get over it."

"I'm not over it." My voice breaks and I quickly clear my throat. I'm hit with this heavy feeling of missing her. And just as suddenly, I'm relieved that she has friends in Free Verse to take care of her. William, with his thick English accent and obsessive love of poetry. And savage Swan. And even CJ, nerd supreme. They're not so bad after all.

"I hurt her. Really bad," I say. "And it's not gonna happen again. So. I'm done."

I pick up my bike and when I turn around, Henry's eyes are wide.

"What?" I ask.

"Do you, like, love her or something?" He immediately shakes his head, throws the question away.

I jump onto my bike, the question ringing in my head. *Do you love her or something? Do you love her?* I look at Henry. "Don't bother coming to my house. We moved out months ago."

A knot forms in my throat as I pedal away as fast as I can, leaving all the friends I ever had behind.

Explore the thoughts that are worth your time, I tell myself. Because even though everything hurts, I don't have time now to dwell on it.

A few houses down, I jump off my bike, pull out my phone, and call Mr. Oakland, glad I actually saved his number before tossing the business card. "Sir, I'd like to see you," I say when he picks up. "No. It's not about that."

CHAPTER FORTY

Uncle Rowan is sitting in his white recliner in the living room, a newspaper spread over his crossed legs. He likes to sit there beneath those dripping chandeliers with a cup of evening coffee.

He looks up at me briefly and then does a double take, his eyes lingering on the stack of papers in my hand. He makes a big production of sighing and closing the newspaper and rubbing his eyes beneath his glasses. "Sit down," he mutters.

"How long have you had these?" I ask.

"Sit down."

I walk around the coffee table and lower myself onto the sofa. "When did he give these to you?"

He purses his lips and sighs. "A couple of weeks after I found him in your room," he says, his voice full of accusations.

My jaw falls open. "Seriously? That long ago? Why'd you keep them from me?"

He huffs. "Need you ask?"

"You said we have to stay away from each other. You didn't say we can't communicate as long as we're both alive! Were you ever going to give them to me?"

"When the time was right."

"And when would that be?"

He gives me a stern look, beady-eyed. "When I decided to give them to you."

I want to scream at him, but it would only make him feel justified. A lovestruck teenager who can't control her emotions. I won't give him that. I take a slow breath to collect myself.

"You say I'm smart. But you don't think I'm smart enough to handle this. Him."

"It's not about handling it, Janelle. It's about protecting you from all the bullshit."

I straighten. I've never heard Uncle Rowan cuss.

He lays the paper over the armrest and lowers his elbows onto his thighs, leaning forward with his eyes fixed on mine. "Janelle. Sometimes love is just bullshit. It can't feed you. It can't put a roof over your head. It's a distraction from your main goals. Focus on your *goals*."

"Are you speaking from experience?"

His eyes widen. "You're not gonna psychoanalyze *me*." He picks up his paper again, opens it noisily over his face. "By the time that poetry night is over, you'll have forgotten about that boy. Outta sight, outta mind."

"This proves otherwise." I hold up Derek's papers. "You said we couldn't see each other. I was still thinking about him. He was still thinking about me."

"I hope that makes you feel warm on a cold night. Now, let's drop it."

I clench my teeth. Swan's voice is in my head, insistent. *No more hiding*. Not even from Uncle Rowan.

"No," I tell him. "I'm not gonna drop it. Because it's not even about love. It's about having a choice. You are constantly taking choices away from me."

"Now. That's not true. You had a choice to stay here or go back to Atlanta. You had a choice to stay in that club or let Derek stay."

"That's some choice. Thank you so much."

"Don't get sassy. You're living with *me* now. It's *my* job to protect you."

I have to breathe deep to calm myself, because I'm starting to feel that tightness in my throat, that shakiness in my voice. "It's your job all of a sudden? Where were you all those years? You talk about Dad leaving like it's the worst thing a man could do. How about you?"

He shakes his head. "You don't—"

"You just stopped coming around. You stopped visiting. Why didn't you call me? I missed . . ." I stop. I'm not ready to say those words. *I missed you*.

He draws in a long breath and rubs the top of his bald head, not saying anything. The ticktock of the wall clock grows louder and louder in our silence.

He removes his glasses and busies his hands over the frames. "Word on the street was your father had another family. I confronted him about that, told him to tell your mama or I would. I was trying to look out for both of you, but the truth was something she couldn't deal with. She blamed me for him leaving. Wouldn't have any contact with me. Told me not to call."

For a moment, the news stuns me into silence. Uncle Rowan knew about Dad before we did. I breathe deep and let that old pain go.

“Is that all it took?” I ask him. “She said *don’t call*, and you didn’t? I wasn’t worth fighting for? You told Derek he couldn’t see me. And this is what he did.” I hold up the papers. “Looks like he’s fighting harder for me than you ever did.”

For the first time, I see something different in Uncle Rowan’s face. Uncertainty? Shame? He clears his throat. “I should have been there for you. I’m sorry I wasn’t.”

I blink away the sting in my eyes. “You think I just had a baby. That’s not it. I had a part of me torn away. Do you think that just because I was young it didn’t hurt? That I didn’t need anybody? I needed somebody. *Some*body. And no one showed up.”

“Janelle.”

“She was gone and my milk came in. So much. And no baby. Milk and no baby. It was for her. She was supposed to be mine.”

“Janelle.”

“She was supposed to be *mine*.”

“Janelle.”

Uncle Rowan’s voice, calling me again and again, finally pulls me back. His hands are on my shoulders and he’s pulling me up from the sofa. I let the papers fall from my hand and wrap my arms around him. My tears wet his shirt. His heart beats against my ear. He’s warm. Big and broad like Dad.

“I didn’t know,” he says.

“You never asked.”

“No, baby girl, I never asked.”

When my breath stops shaking, he lets me go and takes a step back. He places his hands on his hips and examines my face. "I didn't do a good job of taking care of you back then. But you're here now. I can't just sit back and let another person break your heart. Do you get where I'm coming from?"

I nod.

"Now, I saw that boy's living situation. And I know what kind of family he comes from. Things won't be easy for him."

"They weren't easy for you, either."

"And that's how I know. I fought hard for the life I have now. Blood, sweat, and tears is not a metaphor for me. Most people aren't willing to put in the work. Those friends who grew up with me? They're still in the projects, too scared to fight for better."

"That's not him." I shake my head. "It's just not. He's good at so many things."

"It's not talent, it's tenacity. Fighting for what you want."

I grab the papers again, hold them up. "He is fighting. And he's trying not to disrespect you in the process. That counts for something, doesn't it?"

He sighs heavy, rubs his eyes. "I appreciate that. Yes, I do. I think at his heart, he's a stellar kid. He communicates. That's important." He gives me a stern look. "But that doesn't mean you're right for each other. Or that it's even the right *time*. The fact that you've both had it hard doesn't mean anything. From my experience, it makes things more difficult."

I frown, realizing then that the only thing that's ever been difficult for me and Derek is other people.

"You were wrong," I tell Uncle Rowan, "for leaving my life like that. You're wrong about this, too. I'm not saying Derek and I belong together. I'm saying you need to give me a choice. And Uncle Rowan, you need to call me Jae."

He turns his head and looks at me sideways. And for the first time since I moved here, his eyes tell me I'm right.

"What did you want in my office in the first place?" he asks, scowling.

"A pen, what else?"

CHAPTER FORTY-ONE

Jae

I walk up the stairs almost lightheaded. From Uncle Rowan's apology. From his hug. From what feels like love. I lie down on the bed, sink into it with deep breaths, and stare at the ceiling. Maybe I could use some stars.

My phone buzzes.

Just checking on you.

You don't have to respond if you don't want to.

The house is so empty without you.

I stare at the messages that go way back, unanswered. I picture her sitting at the kitchen table, only one chair occupied, the sunlight from the window illuminating dust and emptiness. I wonder if she still watches our shows in front of the TV. I wonder if she steps into my bedroom, seeing all the old treasures I left. School trip photos and friendship bracelets. I hear the quiet plod of her feet down the hall.

I put the phone on speaker, hear the ringing and my heartbeat.

"Jae!" she answers, almost breathless. "Oh, Jae." She sighs into the receiver. "Jae."

CHAPTER FORTY-TWO

Derek

I'm on the beach. Same spot I came to with Jae. I cover my feet with mounds of wet sand, wiggle out and start over again. My mind flashes back to a memory of Dad swinging me upside down, me laughing hysterically. My head swoops close to Mom's toes. I remember her tan skin. Her nails bright pink.

Now, a seagull screams and dives low and I duck. It stops at the edge of the water and takes a short stroll before flying off again over an ocean of rippling glass.

The beach is quiet, and I look over my shoulder to see I'm alone, except for one person standing in the distance in a bright red shirt. I wonder how long he's been standing there watching me. I wave and he walks over.

His shirt makes his copper hair look even brighter. The sun is a harsh beam on his glasses so that I can't see his eyes. His lower lip is tucked in, making him look perplexed. I can tell he didn't expect to find me here alone.

"Swan and William are parking now," I tell him, holding up the text message I just got from them.

"Okay." CJ sits down beside me and crosses his legs. His jean shorts reveal legs much hairier than mine. For a nerd, he has calves built like a warrior's, and I wonder if he's secretly some martial arts master like in the movies. He stares at the water, avoiding my eyes, and clears his throat.

"Thanks for meeting me," I say. Even if this is a one-time thing, it's nice to have someone to talk to.

"Bygones," he says, pushing up his glasses. Then his face turns bright red and he turns away and takes deep breaths.

I breathe deep too, matching his rhythm. He turns around. Grins.

"I just found out my fish has anemia," he offers. "She's been kind of gray around the gills. I have to buy her folic-acid-fortified food. Try saying that three times fast."

"What's her name?"

"Juniper."

"I hope Juniper gets better."

"Thanks."

I push more sand over my feet and draw beady eyes and a smile on the mound. I wonder why CJ told me about his fish out of the blue, but I figure it's a good ice-breaker.

"I have a sticker constellation on my bedroom ceiling," I say. "Like the ones from the nineties." I give him a sideways glance and wait for him to laugh, but he doesn't.

"I have a birthmark next to my belly button that looks like my belly button," he says.

"I hope I get abducted by aliens one day. As long as I can survive it and make a movie about it."

"I wouldn't mind learning how to belly dance."

"I do belly dance." I lift up my shirt and wave my stomach.

CJ smirks. "Impressive. I can burp the alphabet." And he does, and by the end of the loud and extended *zeeeeeee*, we're both wiping tears from our eyes. CJ's smiling so hard his braces almost blind me, and something about that makes me happy.

I hold out my hand and he shakes it. "I'm Derek Patel, nice to meet you."

"Christopher James Tillman. You can call me CJ or book freak."

"I guess you can call me book freak too."

We both turn our heads when we hear a resounding bang behind us. Swan and William are walking toward us, followed by two men, one who's wearing a red, black, yellow, and green hat beneath long, thick dreadlocks.

Swan waves. "I think I found your guys!" she yells.

I jump up and dust the sand off my jeans. "Yah man!" I yell in my best, or worst, Jamaican accent, and pump my fist in the air.

CHAPTER FORTY-THREE

Derek

It's December. The pavilion is draped in lights. Bright bulbs like constellations over the railings and across the wooden buttresses. The ocean is roaring, water rushing over water until it laps up onto the sandy beach.

There's a buzz. People are sitting on benches or marking their territories with their bags as they flit around to mingle or grab punch. Some faces are familiar. Bellwood students and their parents, some teachers. Some could be neighbors, but I'm not sure. We're not a *take over a Bundt cake* kind of family. I invited my boss Gina from the diner, but I don't see her yet. Of course I didn't ask Mom to come. You never know what version of Mom will show up.

CJ and Swan are walking around with a sign-up sheet for performers. He's in a snazzy blue suit, much nicer than my button-up shirt and jeans. Swan's in a lingerie-looking top and blazer, a frilly skirt, and tall army boots. All black except for red stockings.

A hand taps my shoulder.

"Here alone?" William asks.

I nod. "You?"

He points across the pavilion to two statuesque blonds settling onto a bench. "My mom. And Stepfather Number Five, Mr. Archer."

"You said five?"

"Yessir! Number five. He's a pilot, so he's gone half the time. That means this one might actually stick."

I laugh, feeling a tinge of loneliness being here without family. "You ready?" I ask.

He pulls out his notebook from his jacket pocket. "Not sure, to be honest. I'm stuck between two poems."

"That means they're both good. Just flip a coin."

"Yeah, you're right. Uhhh . . . speaking of being ready." He nods behind me. "Are you? Jae's here."

I turn around. Jae's walking toward us, and—I'm not being hyperbolic—I can't breathe. She's so damn pretty. She's wearing a white shirt that cuts off a little high, and a high-waisted skirt that might be African print. All those colors against her skin. She is otherworldly.

I try to smile but it wobbles on my face. The last time I talked to her, she was so angry she could have launched me into Ursa Major III.

She waves. Smiles. Bright teeth. Dimples like a tiny mouse took a bite out of her cheeks. "Hey, William. Hey, Derek."

My heart skips when she says my name. Those lips. The sweetest shade of pink. I actually got to kiss those lips. I tasted her tongue. I—

"Hi, Jae. Glad you made it," William says, stepping out from behind me. He gives her a very audible bear hug and I'm instantly jealous. "Oh. Is this—"

"My uncle." She turns around and gestures at Mr. Oakland, who's dressed like I've never seen him before, a plain T-shirt underneath a tan bomber jacket.

He extends a hand to William. "Nice to meet you."

"You too, sir."

Then he shakes my hand, maybe a little harder than necessary. "Derek," he says.

"Mr. Oakland," I respond.

He stuffs his hands in his pockets and walks away to find a seat, right next to the benches reserved for Free Verse members.

"Man," I say in disbelief. "He looks . . ."

"Cool?" Jae cringes. "I know. Weird, right? I told him he didn't have to stay, but he insisted."

"It's like *Invasion of the Body Snatchers*. So, are you—"

But she's already hurrying past me, squealing at CJ and Swan like they haven't seen each other in ten years. I feel a gnawing emptiness.

Just then, Mrs. Aldana pulls away from a conversation and makes a beeline for me with her hands outstretched. She grabs my shoulders. "I am so happy to see you, Derek! I could burst into a million butterflies." She's traded her gold shawl for an ocean-themed one with pale blues and browns.

"Nice to see you, too," I say. And I mean it.

"Your poetry has blossomed these past few months. Smart and insightful and sincere," she says.

My face grows warm. "Thanks," I say.

She pats my shoulders. "I was right, wasn't I? You do belong with us." She floats away to gather the others and lead them to our special reserved bench.

You do belong with us. I almost laugh. If someone had said months ago that I belonged in the poetry club, I would have called them crazy or worse. But I agree. I do belong here. The creative power of the universe is here.

"Looks like things are about to start," William says. He pats my shoulder and heads over.

I pull out my notebook from my back pocket and glance over it. I get a nervous flip-flop in my belly at the thought of standing in front of all these faces and reading something I wrote. I'm even more nervous about how Jae will respond. I turn away and give myself a moment to close my eyes and breathe. *In—four. Out—six. In—four. Out—six.*

When I'm ready, I head over. But I stop in my tracks, like I've hit an invisible wall.

All the members are sitting on our reserved bench, except for Jae. But she's sitting with her uncle on the bench right next to it. There's one seat left on the Free Verse side, so I take it. CJ on my left. Jae's body just inches away on my right, dripping with something so sweet it reminds me of nectar. I lean my head millimeters closer. And closer. Passion fruit? Guava? Something the gods just sprinkled on her this morning for good measure?

Mrs. Aldana claps her hands to get everyone's attention. Like an experienced teacher, she glances around and commands silence. "Welcome to Bellwood High's Poetry Open Mic!" She wiggles jazz hands and the audience laughs. "This special event is hosted by our small group of outstanding poets, The Free Verse Society. For those of you in the audience who are Bellwood students, we invite you to join us next semester. Now, we'll begin our reading with poems by our members, after which the audience is free to participate. You'll find all the rules for performing on the sign-up sheet."

She pauses, glances at Jae. "Before we begin, I'd like to share that our club as a collective is dedicating this event to Sarah, or June Baby, who's the daughter of our member Jae. We are so proud of

Jae, and we hope you'll join us in celebrating her bravery in placing her daughter with a beautiful family. June lives in Georgia and she is almost six months old!"

There's a smattering of applause and *Awwws*, and when I peek over at Jae, she looks positively smug. I see her future as a bumper sticker mom: MY KID'S AN HONOR STUDENT.

Mrs. Aldana continues. "Now. First up to read! We have our club president, William Shakespeare Huntington."

There's delayed applause as everyone's probably wondering who would name their kid William Shakespeare. Mr. Archer blows a sharp finger whistle as William makes his way to the front. Instead of a piece of paper, he's holding a pen, and he raises it dramatically as he looks over the audience. "'A Call to Arms,'" he says evenly, and clears his throat. And then he's pointing his pen at the audience, his voice rising.

This is a call to arms, you sluggards,
You lowly, friendless "freaks,"
You nerds, you geeks,
You bespectacled dreamers.

If you've no voice, no matter.
Your pen is all we need.
Rise up! And tell your story.

You are filled with a magic only you can see,
But it takes time,
So breathe,
And let your inner light guide you.

Go the path less traveled,
If you must go a path at all.
Find the hidden worlds beyond
Insurmountable walls.

Be an outcast if you must,
But be yourself!
That you must.

This is your time,
The time is now,
If you haven't the strength to fight,
Then take up your pen and write!

William thrusts his pen into the air like a sword, and then tucks it into his pocket and takes a deep bow. I almost jump at the loud applause and whistles that follow. People are pulling out their pens and raising them in the air. I laugh. He sure knows how to work a crowd.

I feel Jae's body lean away from me as Mr. Oakland says something in her ear. I see her in my periphery still clapping profusely for William, and then she leans back my way, her body closer than before. Did she mean to shift over like that? I could feel the difference in millimeters, and this is like an inch.

Mrs. Aldana approaches the front clapping. "A call to arms indeed. Next is Christopher James Tillman."

CJ breathes in deep. Wipes his hands on his lap. "I have to follow that," he mutters, standing up.

"You got this," I say, clapping him on the back. "Do it for Juniper."

He looks down at me with a metallic smile, green eyes dancing, then walks off. Stands in front of the crowd and adjusts the collar of his shirt, ears glowing red. He wipes a bead of sweat off his forehead with the back of his hand, then he takes in a deep breath, looks down at his feet, and blinks up at everyone. "This poem is called 'Attic.'"

Something settles in the crowd, and I suddenly realize CJ's superpower. He shoots out gentle rays of empathy that make you just want to hug yourself. I think Jae feels it too. She sighs.

CJ reads.

After the sun rises
Behind
Crystalline clouds,
Daylight breaks and
Enters the cracks of the
Fractured window blinds.
Gliding rays,
Hovering lights,
Inching their way across the
Jagged attic ceiling where we
Keep boxes and boxes of
Little
Memories
Never
Opened.
Piles of books and newspaper
Quotes,
Remembrances we
Silence up there with packing

Tape.

Unopened

Vaults of past joys,

Weathered edges,

Xanthic

Years,

Zygotic pasts: love and pain.

Time moves slow as CJ reads. I feel every hair of wind. Hear every murmur of the ocean. The space between Jae and me is like a canyon, but still, so, so close. I'm so close. I could touch her skin again. If she would let me. If I just leaned over, just a little.

She moves too. Slow. And then, our shoulders touch. And touch deeper. We're leaning against each other. I hear her breath. If she turned her head, I would feel it on my skin.

I drop my hand from my lap, let it dangle in the space between us. She drops her hand. Touches her fingertips to mine. I'm breathing too fast. It's too much. Our skin brushing, brushing, brushing against each other. It's undoing me. It's a hundred tiny kisses.

And then it ends. CJ finishes. We sit up straight.

"I feel like a proud mother hen," Mrs. Aldana says to the crowd as CJ sits down again. "Next, we have our club secretary, Su Hwan Cho."

There's polite applause as Swan makes her way to the front. She adjusts her blazer over her lingerie top and waves at the audience. "This is a poem about me. But it's really about everyone who ever expected me to be silent because of how I look."

Someone in the audience coughs. A gray-haired Black man says, "All right," and leans forward with keen eyes. A lady sitting next to him stops her coffee cup halfway to her lips and sets it back down.

Swan clears her throat.

you made me invisible
gave me The Dream in exchange for a quiet, unseen
life
chose only the best and made me a model
of success

you made me invisible
to build up your railroads and your neighborhoods
but after generations:
"where are you really from?"

still not American

you let me stand on a pedestal
with a gag around my mouth
so I won't talk about
Japanese internment
Chinese Exclusion Act
"Hindu Invasion"

I am not invisible
I wear all the colors
and the rainbow belongs to me
I won't submit
I'll talk when I please
to hell with your model minority

"*All right!*" the gray-haired man shouts, jumping to his feet and clapping. CJ lets out a loud whistle and a *whoop!* and the audience follows in applause. When Swan sits back down, I lean over to give her a fist bump. Jae grins at her with the cutest little thumbs-up.

Mrs. Aldana's talking to the audience again and suddenly I'm lost in the panic of reading next. I don't know how much time has passed before I hear, "Derek?" She's staring at me with arched eyebrows. CJ's nudging me with his elbow.

I stand up. My heart thunders with my footsteps. I take the deepest breath and then turn back to the audience. My hands shake and I flex them, trying not to let the tremors show.

"*Derek!*" someone whispers sharply.

All the way on the other side of the pavilion is Gina, blond curls piled up high, lashes like giant fans. She waves.

This might be the loneliest year of my life, but today, I get a glimpse of what it feels like to have real friends. People who want to listen to the words I have to say. I wave back. *Okay. I can do this.*

I wipe my sweaty hands on my jeans, then pull out my notebook. The page is full of smudges, a hole where I erased too hard. But the words that matter are still there. I breathe again. I read.

I couldn't write an epic poem like I wanted
But I looked at the sky and saw your smile in Orion's bow
And a poem wrote itself.

We are
The smallest of the smallest of the smallest fraction

Of millenniums of small, small lives
A grain of sand in an oceanic universe
But the phenomenon of You is what trips me up

That little glimmer in your iris is
The light from a half-gone star 4.5 billion years old
That traveled through millions of miles of emptiness
Just to kiss the aperture of your eye, like it wants to die
There

Your face is more beautiful than Saturn's rings made of
Ice and dust and obliterated moons
You are just that glorious

You make me dizzy wanting you
Wondering if I'll see you soon or if you're just
The far side of the moon
And I will never
See you again

You spread your stardust over me
Make it hard to breathe
Till I am
Transformed beneath your skin into something
Ravenous
That could destroy us both

You are the stars aligned
The glory of a galaxy times nine

I could kiss you a million and a million times and still

Ask the universe for just

One

More

I close my notebook. It's like someone took a giant broom and swept everyone away except for her. I can only see her. Her mouth hangs slightly open. She's unmoving, made of wax, except her eyes are blinking wildly. And she won't look at me.

Look at me.

I'm hungry for just one glance. Greedy. Because she touched me today, and I could never stop wanting more of her.

Look at me.

Please.

Look at me.

CHAPTER FORTY-FOUR

Jae

Whoa whoa whoa. BreatheDeepBreatheDeepBreatheDeep.

What just happened?

I'm in the water. Gone. Submerged. I've fallen for Derek Patel in every way and my insides are knotted up and taut and—if I could just breathe right! If I could just—*BreatheDeepBreatheDeep*.

I can't look at him. I have to read next, and I'm a mess inside.

Derek starts walking back to the bench, and I look away toward the big trail of sea grape trees leading to the pavilion. I pray for my heart to quiet, but my heart isn't stopping for anything. It's beating its own Morse code. *Tack-tack-tack-tack-tack-tack-tack. Done in. Done for.*

I want him more than I've wanted anything.

Uncle Rowan breaks the spell. "Who does he think he is, Casanova?" he mutters, shaking his head. He crosses his legs and crosses his arms and grunts. Mrs. Aldana's talking and he's still muttering to himself. Then he pokes me in the leg. "You're next. Pay attention."

I jump to my feet before Derek even sits down, which is a mistake because now he's in front of me. My eyes are level with his chest but wander up to his neck, to that smooth Adam's apple that bobs. I am all tingles. Exposed nerves everywhere. I can't touch him. I can't look at him. But I sure as hell can smell him, and he is delicious. What is he wearing? I want that scent all over my pillow.

I step right, he steps the same way. I step left, he does too. Right. Again.

He lets out an embarrassed laugh. "Go ahead," he says, waiting for me to step around him. *Don't look at him*, I warn myself. His voice alone. God. His voice alone.

I want to be improper. I want to do things I've never done. I want to break every single promise I made to Uncle Rowan.

I'm thankful when I get to the front and look out over the audience. Anything to get my mind off this incessant heat inside me.

Mrs. Aldana is giving me a small, lopsided smile. Like she's Auntie Aldana and she knows my business. I blush, stare down at my notebook.

Glancing over the words, I try not to think about anyone else except her, sitting on one of these benches, tiny feet swinging in sandals, skinned knees, ashy legs, and wispy arms aching for a hug. Her eyes full of questions. Questions I still ask Mom and Dad. *Why did you leave me?* I take a deep breath and read. To Sarah.

Mothers are not masterpieces
Notes written in perfect key
Poised Mona Lisas with hands perfectly
Perched

Mothers are miracles
Notes not right but beautiful
Melted clocks that keep on ticking

She gives smiles when she has no joy
Consoles when she has no hope
That's what you should know:
Mothers are vessels
That can be empty too

They stand with mouths open
Begging for rain
So they can pour
Themselves out for their children

My mother was full
Until she broke
And lost all she could hold

She had nothing to give me
And I had nothing to give you

I set you out on the river between the reeds
Like baby Moses
Waiting for Pharaoh's daughter to pluck you out
And give you the world
She gave you a name

This is my joy:

That you were chosen and cherished
That you will be filled
Because someone

Has so much to give

Mothers are not masterpieces
Far from perfection
But my greatest work was to give you a home

A place with everything you need
To paint your own picture
With your own colors
With your own strokes

So I could watch you grow
From a small. dark. plum.

To a tree
that can
stand
on her
own

I'm not paying attention to the applause. I'm in my feelings. Submerged in them. Pain and longing and happiness and hope.

Derek's eyes are on me. I can feel them as I head back to my seat, and I wonder what he's thinking. Am I still his destiny? The glory of a galaxy times nine? Or did I just bring him back to Earth?

Mrs. Aldana announces the floor is open to everyone, and she starts with the first name on the sign-up sheet, a Bellwood sophomore I've seen around but don't know.

I sense Derek's hesitation as he leans toward me. "You did good," he whispers, minty-breathed. My skin tingles, remembering. *Transformed beneath your skin into something ravenous.*

Ravenous.

"Thanks. You too."

"*Shhh!*" Uncle Rowan hisses. "Don't be rude."

So we straighten up and pay attention.

But when Mrs. Aldana calls the next name, *Mr. Rowan Oakland*, I nearly keel over onto the floor.

He stands up, back tall, snaps his jacket straight at the waist, and walks smooth and slow to the front, bald head gleaming.

"No," I whisper. I grab the nearest thing to me, Derek's arm. Death grip. "Stop him. Somebody stop him. *Swan! CJ!*"

I'm hoping they tackle him, but nobody moves. William leans over, cheeky grin. CJ gives a thumbs-up. Swan, a sympathetic *uh-oh* smile.

"He's gonna do fine," Derek whispers, patting my hand like I'm some old lady he's charged with taking care of.

Uncle Rowan clears his throat. "We had a little Romeo up here earlier." The crowd laughs and Derek chuckles. Everyone claps for Derek again.

"I gotta say," he continues, "I wasn't expecting that. He surprised me. You all surprised me. But let me show you what a grown man can do."

"Oh, no," I groan, as he rubs his hands together, licks his lips, and becomes this character I could only call the Prowler. He's doing too much. How did it get to this? Was it my fault for not making him leave? Is there still time?

I sink down into the bench as he begins.

Love ain't it.

He pauses. Looks around at the crowd.

I said, Love ain't IT!
I do believe it
to some extent
If I'm being ho . . . nest.
But if I'm being ho . . . nest
Then I should probably add this:

I'm mortified. He's bending the vowels to make them rhyme with *it*. He's been watching slam poetry on YouTube, it's obvious.

I could never forget That Girl.
You see
We lived in Apartment Number 13
Brought up by Aunt Marlene
'Cause Papa died in the war and
Mama was always
Gone.
Rehab. Jail. Rehab. Jail. Rehab. Hab. Hab. Hab.

I'm pulled out of the poem again, thrown onto my bench. I sink deeper. Is embarrassing me some rite of passage? Does this make him my uncle *forreal* forreal?

Aunt Marlene worked most nights
Sis and I alone most nights

And then one night
The girl from Number 23 came down the stairs and said
Papa wants you over for dinner
And the next night, and the next night, and the next

That house was like heaven with
Two parents and
Two grandparents
Cramped up together in a space that felt like
Looove.
They were called the Kings
But they made us feel like royalty
Even though we had nothing to speak of.
Meaning, possessions.

She was always destined to be something
At least something more than me
She left at sixteen to New York to chase a dream life
But she was my dream, and I chased her
Through books, and pages, and degrees
Got all those letters after my name (Did you see that shit?)
Built a house
Got a car (Did you see that shit?)
And found her one day
On a billboard
Gone and married to some big TV exec (Ain't that a . . .)
And I had everything in the world and I didn't have
Love

So don't wait on love
'Cause love won't wait on you

My mouth is just open. I can't close it. Shocked, like being thrown out of an airplane into Arctic water. Uncle Rowan just read a poem. In public. About love. Or maybe, anti-love? He walks off to applause and gives Derek and me this look and this nod, like he's saying without saying, *And that's how it's done.*

CHAPTER FORTY-FIVE

Derek

The open mic ends and the pavilion turns into a beehive of activity with *Oh my God* and *Did you hear* buzzing around us. Gina comes swooping in with a floral-scented hug.

"*So* proud! *So* proud!" she says with such gusto, I wonder if she was a cheerleader back in the day. "*Mah gawsh*," she drawls, "if a man wrote a poem like that for me, I don't know what I'd do. I just don't know. Who's the muse? I saw you looking at somebody. Good God, I wanna lay my eyes on that lucky girl. Where is she?"

I point across the pavilion to Jae, who's leaning into Swan, giggling. "The short one," I say.

"Now, she is *cute*," Gina says. "I can see why you'd write a poem about her. Thank you so much for inviting me. You made my week, my month! I am so proud of you. Now, let me go say hi to your amazing teacher before I head on out. And Derek, you don't have to be on the clock to come by the diner and see me. I'm always around." She squeezes my arm and hurries off, and I stand there and laugh because I only got three words in.

I turn back to the group and almost fall over at the sight of Jae. She's talking to Henry. When did he get here? I nearly sprint over, plant myself between them. "What's going on?"

Henry takes one look at my face and steps back.

"It's okay," Jae says, grabbing my arm and giving it a small pull. "He was apologizing. And I appreciate it. Thanks, Henry."

"Long overdue," he says, nodding, then looks at me. "Disappointed to see me?"

I look him over—his Mohawk is braided down, and he's dressed in a checkered black-and-white shirt—and I'm trying to decide exactly what I feel. I can't be a hypocrite. His apology is as good as mine. But when I rode away from Miguel's house a month ago, I was sure I was leaving all of them behind.

"Just surprised," I answer.

He holds out his fist. I bump it.

"How'd you find out about this?" I ask.

"Was on my way to the principal's office." He gives an embarrassed shrug. "Saw the sign on the bulletin board. Figured you'd be here."

"Man. You care about me." I laugh at his grimace and clap him on the back. "Thanks."

"Of course, man. Hey, uh . . . That was kinda cool. I mean, you're a good writer."

"Yeah? You should join the club."

"Ehhh." He shakes his head. "Hey, why don't you come over tomorrow? *Call of Duty*? Just you and me."

"Yeah. Sure. Cool."

"Yeah. See ya later," he says. "And good job."

And that's it. He stuffs his hands in his pockets and leaves.

Mr. Oakland offers me a ride home. He makes Jae sit in front. Then we fold my bike into the trunk and I get into the back seat. I sit behind him so I can watch the streetlights and shadows roll over her face. On our way to the pink bungalow.

I wonder what Mom's doing tonight, or what she did while I was standing in the pavilion, staring at the faces of people rooting for me. It hurts to think that I lost her completely, the mom that she was. But I have something too. People who care. And there's a girl, and my heart beats for her. Maybe that's happiness enough.

"I think it's cute you ride your bike everywhere," Jae says, and her voice breaking the quiet rattles my insides, makes me flutter.

"*Cute?*" I say, in mock offense. "Then I'm glad I didn't get that Ferrari they promised me."

"Ferrariii," she says, impressed. Then she turns in her seat to look at her uncle with a very serious expression, eyebrows furrowed. "Uncle Rowan. Your poetry career. We can bury it, burn it, or cast it into the ocean. But it ends today."

"What are you talking about?" he objects. "That was some good stuff!"

"I will never be the same."

"You got jokes. But I bet you learned a thing or two."

"Before and after your poem, maybe."

"Be for real, now. What did you learn?"

"Don't get too comfortable."

I haven't heard a laugh so loud from that man before. He laughs until I see him wiping away tears in the rearview mirror. And I'm laughing too, watching this back-and-forth Serena-versus-Venus match.

"Okay. But seriously, though? You don't believe in love?" she asks him. "You almost made me cry."

He grunts.

"She might be your soul mate. That girl from apartment twenty-three," she says dreamily. "I mean, like, I don't think you could love another person. You might be incapable."

"Incapable?"

"Have you looked her up recently?"

"No."

"What if she's divorced?"

"What if she's not?"

She gasps. "Uncle Rowan. You went after everything but the girl." She shakes her head and looks out the window. "I think this proves adults don't know what true love is."

Mr. Oakland sucks his teeth but doesn't say anything. He looks up, his dark eyes in the rearview mirror, light bouncing off his glasses. There's something he's not saying, but I can read it, and it makes me flush, ears on fire. It's like he can see inside me, sees what I am, or what I've always wanted to be, and he thinks I'm all right.

It feels good being here. With this family. The girl who cared enough to come out of the stall and ask if I was okay. She was soft when everything around me was hard.

I could, as Mrs. Aldana said, burst into a million butterflies.

CHAPTER FORTY-SIX

Jae

Derek: hey

Me: hey

Derek: ur poem was amazing

Me: thanks

Me: your poem was . . .

Derek: ?

Me: I felt things

Derek: 😈

Derek: what kinds of things?

Me: not gonna say

Derek: u wanna give us another chance?

Me: we were never together

Derek: u know what I mean

Me: I'm not ready

Derek: even though u felt things?

Me: because I felt things

Derek: ?

Me: this is one of those it's not you it's me situations

seriously, it's me

Derek: not tryna push u, just saying, I think ur perfect

Me: see? you are too smooth. can we even be friends?

Me: are you still there?

Derek: yeah. it was nice seeing u today jae. gnight

CHAPTER FORTY-SEVEN

Jae

There were clues. The first clue was that Ms. Rosette was in a frenzy and platters of food multiplied on the kitchen counter. The next clue was that nobody from Free Verse wanted to hang out. *Homework*, they all said.

But now it's late afternoon on a Sunday, only days after the open mic, and when I pass the kitchen, there's William and CJ in the garden past the pool, stringing icicle lights onto bushes. Swan's looping calla lilies through the ornate iron bench. And Derek is coming from the side of the house, carrying folding chairs we don't even own.

I step out onto the balcony, into birdsong and whirring insects. "What are you guys doing?"

"Just a little party," Derek says, head tilted up, eyes dark beneath his white visor, and everything inside me stirs. I haven't been able to purge his voice, or the fire in it. *I could kiss you a million and a million times.*

After hearing that poem, everything in me needed Derek, and I never want to need anyone more than I need myself. Not again. So right now, Derek—the boy who makes me feel everything—can't be my everything. Even with a voice I can't purge.

I hold the warm balcony railing like I'm trying to ground myself. "How come I didn't know about this party?"

"Because it's a *surprise*." He rolls his eyes and laughs, saunters away with chairs in both hands, doing the farmer's walk.

They're throwing me a party? For what? Surviving a semester with Uncle Rowan? I'm dying of curiosity, but I'm not anxious. If this were a trust fall, I could count on each one of them to catch me. So I decide to enjoy the mystery, watch them like I'm watching a colony of ants. How cute. How diligent.

Back in the kitchen, Ms. Rosette is singing loudly over South African praise music. I get close enough to see ginger, garlic, and pepper sitting in the blender, yams submerged in oil, browning in the deep fryer.

"Koliko?" I ask, excited to see what has become one of my favorite Togolese dishes.

She nods. Nearby is a plate piled high with zowey, which reminds me of Dad's trips back from Ghana, suitcases full of fruits and things he couldn't bear to miss, US Customs be damned.

"But for what?" I ask.

She looks up, peels the wrapper off a bouillon cube, and crushes the yellow seasoning between her fingers. She's too busy for my questions. Or she's decided not to conspire with me any longer.

"Can I at least help?" I ask.

"It looks like I need help?" She pats my cheek, then turns on the blender. It screams, spitting green liquid throughout the glass.

I drag my feet through the house, looking for Uncle Rowan, but he's nowhere. His car, gone. Resigned to my room, I stand in front of the closet and assess the situation. A party's a party, and even if I don't know what it's for, I can still look nice. The yellow dress I wore on the yacht ride is hanging wrinkle-free. I throw it on, give myself a high ponytail à la Janet Jackson, and apply crimson lipstick with a layer of gloss. They might think I'm the goddess Oshun.

When I step outside, Derek takes longer than necessary to watch me descend the balcony steps. I'm blushing, conscious of every muscle that moves beneath my dress, every angle of my silhouette, and finally breathe easy when he goes back to stringing lights with CJ and William. They both give me a quick *hey*, and William's blue eyes are bright and filled with secrets.

Swan's putting finishing touches on the bench. All the flowers are perfectly placed, with petals like wells for rain. She looks up at me and squeals, clapping. "I'm so excited!" Skipping over and grabbing my hand, she says, "So. I'm gonna MC this thing."

"What thing exactly?"

"Oh, it's just a thing." She hooks her arm through mine, just in time for Mrs. Aldana's voice to sing from the gate, "Helluuu!"

I frown at Swan, but I don't bother asking again what's going on because I know she won't say. It's fine, I tell myself. The day has been all sun, the grass dry from earlier rains, the air fresh and sweet. I feel like a cat, stretched out, luxuriating in a warm winter.

And dying of curiosity!

Swan runs to grab a bag from Mrs. Aldana—who sends me a wink—and carries it to a collection of gifts I didn't see at the base of the balcony steps. Uncle Rowan enters the gate next, says goodbye into his phone, and yells across the yard, "Are we done, kids? It's getting late!"

My phone says it's only five.

"Done!" Swan calls back.

"Great, do I get to know now?" I ask, looking around. "Or am I about to be sacrificed?"

Derek looks to Uncle Rowan for a nod, and I feel the gravity of the unknown. He comes close enough to fix the twisted strap of my dress, letting his fingers linger before they slowly fall away, dragging across my skin. "You said you didn't have an entrustment ceremony," he says. "I thought, it's never too late, right? So I talked to your uncle about it."

The words float around me like dandelion petals bleached white in the sun. *Entrustment ceremony.* Two words, drowned in my deluge of anger and so easy to miss. He'd plucked them out. He'd kept them. I feel, maybe for the first time, the burden of being cared for, the weight of a full heart. That he would plan this for me, even when he wasn't allowed to see me. What do you call that? I think I know. I know.

Derek pauses, licks his lips nervously. "I mean, I hope we didn't overstep."

I throw my arms around his waist to stop him talking, squeeze him tight so I don't unravel, so the feelings don't turn into rivers.

"It wasn't just me," he says, rubbing my back. "We all planned it together. Everyone helped."

"I didn't think you were listening."

"Had to. You were yelling." He chuckles, brushes a hand over my hair, tugs on it, and I'm enchanted, breathing in his woodsy scent, feeling the warmth of his chest and the tremor of his voice.

I quickly let go.

Tired of our display, Uncle Rowan is already settling into one of the folding chairs. They're arranged in a semicircle around the bench decorated with calla lilies. Everyone follows suit and grabs a seat, except Swan. She leads me to the bench in the center, tells me to sit down. Then she stands beside me and folds her hands, as solemn as if she's about to pray. She does look churchy, but only from the waist up. A white chiffon blouse tucked into tight, glittery lime-green shorts.

"We're here to celebrate family," she says. "The family that Jae created, an extended network of love that holds one child. A human banyan tree, if you will. I'm honored, as her new friend, to MC the ceremony. Jae," she says, reaching for my hand, and I've never seen Swan so full of softness that it pools in her eyes. "I thought you might like another chance to share Anne's letter. On your terms. But only if you want to."

I've read the letter a hundred times, but not once after the Halloween party. That night, it became something else, a monster Valeria had created. Now there's a chance to make it something new again. So I nod. Uncle Rowan goes inside the house and comes back with the letter and a pat on my shoulder. He sits down.

I unfold it, look over Anne's slanted, delicate writing, and bite my lip, remembering what it felt like to read it for the first time. The anticipation, the fear, the guilt. It's not just a letter from Anne to me. It's a reminder to forgive myself, to find happiness in someone else's joy.

"You got this, Jae," CJ says, adjusting his glasses.

I nod, and I start. "'Dear Jae.'" But when I get to Sarah's name, my voice breaks, the paper rattles. I'm overwhelmed by this moment. By the moments I've missed. By a given name that I didn't give.

Mrs. Aldana eases herself onto the bench beside me and leans in. She smells like a cozy cottage might. Earth and cinnamon and baked goods. "I'll read with you if you like," she whispers, and she wraps her arm around my shoulders. I'm tucked inside a maternal warmth, reminding me I'm someone's daughter. I long for Mom and the closeness we once had.

We read together, Mrs. Aldana's voice a scaffold. We read until *We will love you forever. The three of us.* She gives my shoulders a final squeeze just as a burst of wind shakes the palms. A stir like the sound of shifting sands.

They give me gifts: storybooks I can record for June; a giant plush stork with WORLD'S BEST BIRTH MOM stitched on its foot; and a necklace with a silver moon pendant and June Baby's birthstone embedded, from Uncle Rowan. Derek says it's moonstone, the most magical stone in the world, sacred in India, and that it'll bring me luck. Uncle Rowan dismisses the thought with a wave.

"I have a gift too," Derek says, bashfully. Then he and William disappear to the side of the house and come back hoisting a potted tree, almost as big as they are. It's in flower, and when they set it down with a thud at my feet, purple petals scatter on the ground.

I hold my face to contain my smile. Wisteria. I've seen them mostly as winding vines consuming oaks, reaching fingers across red bricks and windows, embracing trellises. But this one, trained as a tree, will tower like a giant umbrella.

"Had to find one with flowers on it already," Derek says. "So I could make sure it was purple. You like the purple ones, right? You looked for them everywhere. Now you can just look out your window."

I breathe in the intoxicating sweetness of the flowers, a smell that feels like Sunday walks with Mom through gardens. "It's a lot," I say, gently touching a stem with velvety petals. "Thank you."

Uncle Rowan sighs deep and frowns, takes off his glasses and wipes them on his shirt. "Jae." He's hesitant, stumbling before he finds his next words. "We all discussed this and thought it would be a welcome surprise," he continues, "but if it's not, you just let us know."

"Okay? What's going on?"

Derek takes in a deep breath and grabs my hand. "Your mom's here. And so is the baby. Anne and Jermaine, too. But listen. They're gonna be in town all week, so if it's too much tonight . . ."

I'm floating somewhere above all this. Derek's voice is replaced by a ringing in my ears. I feel like I'm up there in the blushing sky, looking down at this scene that was never supposed to happen. I was always alone. How did I get here? How did they all get here?

I must have nodded, because soon a shadow passes through the kitchen in the house. The shadow opens the balcony screen door and the bright light at her back creates a silhouette so familiar it's unmistakable.

Mom is bounding down the steps and before I know it, I'm smothered in a scent I've almost forgotten, of sweet almond oil and cocoa butter. She puts me at arm's length, examines me from head to toe, and cocoons me again. My name is a constant syllable on her lips, a mantra.

All that I have been, she has known, and we are tethered. We're not the same as before, but time will close the gap. Forgiveness will seal it. I am her daughter. I am her June.

We stand still like this, feeling heartbeats and names and dying daylight. Then a baby whines. And I look to the gate. And there she is.

CHAPTER FORTY-EIGHT

Jae

We're all sitting in the outside kitchen in the cabana. Our plates are piled with food, our conversations brimming with laughter. We heap praise on Ms. Rosette like she's a Michelin chef, and she says the food would have tasted better if she'd used ingredients from back home. Derek tells the *real* story of how he ended up in the club, which involves an embarrassing uniform and jumping over Mrs. Aldana's gate. I watch Uncle Rowan's face for disapproval, but he only chuckles. "That's nothing. One of these days, I'll tell you what kind of mess *I* got into."

I don't eat. Tonight, my hands are for holding, my lips for cooing. I want to bottle up every waft from her curly hair, every giggle, every glint of light on her eyelashes. *That little glimmer in your iris is the light from a half-gone star*, I whisper to her. She cackles.

Everyone busies Anne and Jermaine in conversation so I can have Sarah June to myself. I decide that's what I'll call her. I can do Sarah June.

She's standing on my lap and batting at my lips. I make a popping sound and it sends her into hysterics. Over and over again. Mom's sitting beside us, taking us in, and her eyes are drowning in love and memories and lost things.

"We knew she'd love you," Anne says. She looks tired, her straight brown hair in a messy bun, and I realize how much work she's done taking care of our baby. How she's the strongest shoot of our banyan tree. Jermaine places a hand on her shoulder and squeezes. I know it's not easy for any of us. But this is us.

In the sky you can already see a few bold stars, and the moon spreading its Cheshire cat smile. The wind is soft like velvet, and warm. It's the kind of wind that wraps around memories and brings them back to you again and again in different seasons. This day will come back when I least expect it. The smell of it, the taste of it. The air.

CHAPTER FORTY-NINE

Derek

The night is almost done. Anne says they'll take the baby back to the hotel soon, and Jae clenches her jaw. She looks on the verge of tears, but no one else seems to notice. I get it. They're feeding off the joy of the moment, laughing at William's Jim Carrey impression—which, seriously, is so spot-on, it's eerie. I wonder what other sides of ourselves we haven't shown each other.

But for me, the night is all about Jae, and I make my way around the table, ask Mr. Oakland to move down, and pull up a seat next to her.

"Hey," I say, almost lost in the scent of citrus and sweetness coming off her skin. "They'll be here all week, remember? You'll see her again."

She nods, and when she looks at me, she whispers *Thank you*, like that's all the voice she has.

"How do you feel?" I ask.

She blinks at the empty plate in front of her, the unused fork, and puts her cheek to the baby's hair. "Her breath smells like milk. I'm glad I didn't miss that." She breathes in the baby again. "I'm so happy, Derek. You're the sweetest friend."

Sweetest friend. I chew on the words, not sure I like the taste. But I swallow them, and tell myself that's good enough. *Jae's happy, and we're friends. That's good enough.*

The phone buzzes in my pocket, jangling my house keys. I pull it out, turn away from Jae, and answer it. "Yeah? Awesome! Come through the back." I hang up, and she clicks her tongue.

"What now?" she asks.

Before I can say anything, the gate opens, and Walter and Ash walk through the yard carrying drums.

"We know those guys!" Jae almost yells, elbowing me.

They wave at us, leave, and come back with more drums and percussion instruments, as Jae rambles excitedly to everyone about the drum circle at the beach.

The baby whimpers for Anne, and Anne rushes to get her. Jae breathes in deep as she lifts the baby up and lets her go.

I take her warm hands and pull her up from the table. "She's not gone yet," I remind her.

"I know. I'm all right," she says, smoothing out her yellow dress, which I'm so glad I get to see again.

Jae's mom turns to Mr. Oakland. "Rowan, aren't the neighbors gonna complain? Drums? In the suburbs?"

He stands up, stretches his limbs, and pats his full belly. "They've been told," he says as he walks away. "Just have a good time, Paula. Can you manage that?"

Jae's walking ahead of me to the gathering group, and I don't know how I'm going to do this. How I'm going to be a sweet friend when I don't want to be sweet. Not with her. CJ, Swan, and William are already sitting in front of their drums. Jae's standing back, watching them, and I take my spot in front of a djembe.

"Grab an instrument," I say, and Jae picks up two tambourines from the pile and hands one to her mom, who starts doing what looks like choir choreography while she hollers a few lines of praise music. Mrs. Aldana and Ms. Rosette laugh at this and join in with maracas. Then everyone laughs more when the baby crawls over and grabs a maraca for herself and gums it.

Mr. Oakland pulls up his pants at the crotch as he sits in front of the last djembe beside me. "I'll follow y'all," he says to me.

"That would be best, sir," I reply. "You wouldn't wanna hurt yourself."

He chuckles. "You got jokes."

Ash, the Lenny Kravitz look-alike, adjusts his suede fedora. "We heard your daughter likes Bob Marley," he says to Jae, and she turns and smiles at Anne. Then Walter, with the giant dreadlocks, counts off, quiet taps on his drum. And his voice, loud and raspy like a blues singer, shouts, "Don't worry!"

The rest of us join in, carefully tapping out the rhythms they taught us at the beach. CJ looks up from his drumming with pleasant shock, like he's saying, *It's working, guys! It's really working!* Jae's looking at the grass, and then she sets her tambourine down and starts walking away, lights and shadows passing over her as she moves through the garden.

For a moment, they stop drumming. They call her name.

"I got it," I say, waving my hand for them to continue as I slide out of my seat and run after her.

I grab her hand at the balcony stairs and pull her toward the side of the house, where we walk the white path made of pebbles that crunch beneath our feet. I stop and face her.

"What's wrong?"

She's blinking fast, gaze down. I gently lift her chin, and I'm lost in all the angles of her face, in the fleshiness of her mouth. Her eyes meet mine, and my heart is completely rended. They're dark and shimmering and wet.

I know what I'd do if I could. How I'd hold her face just like this, tilted up at the stars, how I'd press my lips against hers and melt, melt, melt into her. Just like that night in her room. Except this time, I'd kiss her until we were both out of breath, until the universe said *Enough*.

She sniffles, then scrunches her nose like the cutest rabbit.

"You feel like crying?"

She shakes her head.

"You can cry. I'll stay with you."

"I don't *want* to cry." She laughs through tears and wipes them away with the back of her hand. "It's just . . . I feel so . . . I dunno."

"Overwhelmed?"

She nods, shaky breath. "Yeah. That's it. But not in a bad way. It's Sarah June and all those people—I can't believe I have so many people—and it's you, and what you did for me. And . . . it's you. It's you."

Her lips are trembling, and I brush my fingers against them, mesmerized by her mouth and how soft it is. My heart twists when she closes her eyes and parts her lips. And then her warm tongue grazes my finger, sending electric surges through my body.

"Hey," I warn her. "Don't do that."

Her eyes open, and she blinks at me, and she says, "I like you so much."

My heart flutters madly in my chest. "I like you, too." But that's not true. *Like* doesn't feel this way. It doesn't make you ache this way.

"It's like you said in that poem. Something ravenous that could destroy us both? I feel that with you."

"Me too."

"Sometimes it's too much, though. It's like I'm not even human anymore, I'm just *hungry*."

Those words on her tongue. *I'm just hungry*. The memory of her touch is all over my skin now and I want more. More of her on me. Teasing me with her eyes, her voice, her wet mouth on mine. I want to be *hers*.

"Destroy me, then." I grin and step closer.

For a second, there's a spark, a glimmer in her eyes, a tug at her lips. My breath is straining.

"Jae. Don't take this the wrong way. But I want you more than I've wanted anything. Every piece of you, I want it."

A small gasp. Something in her wavers. Then she steps back. She's quiet. Looks at me with lamplight glowing in her eyes. "Be my friend," she says.

"What?"

"Tell me that's enough."

I laugh, and my voice comes out in a whisper. "You're killing me. Seriously, Jae, you're killing me." I turn around, take a few steps down the path. Everything inside me is straining, pulling itself apart. I've never wanted anything so much in my whole life. "Why?" I ask her.

And then her words come out slow, like she needs for each syllable to be understood. "You said I'm perfect. I'm not. It's like a cut that hasn't healed yet. It keeps opening up. It's so much! All of it. And I need time. You know what I mean?" She looks at me intently.

"I think so."

"I don't want to lose you. So please. Be my friend."

I close my eyes, take in as much air as I can. Let out a long sigh and let the tightness inside unravel. I don't know how to do what she's asking, but I nod anyway.

She takes a few steps down the pebbled path, then turns back when she doesn't hear me follow.

"For what it's worth," she says, "I've never wanted anything more, either." Her smile is empty, and she walks away toward the drums.

I've missed her, I've wanted her, I've craved her. And now that she's back in my orbit, I can't get too close. It's like a chisel is pressed against my heart, and each second, it's struck deeper. And deeper. And deeper.

Be my friend. Tell me that's enough.

If she asked me to, I would lasso the moon, pull it close enough for her to hold it in her hands. But being her friend—just her friend—feels like something I can't do.

But I will.

For Jae?

Anything.

CHAPTER FIFTY

Jae

With my heart thundering in my chest, I listen to the *shwoosh* of car tires against wet pavement as I wait at the corner of First and Swinton.

It's the first day of summer vacation and another therapy session with Dr. Awad, an old friend of Uncle Rowan's from Howard University. He was eager for me to start therapy because *You need someone you can always talk to*. I liked Dr. Awad the moment she opened her office door wearing a hot-pink hijab and a T-shirt that said YOUR SILENCE WILL NOT PROTECT YOU. She reminded me of Swan, if Swan were Syrian and middle-aged.

I'm standing in front of that nondescript yellow building that looks like it should be full of flowery sofas and doilies but is a magical garden in the heart of Delray. On most days after therapy, I walk down to the Sundy House and sit in the gazebo to fill out my journal for Sarah June. Then I walk through the bamboo groves and dip my feet in the pond.

Today I told Sarah June that life was about to change. That change is inevitable. That it's hard to believe how much this city feels like home. That I will see her again and that I will always want to see her.

The patter of rain on my umbrella gets louder. It's one of those Florida rains that come down hard and fast, and in a few hours, the rain will dry up and the trees will take in the water and grow greener. But for now, the way is hazy with rain, and a small black Honda suddenly materializes. Headlights like two bright eyes approach.

I hear Dr. Awad's voice in my head, so I try to turn my anxiety into excitement through positive thinking. The butterflies, the fluttering. They're a good thing. *Not anxious, excited.*

The car slows down and pulls up to the curb. I open the passenger-side door and slide in, shaking out my umbrella and pulling it in after me.

"Were you waiting long?" Derek asks, reaching over to brush away a water droplet from my forehead. My face warms.

"Just a minute."

"Good."

He's giving off an intoxicating, just-bathed-in-wood-chips-and-moss smell, and I find myself leaning in closer.

He looks into the rearview mirror and adjusts his white cap, brushing a tuft of dark hair behind his ears. Then he puts the car into gear and drives off, filling the air with questions about therapy and what Dr. Awad wore today. We talk about last week's graduation party for Swan and Ade, a Nigerian boy who transferred to Bellwood the last semester of his senior year. But there's still something hanging in the air, and after a few minutes, I finally bring it up.

"You did it?" I ask.

He nods.

"How do you feel?"

He doesn't take his eyes off the road, but I can see him squinting, which means he's trying to sort through his feelings. He reaches into the cup holder for a stick of gum and pops it into his mouth. He has an endless stash of gum. In the glove compartment, in his backpack, in his locker, on the windowsill in his bedroom. He reaches for it anytime he's stressed or nervous or thinking or feeling too much. It helps him not to smoke.

Just before picking me up, he dropped his mom off at a rehab center minutes away. It took little convincing to make her go. I think she noticed how much he changed this year. How he stopped fighting with her and instead left the house with his notebook anytime things got heated. How he increased his hours at Old-Timer so he could buy a used Honda from Mr. Tillman's dealership. How he started to talk more and more about college. I think she saw how he was changing and decided she could too.

"I'm relieved. Hopeful," he finally says. "But rehab doesn't always work—"

"It will," I say. And I say a silent prayer to the universe that it will.

Since the entrustment ceremony, Derek and I tell each other things we wouldn't tell anyone else. I know his feelings like I know flowers. I can identify every emotion that flits across his face. The little flare of his nostrils when he's about to laugh. The way his mouth twitches when he's trying not to. The way he bites his lip at our goodbyes. I know him, and he knows me, and he hasn't asked for more.

I haven't asked for more. Not yet.

"What's for dinner?" he asks, and I shake myself free of tangled thoughts and roving butterflies.

"I think it's Uncle Rowan's turn to decide."

I don't know when it was that Derek became a regular at dinner, but at some point, Uncle Rowan just expected him to be there. *The kid's working hard. The least you could do is make sure he gets a good meal*, he scolded me once when I didn't invite Derek to eat. I think Uncle Rowan likes having him around to talk sports with, and even more when Derek brings Henry along.

The car jostles as we pull up to the curb. The black gates are open and we roll into the driveway and park behind Uncle Rowan's black Cadillac.

I'm looking straight ahead, but I can feel Derek's eyes on me, can almost hear him smirk.

"You have something you wanna say?" he prods, his voice whispery and cool.

"Not yet," I say, nerves buzzing.

"Not yet?"

"Not here."

I step out of the car. The rain is just drizzling now—I don't bother grabbing the umbrella. I walk until I notice I'm walking alone. Then I turn around, and I'm standing in the stream of bright headlights. Raindrops glimmer like a million falling stars. Derek sits in the driver's seat. His body is still. Through the dashboard speckled with rain, I find his dark eyes watching me like I'm the most amusing thing he's ever seen. His lips slide into a slow smile.

He turns off the engine and steps outside. The headlights are gone and we're under gray sky, and the rain falls with quiet pin drops on leaves and carries the sweet smell of earth.

"Why are you looking at me like that?" he asks in that voice that makes me feel like he sees every inch of me.

"You're nice to look at."

"Yeah?" He squints and stuffs his hands in his jean pockets. "So does everything have to be on your time?"

"What do you mean?"

"Can't you tell me now?"

I breathe, trying to temper the feelings roiling inside. Instinctively, I take a step back, because I know him—I know us—and even this far apart, I feel the pull, and there are words I need to say.

"It was a few months ago. Dr. Awad asked me why we weren't dating if we both had feelings for each other."

His eyes suddenly brighten and he looks smug. "You talk about me often?"

"Maybe," I tease.

"And what did you say?"

"I told her I didn't trust myself."

"Why not?"

"Because of Austin."

He huffs, wrinkles his nose in disgust.

"I know, I know. It's not about him. It was never about him. I just hadn't *forgiven* myself for him."

He nods slowly, moving the gum around with his tongue.

"I was stuck on that mistake, still ashamed of it. Still afraid of my feelings."

His eyebrows furrow in concern. "It wasn't your fault. He—"

"I know." I hold up my hand. "But it's my turn to pour out my heart now. Okay?"

He looks confused when I reach for his hat and turn it backward. Drops of rain speckle his black lashes, his freckled nose, his lips, his cheekbones. I run my fingers along his wet jaw, kiss him at the sharp corner of it, taste the rain and his skin. I relish the soft sigh from his lips.

"What are you doing?" he whispers, mouth against my ear.

I hush him, and I say, my cheek caressing his, "I'm allowed to want things. And I want you."

He pulls away, shaking his head like he's in a daze.

"You're more beautiful than Saturn's rings." I grin.

He laughs. Soft. "Those are my words."

"I like your words. What was the other thing? Destroy me?" I give him a teasing smile and he blushes, looks down at the ground, and bites his bottom lip.

"You want me?" he whispers.

"More than anything."

He looks up at the sky. Laughs. Curses. Then he leans down toward me, and those seconds are like the stretch of sunset: I study every light and shadow, every angle of his face. This moment feels like forever, and his beauty will never get old to me.

He presses his lips against mine, and my heart sings like it's the first time, like we're in my bedroom, putting our wounded pieces together. His warm hand cups my face, his fingers stroke my skin, and I ache and I tingle, like I'm merely a bundle of nerves, all exposed. His lips are the softest things, begging to be soothed, and I lick him and I tug, and we are breathless.

He explores me, wet-mouthed, and I'm like a cat, arching and purring under his touch, and every gasp or quiet moan is like a spark that ignites him. His voice is cool and gravelly when he says my name. "Jae." And again, when my tongue brushes his lips. "Jae." He grasps for me, desperate, like he's trying to grasp water, like I could slip away from him forever.

Against my ear is a moan, a wet tongue, a warm breath that sends shivers down my spine. I reach under his shirt, run my hands along smooth muscle, and feel his breath stop as I trace a line down his jeans. His strong arms pull me against him.

My legs, and everything inside, go soft.

I grab his belt loop and pull harder.

He traces the skin beneath my shirt, his fingers as soft and as light as a breath. I am aching.

"You're too much," I say, grabbing his hat, raking my hand through his hair, tugging, feeding off the wild look in his eyes, the catch in his breath. I want him to melt in my hands.

"Jae." He's pulling away.

"More," I say. I reach for him, because this is not enough. Not yet.

"Jae."

"*Derek*." And I open my eyes and follow his gaze to the front door. My stomach drops.

There's an eerie silence, like there would be just before the world ends. And then Uncle Rowan is yelling at us.

"*Where is your sense of decency?*" He's in the doorway, frowning in a new gray suit, arms tightly crossed in front of him. "This is not a Hollywood set! Are you trying to get sick? I don't know the last time I saw something so foolish."

We have the long walk up the driveway and up the steps to cool down. Uncle Rowan's eyes are a death glare, but when he steps aside for us to pass, he playfully tugs on my loc and gives Derek a handshake. It's some West African thing that Ade taught Derek, and every time Uncle Rowan does it, with his fingers snapping, he giggles.

I hold Derek's hand as we walk down the hall to look for Ms. Rosette, and I pass a picture of me holding Sarah June by the wisteria. I miss her so much. But on days like this, I feel like there's love pressing in on all sides, and there's hardly a moment to sit in sadness.

"Are you packed up for your trip?" Uncle Rowan asks me at dinner.

Swan has decided to look for her birth parents in Korea and wants me to go with her.

Derek squeezes my hand under the table. I know what he's thinking. We won't be together most of the summer.

"I still have three weeks left," I say to Uncle Rowan, and I squeeze Derek's hand back. "I already got a Korean phrasebook, though. Annyeong haseyo."

"You'll call me, right?" Derek asks.

"Every day. You'll get so sick of me, you'll change your number."

"You need to let the young man focus," Uncle Rowan scolds me. Then he says to Derek, "Your portfolio isn't going to materialize out of thin air."

"Yes, sir." Derek nods.

Ever since Derek said he wanted to go to film school, Uncle Rowan has been nagging him nonstop. Better him than me.

"And how's your mother?" he asks.

Derek shrugs. "She's starting the program today."

"That's good." Uncle Rowan nods. "That's a good thing. Keep your chin up. She'll be okay."

"Thanks, Mr. Oakland."

After dinner, the three of us sit in the living room to watch *Koi . . . Mil Gaya*, the movie that started Derek's obsession with space. It really is the corniest thing I've ever seen, but we can't stop laughing. And when Uncle Rowan says, "Now, this is good, wholesome TV," Derek and I roll our eyes at each other.

Halfway through, Uncle Rowan falls asleep, so we pause the movie and head upstairs to my room. We follow the rules and keep the door open.

Derek lies down and I snuggle into the crook of his arm. He sets an open book on his chest and I lean in to read the pages. He reads aloud from *The Disordered Cosmos*, which he borrowed from the library after I said one too many times that I didn't "get" space science. And when he reads the opening benediction to the universe, I feel goose bumps rippling across my skin.

The heartbeat. The breath. The soft turn of the page. We stir, quiet, until I forget we are separate bodies. Then his fingers brush softly against my shoulder and I remember. I think of Lucille Clifton's poem "won't you celebrate with me." Derek reads, and I silently celebrate my life, my self.

Something moves outside the window.

I sit up on my elbows and jump out of bed and make my way across the room. When I pull aside the curtains, above and below, the night is calm. Garden lights glow over short bushes, over towering palms, over portulacas and pink clusters of pentas. Over a small wisteria tree that will one day grow into a giant canopy of weeping purple petals.

Derek comes to stand beside me, and he's quiet, as captivated by the darkness as I am.

I push open the window to let the cool breeze in. A collection of mingled breaths from past to now. Strangers. Lovers. Mothers. Daughters. I breathe in deep and close my eyes. I breathe out slow and take Derek's hand.

Light, shadow, rain, sun.

Breathe deep.

Carry on.

ACKNOWLEDGMENTS

To Dad, for being the first Uncle Rowan; for believing there was greatness in me. Your ~~nagging~~ encouragement pushed me to query this book, and look where it ended up. Now, please don't read it.

To Daniel, for making every milestone feel like I had slain giants. You've seen my tries and my fails, and you've always given me a safe place to land. You are part of every beautiful thing I know.

To Mom, Theresa Adzewoda, for pouring yourself out for your children. There is no one more deserving of freedom and joy.

To Elsie, for sharing the name Aƒenyo with me. For sharing the woman who couldn't turn down a good beat, whose boogie shoes were always ready. Auntie Rita is forever in these pages. And to Pamela: I hope this is a joy-filled surprise.

To my little one, for reminding me there is life and beauty beyond the page. (Stop screaming, please. Mama's coming.)

To my unfailing agent, Lindsay Auld, for being wisdom incarnate; for being the partner I needed; for putting my heart so much at ease.

To Ashley Hearn, the plot whisperer, for seeing the diamond in the story and helping me to shape it. I cannot imagine beginning my writing career without you.

To Lily Steele. Thank you for your expert design, your collaboration, and for literally moving the heavens.

To Kei-Ella Loewe. Thank you for capturing the mood of this moody book so beautifully. The wind, the shadows, the stars, the moon—it's glorious.

To Farah Géhy, for sharing my story in such faraway places. I'm so grateful.

To Stephanie Pando and everyone at Peachtree/Candlewick/Walker/Holiday House who has worked endlessly to spread the word.

To Roisin Heycock, for your graciousness and belief in this story. You encouraged me to aim high, and I'll never forget that. When I think of this journey to publication, it often begins with you.

To Amy Bishop-Wycisk for your thoughtful feedback, to Alexandra Levick for pulling Jae and Derek out of the slush pile, and to Brianne Johnson for loving them.

To Barbara Perris and Regina Castillo, for your sharp—er, keen eyes.

To Mawunyo and Eyram, for being my sounding board, especially when I was in a panic.

To Namita Matharu and Kajal Patel, for sharing beautiful cultural insights with me. I hope you like what the story has become. (Any mistakes are my own.)

To Monica Connell, for loving Jae and Derek before their story was fully written. You should be here.

To the authors in the 2026 Debuts cohort and my fellow Peachtree authors: What have you *not* done to make this road easier for me? I'm so thankful I did not wander this wilderness alone.

To Linda Spaulding, for your feedback, your love, your friendship. The world will be better for your stories.

To Malika Griffith. For being my way-back friend, and for showing me what support looks like.

To my Korean language meetup and Mr. Hoon, for your time and friendship. You filled my well.

To the readers who love and will love this story—this would go nowhere without you. Thank you.

To all the hands that went into this book that I could not know or name or count: Thank you for your time and expertise. Thank you for making my dreams come true.

ABOUT THE *Author*

DELALI ADJOA was born in Togo to Ghanaian parents but grew up in Canada, where she traded sunny cottons for wool tuques and snowsuits. She has been chasing warmer weather ever since. Delali writes fiction centered on identity, freedom, and family, and loves the American South for the stories it has buried. She is a graduate of the University of Kentucky and Georgetown University.